# Brushwork

Also by John Scherber

NONFICTION
San Miguel de Allende: A Place in the Heart

FICTION
Twenty Centavos
The Fifth Codex

# Brushwork

John Scherber

Any book starts as an idea, and by its completion becomes a joint effort.

Thanks to my readers:
Patti Beaudry, Joan Columbus, Lou DeRonde,
Donna Krueger, and Marcia Loy.

Cover Design by Lander Rodriguez
Interior Design by Jon Sievert
Author Photo by Gail Yates Tobey
Web Page Design by Julio Mendez



ISBN 978-0-9832582-0-9

San Miguel Allende Books
Laredo, TX
*www.SanMiguelAllendeBooks.com*

Printed in the United States of America

## AUTHOR'S NOTE

*Brushwork* is the third of the Murder in México series of mysteries, set in the old colonial hill town of San Miguel de Allende. Other titles will follow soon.

*Daddy's Girl*. A sexually posed murder of a former madame, once a Zacher painting model, pulls Paul into another plot, this one going back years in its origins. Tired of being shot at and kidnapped, Maya hits the wall and leaves, and Cody comes up with a completely different view of who the killer might be--another painter. Working alone, Paul stumbles across the woman who might be the answer to his dreams, or just another nightmare.

*Strike Zone.* The search for a solid gold human skull, cast from the last remaining bullion of the Aztecs and once in the collection of Hermann Goering, pulls the Zacher Group down to Oaxaca. Here the artifact may or may not be in the possession an old alcoholic GI who was charged with guarding the salt mine in Austria where the collection was hidden at the end of World War II. A teachers' strike erupts in lethal violence around them as Goering's illegitimate son and his Panamanian thugs track their movements in hopes of recovering the artifact.

*Vanishing Act* brings the Zacher Group north of the border to track the disappearance of Cody's nephew, whose pregnant wife has been murdered, and their house burned to the ground. Is the nephew a victim or the perpetrator? The search takes them to New Mexico and Colorado as they try to sort out identities that may not be at all what they seem, and in a way they could never imagine.

*Identity Crisis.* Paul and his friends are hired to establish the identity of a man who fears he may not exist. He is murdered before they can help, and they are drawn into a race against time to stop a sinister plot to assassinate the governor of the state, so that his successor can approve a mining permit that will lead to environmental disaster.

*The Theft of the Virgin.* At an exhibition of memorable forgeries of great paintings, Paul spots one that is unmistakably genuine. When he challenges the director, the painting is stolen from the exhibit and the Zacher Group finds itself on the trail of a conspiracy to steal Mexico's greatest national treasure.

See our website, *www.sanmiguelallendebooks.com,* for more details on release dates and availability.

*To Kristine*

# Prologue

## August 11, 1965

Malcolm Brendel had always known he was special, but he didn't realize how special until he rose from the dead at the age of 33.

It happened during a Lamb of God Revival meeting in southwestern Kansas, a gently rolling country of stone houses and solid people. The dense, saturated heat of the day had not dissipated when darkness fell, and lightning crackled in the humid air, threatening a downpour that never materialized.

It was the end of the third day of the revival, the day Reverend Brendel had designated as "Red, White, and Blue God and Country Day," where testimonies of personal salvation alternated with ringing endorsements of America's ever deepening struggle with Godless communism in Vietnam. Prominent Kansas Republicans alternated with noted preachers in a round robin of speeches and sermons that was about to culminate in the appearance of Malcolm Brendel for the nightly baptism of the saved. People had come from as far away as northern Oklahoma and eastern Colorado for the event.

As he descended from the bus that served as his road headquarters, one which he believed was the only retired school bus in the state of Kansas with its own safe, the Reverend Brendel took a last drag from his unfiltered Pall Mall and crushed the butt into the sandy soil under his foot. Adjusting the collar of his sky-blue robe, he headed for the tent, passing between poles supporting a banner proclaiming the three-day revival. Two ushers at the entrance greeted him respectfully.

Reverend Brendel entered between two folding literature tables filled with Bibles, devotional books, and recordings. The capacity crowd immediately sensed his presence and rose from their folding chairs, some saying, "Praise the Lord," others, "Thank you, Jesus." Brendel nodded graciously in acknowledgment. When he reached the low platform at the center of the tent, he turned and stretched out his hands to the crowd, which fell silent. Removing the microphone from its stand, he placed it against his lips, and said in a near whisper that was heard perfectly at every seat, "Know that you are not here to be saved. You are here because you are saved. God himself has said this, and I say it to you again." There was a restrained cheer and a chorus of "Amen."

Next to the platform stood a galvanized steel cattle trough full of water. It had seen heavy service during the previous two nights of the revival and the soil around it was muddy. Two attendants stood behind it to assist people emerging from the trough and present them with towels. Reverend Brendel concluded his remarks and signaled for the first candidate to come forward. She was a woman in her early twenties, short and thickly built, wearing a pair of dark blue slacks and a white cotton sleeveless blouse. One of the attendants assisted her into the trough, and she stood with her hands folded while Brendel stepped down from the platform and stood next to her.

"Karen," he said, finding her name at the top of the list before him, his rich pastoral voice reverberating with great solidity throughout the tent, "do you confess that you have turned away from sin and have placed your faith in Jesus Christ as your lord and savior?" He shifted the microphone toward her.

"I do." Karen closed her eyes in near ecstasy as she said this.

"And do you then promise, as you depend upon the grace of God, to faithfully serve Christ within the fellowship of his Church for the remainder of your days on earth?"

"I do."

"So be it then, Karen, that upon your profession of faith in the Lord Jesus Christ, I baptize you in the name of the Father, and of the Son, and of the Holy Spirit."

Her knees trembling, Karen had already sunk into the trough, and as he finished his words, with his left hand Malcolm Brendel firmly thrust her head backward under the cold water. One of the attendants stood ready to drape a towel over her so that her chilled erect nipples did not catch the light through her blouse and turn God's holy rite into a wet T-shirt contest. Personally, the Reverend Brendel did not object to this, because it reminded him warmly of the nurturing qualities of baptism. But there were the less sophisticated men in the congregation to consider.

Suddenly, his hand still in the water, there was a brilliant outburst at the microphone, like old-fashioned photo flash powder going off, and the Reverend Malcolm Brendel was slammed to the ground, where he lay unmoving, eyes staring sightlessly into the top of the tent, searching for the hereafter.

After three or four seconds of stunned silence, a vast communal groan went up from the crowd. Karen was pulled shrieking, but uninjured, from the trough. A man was heard to shout almost hysterically, "It's the will of God!"

But next to him, a woman whose name was recorded as Mrs. Irene Pavelka, matron of a family that farmed near Hutchinson, Kansas, was heard to say even more loudly, "But it's not my will!" Naively, Mrs. Pavelka did not realize that electrocution is forever.

She leaped to her feet and ran to where Brendel lay dead in the mud and fell to her ample knees. She wasted no time in prayer, but instead pressed her mouth fervently to his narrow lips and began to breathe her own life into his lungs. She alternated this with vigorously pumping his chest with the heels of her hands.

This went on for an interminable minute, while the crowd edged toward chaos. Help could not be immediately summoned because the tent stood in the middle of a pasture and no phones were available. Three or four men had run for the nearest farmhouse.

Suddenly Malcolm Brendel began to cough and gasp as he tried to struggle to his feet. Several men emerged from the crowd and held him down, offering him water, but he would have none of it. Irene Pavelka slumped back in exhaustion, leaning against the cattle trough, her chest heaving.

Thirty-five minutes later, after an ambulance had arrived and Brendel had been removed for treatment, one of the visiting pastors, who had already preached during the day, rose and addressed the audience. He was careful to select a different microphone and avoid the mud around the trough.

"We," he began, in a voice that boomed through the crowd and brought it back to attention, "have been privileged tonight to witness the awesome power of almighty God, who has seen fit to raise our brother Malcolm from the grip of death. Let us kneel and give thanks."

Gradually a sense of incredible privilege permeated the worshippers, that of an opportunity never to be repeated, and hundreds came forward to be baptized and link their personal salvation to the night of the miracle. The very presence of God could be felt throughout the tent.

Unknown to the crowd, this was the final night of Malcolm Brendel's lay ministry. Upon his release from the hospital in Garden City, he was diverted to a different, if not higher, calling. Like Paul on the road to Damascus, the Reverend Malcolm Brendel embarked on the fork less traveled, a path that would ultimately lead him to the office of vice president of the United States.

Amen.

# Chapter 1
## Forty Years Later

The line stretched for nearly two blocks over the wet cobblestones. Despite the light intermittent rain of late morning, both locals and gringos waited to get into the estate sale. It didn't matter that all the major pieces had already been shipped to México City for auction; the main attraction was the house itself. After standing vacant for years, the three-story, 1740 townhouse had been flawlessly, even sensitively, restored to its original glory. The tan stucco was seamless and free of cracks and pockmarks from the random gunfire of past revolutions. The weathered stone at the lintels and door frame had been crisply replaced. Fresh varnish gleamed on the double doors of the entry.

The owner and overseer of this flawless restoration, John Schleicher, formerly of Short Hills, New Jersey, was dead. In addition to being a drug dealer who had narrowly avoided prison in the States, he had also been a sophisticated collector of ample means who prudently guarded his privacy, and few of the expatriate community in the middling Méxican town of San Miguel de Allende had ever been allowed inside his home. Even so, his final acquisition, a priceless Mayan codex, one of only five known, had cost him his life. I had already been in the house twice, both times as an uninvited guest. He hadn't been home either time. When I'm not painting pictures, a task that can be sustained for four or five hours a day at most, I moonlight as a detective. Schleicher had moved in and out of my sights several times.

I'm not a collector, except involuntarily. When one of my own paintings doesn't sell I add it to the collection hanging in my house, which over the years has naturally come to illustrate the less commercial side of my work. But I knew that on the top shelf in the library of this mansion, so high up you needed the sliding ladder on its brass rail to reach it, was a three-volume set of *Don Quixote* bound in ribbed green leather that I wanted to own. I believe it's eighteenth century, like the house itself. I doubt that John Schleicher had ever read it; it was merely part of his upscale decor.

From further up the line I heard my name. "Paul! Paul Zacher."

Bill Frost left his wife, Brynn, in place like a bookmark, and walked back toward me. He didn't try to shake my wet hand. "Did you notice that the 'For Sale' sign is down?" Bill was a retired investment banker from Toronto and not the first person I would have expected to see in line at an estate sale. I looked up at the window on the second floor where the sign had been. "I didn't notice. Are you saying it's been sold?"

"Yes, and who do you think is moving in?"

"Presidente Fox?"

"Close. Malcolm Brendel."

"Not the former vice president of the U.S.?"

"Exactly. He's decided to join our exclusive little colony."

"Then maybe we're not exclusive enough; a few things about him suggest that he's not the best vice president we ever had. Are you here for the antiques?"

"Not really. I'm sure all the best things have gone to the auction. I just want to see the house. I've heard it's the best restoration in San Miguel. I'll see you inside."

Frost moved back to his place and I turned around to look at the lengthening line.

Immediately behind me stood a tall girl in a khaki rain poncho and blue wide-leg bib overalls. There was a loop for a hammer on one leg. Her hands were in her pockets, and there was a look in her eyes that said she was just about to make a connection. I placed her age at nineteen or twenty.

"I know who you are," she said, suddenly brightening. I could see her flat pale hair on both sides of her head between her cheeks and the poncho hood.

"That's more than I do some days."

"What do you mean?"

"Sometimes I'm a painter and other times I'm a detective."

"A detective? That's an odd mix. I saw you when you were a painter, at Galeria Uno," she said. "There's an easel with photos of all the painters. Then I looked at your paintings. They're all still lifes. Lots of big fruit. Am I right?"

"Ramon does best with still lifes here. I send my figural pictures down to another gallery in Mérida."

"Figural?"

"People doing what they do, nudes, that kind of thing."

She gave me a wry smile. Her lips were thin, not sensual, and she wore no makeup, but her smile was attractive. Her eyelashes were almost absent of color and nearly invisible. She pulled one hand out of a pocket and put it over her mouth, as if she wasn't proud of her teeth, but I hadn't seen anything wrong with them, and I like to think I notice everything. Her fingers were long and slender and veins in the back of her hand were prominent. She wore no rings or nail polish.

"Do you live here?" I asked.

"I came down to take a mystery writing course at the Bellas Artes. I'll be staying with my father when he comes down tomorrow. He has a job here. I'm Lynn Washburn."

As she held out her hand she looked at me with her disarming gaze and said nothing more. Her hair was parted in the center over a broad forehead and her eyes were a pale blue. A touch of cerulean, I thought, maybe a dash of ultramarine, but subtle, in a nearly triangular face. I had no doubt she had looked much like this as a child, and I could see from her hands and face and neck that she was painfully slender. I was beginning to see something compelling in the possibilities of this combination. If she could be placed nude in a strongly suggestive pose, the innocence would play off it beautifully. It was a risk, but with risk often came breakthrough. I don't mind falling on my face now and then. Even at thirty-five, I heal easily and don't bruise much.

"Would you like to pose for me?" I said abruptly.

There's no subtle way to lead into this. Her eyes got bigger.

"Do you always ask that?" she said, as if short of breath.

"Only when I see someone interesting."

"I'm not very interesting." It seemed to be the end of the conversation. I was about to face in the other direction when she turned to look back at the line behind her for a moment, but then faced me again. "What does it pay?"

"The usual. Immortality." Now it was my turn to smile. "That's the going rate."

"Would I have to be naked?"

"Nude."

"What's the difference?" A woman standing behind Lynn had picked up this turn in the conversation and was studying in detail the cornice of the house and pretending not to listen.

"Nude is a painter's term. Naked is anybody's. It involves the same lack of clothing."

"Would you sell the picture here?"

"It would go down to the Yucatan gallery. No one would see it who knows you."

"I'll do it then. But I might not be that good." She grinned, but with the corners of her mouth bent, so that it looked more like resignation. Like OK, here comes another failure.

The light rain returned, but we were near the entrance. "Tell me your name again?"

"Lynn Washburn. I already know yours." She held out her hand.

When we got inside, I discovered the set of *Don Quixote* was already sold.

Two days later Lynn came into the studio carrying a small overnight bag that she set down on the sofa. The rain had left our courtyard garden refreshed, and the morning glowed with perfect light from my north windows. I made a point of walking her around the room to let her relax, showing her the storage racks for finished paintings, my counter for coffee and snacks, and the changing area in one corner with its three-panel screen. I pointed out the hooks where she could hang her clothes. I always had a certain sympathy for new models as they discovered the awkwardness and the embarrassment of taking off their clothes, the general unknown terrain of the studio and the intentions of the painter himself. My manner was always businesslike, but friendly, encouraging. In art school I had done it myself, we all had.

"Are you feeling comfortable?" I asked.

"Yes, I think so. How do we do this?" She stood with her arms straight at her sides, looking around at the easel. As she turned, I examined her profile, which I hadn't been able to see clearly in the poncho. Her nose was straight and started right off the base of her forehead without any dip, like the faces of classical Greek statuary.

"Did you bring a robe like we talked about in line? Something to cover up in?"

"Yes, I've got it right here."

"OK, we can start if you go behind the screen and put it on. Then we'll talk about the pose."

She hesitated a moment, as if about to ask me something more, then walked over to the screen as I watched her. She was built like a wire coat hanger, wearing tight jeans and a filmy top with puffed short sleeves that was flared at her waist. There was the sound of clothes coming off, and she reappeared a moment later wearing a long blue flannel nightgown with a ruffle at her ankles. She was barefoot. I almost laughed, but stifled it. The comfort of the model was always the most important thing, and I didn't sense any great confidence in her about this process.

"I'd like to have you seated on this chair," I said. It was a steel folding chair in a style that suggested church basement suppers. I had never used it for anything but still life setups; other nudes I had always posed differently. I moved it into position to face me at the easel, sitting on top of a platform about 18 inches from the floor. Elevated in this way, when she sat on it, her eye level was just below mine.

"Let's try it." Lynn sat on the chair in her nightgown. "Can you look straight at me, with your elbows on your legs, supporting your head with your palms on your cheeks. Good. Just stare at me as if you've never seen me before. And sit there a minute so the seat warms up."

She was looking at me with mild interest, but not smiling. I sat down before the easel and pulled out some tubes of paint. She was very pale, so the shadows would have to be lighter than normal to keep from overdoing the contrast. Her hair was thin and hung over her hands as if it had been pressed.

"I'm ready," I said.

"Should I take this off?"

"If you're ready. The seat should be warm now." She stood up and pulled the nightgown up as far as mid thigh and then stopped.

"I've never done this before." Her small voice came from inside the nightgown.

"I've done it hundreds of times. Don't be nervous. Think of your body as landscape. I do."

I heard a deep breath from the nightgown, and then she pulled it off the rest of the way. She was like an anatomy lesson; I could see all of her bones. As she sat down on the chair again her hips moved visibly in their sockets. Her breasts were small and pointed, and I knew they would stay exactly the same way when she leaned forward on her elbows. Her nipples swelled slightly and were not fully defined. Immediately I saw a new set of possibilities; the sheer angularity of her body would resolve into planes and hollows in a way unlike any model I'd ever painted.

"Great. Are you still comfortable?"

"I think so." There was a question mark in her tone.

"How old are you?" I wanted to start her thinking about something other than being nude with a stranger.

"Twenty."

"Are you Scandinavian?"

"My mother's family is Norwegian and my dad's is English."

"If you could move your elbows about two inches farther forward along your thighs. Good. Now could you open your knees a bit, maybe six or eight inches? And give me that same look you had before you took off your nightgown."

She didn't move for a moment. "But won't you be

able to see my...?"

This was awkward. "Yes. I want to see it." Her little wisp of straight pubic hair was like a goatee on a fifteen year old boy. It was the color of blanched almonds and thin enough to be nearly transparent. "Without it the picture would seem too virginal. I want some tension in it."

"Well, I am a virgin, mostly." I had seen this before. Posing nude made some people come out of themselves and say very personal things. "Is tension good?"

"It is in painting. Not so good in relationships."

I began mixing some washes to block in her outlines. "Mostly a virgin?" I said. I didn't think I wanted to hear this story, but I didn't want to seem indifferent, either.

"I've tried it a couple times, but I think I must be too small. It just hurt and it wasn't any fun." She opened her knees. The long narrow hollows on her inner thighs were perfect wells of shadow. I felt like her doctor.

"Lynn, sometimes a guy can be too big." So much for businesslike.

"Anyone would have been. It's just me." Resignation. It was clearly not the first thing that was her fault.

"Can you open your eyes a little more?"

I started sketching her onto the canvas, mostly looking at her face, but I was thinking about her chest. I didn't want to paint each rib individually, although I could count them all. Maybe I could do the shadows where the bottom edge of her rib cage curved away from the sternum and subtly highlight the fingers of bone under the skin. This was not going to be easy, but it could turn into a forceful and disturbing picture.

In art lingo, "disturbing" is good, something like "edgy." I usually stop short of "shocking." It calls too much attention to itself.

"Could you separate your fingers a little as they rest on your cheeks? So that the little finger of each hand is right at the corners of your mouth and there's a space between each of the others? It makes good shadows for me. Right. And then your thumbs are down at the base of your neck, like they would be inside your collar, if you had one. Perfect."

"You're so intense, the way you look at me."

"I'm trying to see you. It's what I have to do."

"You know exactly what you want, don't you?" Her pale eyes regarded me coolly.

"Not usually right away, but in your case pretty fast. The way you're made offers a lot of possibilities. Since this is a first sitting, I get to pick the most promising pose right away."

"Do you like it?"

"Very much. For painting. Maybe we could do another one after this. I'm thinking of a side view because I like your profile, with your legs drawn up, arms around your knees pulling them close to your body. Face looking toward me with your chin on your shoulder, hair straight down your back on one side and over your chest on the other."

"My dad would kill me if he knew I was doing this."

"How would he know?"

"He wouldn't. He's got a lot on his mind right now. Did you know he's Vice President Brendel's driver? That's why I was in line."

"Our newest resident?"

"He's driven for him for years; we used to live in Topeka."

"So what is it you like about her?" said my Méxican live-in girlfriend, Maya, as I cleaned up after dinner. She leaned against the counter with her arms folded. "When she is sideways you don't see her unless she moves." Maya had popped into the studio at the end of the session and startled Lynn. She liked to come into the studio, put her hands on my shoulders in a proprietary way, and look over my shoulder at the model.

"That's what it is. I can see her bones even through her clothes. Her skin and hair are transparent. No blood comes to the surface. I don't think she could blush. She's a waif."

"Waif?"

"A lost child. It's the challenge of capturing that quality."

"I think she is strange. She is not beautiful like me or Barbara. I always understood about Barbara because I knew you wanted to be in bed with her. But this one? She is like water; if you touched her she would slip through your hands."

"I can see why you say that, but looking at her I only see the angles and planes. Despite the frail look, there's a real solidity to her. I'm not going to smooth her out and round her over. It's a much different quality of flesh from yours. It's one flat shape laid against another."

"So flat is good?"

"It can be, but not in your case." Neither of us said any more and I was glad to let it go.

After the dishes were finished I borrowed Maya's laptop and plugged into the Internet. I'd been trying all through dinner to remember the career of Malcolm Brendel and especially his fall from power. Maya was no help; being twenty-eight years old and having lived her entire life in México, she had never heard of him. But the Internet never forgets, and it did not disappoint on the subject of the former vice president.

What I learned was that when Brendel started out as a Baptist lay preacher in Salina, Kansas, he had a degree in political science, but no Bible college training, and an inspired gift with words. He rapidly attracted a substantial following. It was during a series of tent revivals in the southwestern part of the state that he was electrocuted by an improperly grounded microphone.

He was later said to have interpreted his revival by a woman in the audience as an act of God.

His resurrection experience, although deeply moving to the crowd, had the effect on Brendel of moving him toward another career, perhaps having also read it as more of a warning than an epiphany. Using a suitcase full of cash contributions to his ministry, he folded his tent, sold his tour bus, enrolled in law school, passed the bar in due course, and went into politics.

Thus reborn, a brief stint on the city council in Wichita, buoyed by his rhetorical gifts, landed him in the mayor's office, and six years later he was elected governor of Kansas.

I printed most of this out to show Maya, because I

could hardly believe it.

At the end of two terms as governor he was tapped as running mate by a Republican former governor of California who was seeking geographical balance for his ticket. The presidential candidate privately regarded Brendel as a gifted buffoon, but an enthusiastic campaigner.

Malcolm Brendel had not been an inactive chief executive of Kansas. Aside from minor duties like managing highway construction, educational reform, and health and welfare programs, he took the greatest pains with the Department of Natural Resources and the State Board of Zoning and Appeals. By the time he left for Washington, state-owned property in Kansas had been reduced by three-quarters and the zoning laws effectively gutted. In the process he became rich. Malcolm Brendel saw himself as a talented facilitator. He was a man who got things done. The Republican president, having experienced Brendel's entrenched egotism and having heard more rumors about the shadier side of his Kansas career, saw him as a pain in the ass, with the increasing potential to become a major liability at reelection. By the end of his first term the president no longer needed any balance in geography; he could do no wrong. Even blue collar Democrats loved him. It was the president's concern for his legacy, and for having a vice president who might be electable to succeed him, that brought down Malcolm Brendel.

At the behind-the-scenes urging of a presidential aide, a decision was made at the Department of Justice. It was not difficult to find contractors and developers and land speculators who had sat across the desk in the governor's office in Topeka and passed him envelopes of cash. A few were summoned before a federal grand jury and the transcripts of their devastating testimony shown to Brendel in a closed door meeting with the Attorney General. All were given immunity for their testimony.

In the face of a string of indictments that would have brought hard time had they gone to trial, the vice president resigned, returned over a million dollars in bribes to the court, and pled guilty to a single charge of mail fraud, a crime he could not actually remember committing. He received a suspended sentence. The other charges were dropped, but he was disbarred. His dream of being the first president of the United States to have risen from the dead was dashed. It would have been a memorable combination.

The detective business, as it developed, had become for me much like eating peanuts, or, in my case, pistachios; you couldn't eat just one. The hand reaching for the next one took on a will of its own. I knew there had to be something brewing with Malcolm Brendel. He was exempt from the normal morality that lubricated human interaction, his eyes perennially fixed on the main chance. He had joined, even while still alive, that cheesy pantheon of disgraced ex-vice presidents, the Spiro Agnews and the Aaron Burrs of history. I knew I was going to have to find out what he was up to, even if it didn't pay anything.

"Maya!"

"What? I am drying my hair."

"I just want you to know who your new neighbor is." I slammed the sheets down on the computer desk.

"You are not going to believe this. It will confirm everything you ever thought about gringos."

"Really? I hope he is not corrupt, because our politics are so clean here in México. It would be a bad example." The bathroom was not far from the desk and she came out as far as the dryer cord allowed. I rolled my desk chair over the rest of the way. There was something about the way she smelled just out of the shower, and she was wearing only a towel. It made me want to nibble her in obscure places.

The following morning Lynn arrived at eight, again carrying her overnight bag. Maya brought her up to the studio and then left for the archive in Dolores Hidalgo. She was researching a book on the role of different Indian groups in the Independence movement of 1810, compared with the revolution of 1910, for a history professor at the University of New Mexico.

"I've got something sweet for you," Lynn said, emerging from behind the screen and pulling off the nightgown with no hesitation. I didn't try to guess what it was. She was much more relaxed this morning. Yesterday's shyness was entirely gone and she gave me her little girl smile as she sat down on the cold metal seat of the folding chair, and then immediately jumped up again.

"Ooh! That's frosty."

"Let me warm it up for you. Sit behind the easel. My chair has a cushion." So we changed positions and I had a chance to see what the sitter sees. I put my elbows on my thighs and rested my chin in my hands. My knees were eight inches apart, and I imagined myself nude. It was not that comfortable.

"The vice president is looking for a portrait! He asked my dad to find a painter for him. You've done portraits, right? He thought I might ask around at the Bellas Artes when my writing class starts, but of course, I thought of you right away. Obviously, I didn't say what we're doing. I only said I'd run into you at the house sale. Are you interested?"

"I've done a ton of them. My portfolio is full of slides. How old is he?"

"Early seventies, I think."

"So he's old enough now to have interesting lines in his face."

"I think so."

We changed positions again and without touching her I got her body arranged correctly. "I can see you're more comfortable today, but let's not have as many smiles. Yesterday you looked like you were amazed that you were doing this. I'd like to have that expression again."

"So you'll do it?"

"I'd like to meet him, so we can size each other up. He may not like me, or I might not like him. It happens."

"Do you like me?" She smiled again.

"Very much. I'm enjoying this, and when I enjoy a picture it shows. I end up painting more freely."

"You don't think I'm too bony?"

"You're all planes and angles. The Cubists would have loved you; I could see you modeling for Picasso."

"But for you?" I wondered where this was going.

"It's forcing me to alter my style a bit, but it's always good to stretch. When I saw you in line I was taken with the innocence in your face, and that's why I wanted to paint you. I didn't have any sense of your body under the poncho and the baggy overalls."

"Were you disappointed?"

There was no answer to this that wouldn't lead to something awkward. "Not at all. In this picture you're going to be beautiful, but not conventional. If I can make it work, your face will have mystery, your hands and feet will have grace, and your body will have intimacy and vulnerability." That seemed to satisfy her. It would satisfy me as well, if I could pull it off.

"Will the vice president be beautiful too?"

"He'll be what he is." I didn't add that I believed I already knew what that was.

# Chapter 2

Lynn's father called for me in a black Lincoln Town Car with smoked windows and the kind of finish that repels dust. I had wanted to walk, since the vice president lived just four blocks away, but apparently you didn't call on him without a minimum of ceremony. The Lincoln was more than a little out of context as a small cart full of *flor de callabazas* pulled by a patient burro plodded past, clattering on the cobblestones.

"I'm Stephen Washburn," he said as he opened the rear door for me." I think you've met my daughter. She saw your work at Galeria Uno. Maybe she told you." He wore an immaculate gray livery with gloves and a driver's cap. It didn't suit his light coloring. He should have had something in a bolder cut and color, with some of the impressive flaps and epaulets that the Germans knew so well how to use in World War II.

I set my portfolio on the soft black leather beside me and we moved off toward Cuadrante. There was good light this morning, but I didn't expect much of it penetrated the vice president's great house on the western edge of *centro,* except in the rear garden. As we pulled through the carriage gate, Washburn turned and said, "You'll find him in a good mood this morning. That's not always the case. Let him do most of the talking; he doesn't listen all that well."

"He's hard of hearing?"

"No. It's a choice he makes. It's his personal style. If you let him, he'll talk right over you."

"Lynn said you've been driving for him a long time."

"Eighteen years. I've seen him in every possible condition."

Stephen Washburn brought me in through the carriage door at the side of the house and asked me to wait in the library. The classic original eighteenth-century furniture of John Schleicher, the previous owner, was all gone; in its place were modern reproductions, expensive probably, but machine-made, and therefore greatly out of character with the house itself. The bookcases, which had been filled floor to ceiling with books in matched sets when I was there before the sale, now had most of the shelves removed. The tongue-and-groove backs were covered with the sort of photographs displayed in restaurants frequented by celebrities.

Here was Malcolm Brendel shaking hands with President Reagan; in another he sat at a long banquet table across from Margaret Thatcher, champagne glasses between them. Below, a much younger Brendel grinned between Peter Lawford and Sammy Davis Jr. Very much in the Kennedy tradition, for a Republican.

On the adjacent panels he posed with Frank Sinatra at the side of a white grand piano, then with Charlton Heston in hunting clothes, and in a tuxedo with an uncomfortable Richard Nixon who looked as if his teeth didn't fit. Next to that he was in a Pebble Beach golf shirt on the tenth green with an amiably dense Gerald Ford. Farther down in the cases was Brendel with four or five impressive Méxican businessmen. Every picture was autographed and identically framed. I wondered if mine would soon be up there. I'd have to practice my signature.

I turned when I heard the door close softly behind me. For this meeting I had put on chinos with a collar shirt and sport jacket, rather formal for me, but the elegance of Malcolm Brendel's wardrobe made me feel like I was wearing a clown suit stitched together from old gym socks. Even the zipper in his pants was probably custom made. He smelled just as fresh as Maya but it didn't make me want to nibble him.

"We won't stand on ceremony here, Mr. Zacher. You may address me as 'Sir.'" He waved me over to one of two wing chairs by the fireplace. "I understand you have a background in portraiture." His voice echoed the richness of the mahogany paneling that surrounded us as he sat across from me. But elegant doesn't always mean classy and his manner was already beginning to grate on me. I sat in a tufted leather chair that had polished brass tacks all around the edges and put my fingers together. The room smelled too new, like a furniture store.

"I've been doing portraits here in San Miguel for about eleven years, although I do a variety of other subjects as well. I've done three of the city's mayors and nearly twenty of the more prominent expatriates here. I'm accustomed to working full length or three-quarter, standing or seated, and it usually takes between eight and fifteen sittings." Before he could answer I added,

"I also recently did a fanciful portrait of Zorro for a book cover." Maybe that would be the hook. I made this entire speech in Spanish, speaking as rapidly as I could. I knew I had him. I moved the portfolio across the coffee table toward him, but he didn't pick it up.

He looked at me carefully for the first time, as if he might have to size me up a little. He had a narrow, aristocratic face and most of his hair, now iron gray, which I thought of as Presbyterian because each strand was in its preordained position. His brown eyes were clear and sharply focused, and the lids did not droop, as if he'd had them done. He shook his head slightly, suggesting that I was going to have to do better than that.

"I wouldn't have come here if I hadn't done my homework, Mr. Zacher. My Spanish is not perfect, but it progresses rapidly. My language tutor comes three times a week, and my valet speaks no English and wouldn't learn it even if I asked him. I normally wouldn't accept that kind of insubordination, but I'm determined to deal with him on his own terms." He had threaded his way through the minefield of Spanish verb tenses perfectly, but not rapidly, pausing just a fraction of a second before each one to be sure of it. For the first time he smiled broadly. "You see, I intend to fit right in here." He leaned toward me as he said this and I could see a flash of the old charm that had made him such a successful preacher and politician, up to the point of his precipitous fall. I wondered what he'd been doing since.

Somewhere in the house a clock began to chime.

"I would prefer to hold the sittings away from this house, so that I am inaccessible to interruption." The magisterial manner resumed. "I assume you have a suitable place, a studio where you normally work. I don't wish to be bothered with fees or schedules; please arrange all that with Washburn." His hand cut though the space between us in a dismissive gesture. "He is also my secretary. I'll say good day now." He hadn't looked at the portfolio and I was now dismissed myself. He got up and did not offer to shake hands. He had probably already touched more than his share of commoners in his time and knew what they felt like.

Washburn appeared in the doorway a moment later and we went out through the wide hallway, which was rag-rolled in the tones of old parchment, and hung with elegant engravings and ancient maps in dark lacquered frames. None of these had belonged to John Schleicher.

Again I wanted to walk, but he had been instructed to drive me, so I had him take me down to the *jardín*, our main plaza. I said goodbye after we had arranged the terms for the portrait and watched him glide back into the traffic. I wanted to sit on one of the cast-iron benches under the sculpted trees for a while and catch my breath next to the fountain. Oxygen had been scarce in the house, and although it usually did not bother me, this town is already at 6400 feet. After a while I bought a Havana cigar under the arches and wandered over to El Pegaso for a plate of their Thai beef salad and a Negra Modelo. As I ate I remembered Lynn saying that her father was worried about what Brendel was up to. Had it taken Washburn eighteen years to reach this point, or was he worried the entire time?

When I got home Maya was still in Dolores Hidalgo and I dialed my friend *Licenciado* Diego Delgado of the Judicial Police.

"I hope your family is well," I said. "I need some help from you today,"

"Always we of the *Policia Judicial* are here to help, *Señor* Zacher. But for you, especially." Information I supplied had gotten him sprung from an undeserved prison sentence back in June, and his family connection to the deputy mayor had helped him recover his place in the branch of the police force that handled investigations and prosecutions. In México, this is part of the court system.

"I am sure you are aware of the American vice president moving here. I would like to know what he paid for the Schleicher house on Cuadrante. The number is 13A. Is there a real estate record office here that will tell you? Or maybe they would even tell me?"

He hesitated for just a second. "I can get that, but you will not have heard it from me, you will understand this?"

"It will be as a whisper on the wind." I didn't know if that was a Méxican phrase, but it sounded like it ought to be. After *twelve* years here I'd gotten a certain feel for the language. I poured myself a cognac, and lit the cigar, and settled out in the garden near the fountain in the perfume of the orange blossoms while I waited. There are worse places than central México. The part of Ohio I came from is one of them.

Ten minutes later my cell phone rang.

"I have that information for you," *Licenciado* Delgado said. "The property at 13A Cuadrante was sold for five-million dollars."

"I'm surprised he could afford that." But I was not surprised at the price. Premium properties in San

Miguel de Allende often sold for millions. The real estate market here was dominated by the expatriates, often funded by Texas oil money. I wondered how Brendel could afford it, after having to pay back much of his bribe money from Kansas. There had to be someone else behind the purchase. I realized that the compulsion to probe deeper had become part of my persona. Maya would have said it was not the best one.

"But it was not the Vice President Brendel who bought this house," said Delgado as I tried to frame my next question.

"No?"

"The purchaser was a large company called Dos Cerros. They are very big all over México; oil exploration and property development, mostly."

"Two zeros?"

"No, *cerros*." He rolled the double R better than I could. "Two Hills, as you would say up in Gringolandia."

"Would they typically buy a private home, even one so historic?"

"No. They would normally be buying undeveloped land, and not usually so far inland as we are here in the bajio. They own resorts in many of the beach communities. Also they are somewhat unusual because the owners are two brothers who are evangelical Protestants. They make no secret of this, even though here we are mostly Catholic, as you know."

"Is there something questionable about them?"

"Perhaps not, but they do business with much *fuerza*. One does not wish to oppose them if it can be avoided; it is said they have the ear of *el presidente*. If you are planning to be a thorn of someone's side again, *Señor* Zacher, you would do well to choose another this time."

"Thank you, *Licenciado*."

"It is nothing."

I blew a smoke ring and sat there for a while thinking of the pale innocence of Lynn Washburn framed by the increasingly sinister aura collecting around 13A Cuadrante. Of course, she was living there now, sleeping in some top-floor staff bedroom in that touchingly faded blue flannel night gown, or moving from room to room among the expensive but unconvincing reproduction furniture. The day I met her in line at the estate sale she had probably been scoping out her new residence. I had told her father that my portrait fee was $10,000, twice the usual, because I foresaw the possibility that Brendel would prove to be a prima donna, and I had the feeling now that I was going to earn all of it.

I had the $5,000 deposit in my pocket, but hadn't looked closely at it when I got it; that would have been bad manners. After all, this was an art contract, not a supermarket transaction. I set down the cigar and pulled out the check. The name printed on it was Dos Cerros, with an address in Veracruz below. On the line beneath it said, "Special Projects Account," in smaller type. It seemed like a good choice of words. The signature was that of Malcolm Brendel, done with a broad flourish in violet ink with a fountain pen. It had the same weight and style as the signatures on the Declaration of Independence.

So Brendel was now associated with Dos Cerros, and he didn't mind who knew it. Was it oil? I couldn't see how that would connect to his past experience, unless he'd been anointing people and needed new sources of supply, but then, neither did property development.

The phone rang again and I picked it up, thinking that Delgado had forgotten something that might help me connect the dots, but it was Barbara Watt, our wealthy and quite delectable twenty-eight-year-old widowed friend from up the hill. Perhaps she was ready to have me paint her again. I certainly was.

"Paul, darlin,' it's me. I've had a great idea. Would you be willing to give me painting lessons?"

"And create all kinds of competition for myself? Would that be good business?"

"Darlin,' anything with me would be good business, you know that." Or risky business, I thought. "I want to do something more serious with my life than just collecting. As you know, anybody with money can collect."

"And taste, there's that. Well, the place to start, if you're serious, is with some supplies. Do you want to go with me to Lagundi this afternoon, say around three? I've got to get some things too. I'm out of medium."

"Great. I'll pick you up."

I had just locked my door that afternoon when Barbara pulled up in her silver Mercedes. She got out and left the driver door open for me while she got in the passenger side.

"Humor me," she said. "I need to be driven sometimes." She was wearing black capris and a silk sleeveless top in a cool shade of pink, but not quite to lavender. It set off her honey blond hair perfectly.

"You need a big strapping guy in your life," I said, closing the door. "I've brought along my travel easel for you to borrow; in case you don't stay with it, you can give it back to me." She slid her left hand up and down my thigh.

"You've got my number."

"That's true enough." I eased into the afternoon traffic and turned toward the *jardín*. "I've got to stop for some cash."

"I need some too."

"I don't think of you as needing cash."

"Do you think I keep it all in bags under the bed?" Actually, I knew she kept it in a drawer in her dressing room.

"If you did you'd need a ladder to get to the mattress."

Under the arcade in the front wall of the bank were automatic teller machines built into the stucco facade of Banamex, the old Canal family townhouse facing the *jardin*. I stood behind her and looked at the perfect skin of her neck. Her hair was piled up to display her pearl tear drop earrings, but a few fine wisps escaped. Suddenly I felt someone touch my elbow and I turned to see a slender Méxican man with a San Miguel map in his hand.

"Excuse me, *señor*," he said, "could you tell me where the post office is?"

"Of course," I said. "You won't need the map. Go straight along under the arches to the corner, turn left, and it's two blocks up."

*"Muchas gracias."* He refolded the map and stuck it in his back pocket as he walked up the sidewalk. My directions had been more precise than a lot of natives would have given him, but even so, why hadn't he asked a native? In my experience in San Miguel, most

Méxicans would not approach a gringo for directions, not because of any mistrust, but only that a lot of gringos didn't bother to learn the language well and giving directions would be beyond their capability. Barbara lifted a handful of peso notes out of the machine and I took her place.

"I like your hair like that. I know it's your work mode now, but I remember it that way from your wedding picture up in the study."

"I wore it like this all through college. But it looks best let down and spread out on a pillow. I'll show you sometime." She gave me an appraising look.

"I'll take your word for it." This had been going on for some time. I didn't mind, keeping a little distance made me feel virtuous.

Lagundi is down about a block on Umaran from the *jardín*, and we left the car around the corner by the bank and walked over. With the help of a college girl at the counter we located a starter set of Winsor and Newton oil paints, student grade, a pack of six 14" by 18" inch canvases mounted on cardboard, and a small palette. I added bottles of brush cleaner, thinner, and medium, plus two palette knives and a spread of eight hog bristle brushes ranging from small to fairly big.

"Aren't we going to need some of the really tiny ones?"

"Save those for later. It's too easy to get ditzy when you're starting out, caught up in the detail."

"No one ever called me ditzy."

"And with the correct brushes, no one ever will."

I picked out a few things for myself and we left.

She held my hand as we walked back to the car

and I carried the supplies. I figured she'd be touching something and my hand seemed harmless enough. The shops around us were painted in shades of cinnamon, lemon, coral, indigo, ochre, and a dozen others. Most had shallow wrought iron balconies at the second floor level, when they had one.

"What are you working on now? This lesson isn't going to interfere, is it?"

"I've got another nude going; it's different from yours."

"But not as interesting as I was?"

"Not nearly, but it has a feel unlike anything I've done before. She's very slender, probably too much so for her own good."

"I know that kind; scared to death of body fat. She probably doesn't even have a period."

"I didn't ask her. I don't have to know everything to get it right. Anyway, it's all because she's so angular. She's blond, but more ashy and pale than you, and her hair is thin and flat. It makes me think of Michelle Phillips of the Mamas and the Papas. That ironed look, parted in the middle. But she's connected too; her father is the driver for Malcolm Brendel. I suppose you know he bought John Schleicher's house."

She nodded, but with a funny look on her face.

"So it turns out that Brendel wants a portrait," I went on, "and guess who's been asked to do it?"

"Not the Leonardo of San Miguel?"

"Exactly."

"Well, I've got a surprise for you too, then. The American consul called me and asked if I would be willing to host a dinner in the vice president's honor.

I was thrilled because I thought with all the scandal about Perry I might be left out of the social loop for a while."

We reached the car and drove off on Correo to go up the hill.

"Will you and Maya come?" she continued. "It'll be great that you already know him. And I thought I'd ask Cody to co-host it with me, since I don't have anyone right now. He can sit at the other end of the table. It's going to be a week from Saturday."

Cody Williams was my retired detective friend from Peoria. Vice presidential dinners were probably a bit rarified for his social experience, but at six-foot-three and around 240 pounds, he was sufficiently imposing to pull it off, given the right outfit.

"Can I wear my dark blue tee shirt that says STAFF on the back?"

"Not even if you work in the kitchen. But it's not formal at all. Any jacket is fine. Won't it be fun? The consul mainly wants to introduce Malcolm Brendel into the expatriate community."

"Didn't the consul think you might still be in mourning?"

"He did ask me that, but I said it had been more than eight months since Perry died and I was ready to gradually start coming out again."

"Right. Something small and intimate. How many can you seat in the dining room?"

"Just twenty-six. I suspect that's why he asked me. But you've already met him, right? Brendel, I mean."

"I spent part of this morning with him. He's very taken with himself."

"Wonderful! It'll be like when Perry was alive."

"Even more so, I think. Did you know that he rose from the dead?"

"That's certainly impressive." Her delicate eyebrows went up.

"Of course, he was much younger then. Be tougher to do now. He's seventy-three."

In Casa Watt, Barbara's massive neocolonial mansion in the Los Balcones neighborhood, we walked through the second floor rooms. I counted six bedrooms and six bathrooms, as well as the study, a laundry, room-sized closets off the main hallway for linens, off-season clothes, and furs. Barbara was not politically correct and a variety of animals had given their lives to keep her decent, not that it always worked. Any room bright and cheerful with the sun streaming in, I rejected. Because the long walls of the house faced east and west, there was only one bedroom on the far end with north light exclusively.

"This will be the best light for a studio," I said. "There's about a month in early summer when you'll get some direct sun in here, otherwise it's perfect."

"We never used this as a bedroom, even for guests, because it's the farthest from the staircase." She was looking at it doubtfully. Instead of a large four-poster bed like most of the others, it had a day bed along one wall. "But let's give it try. I can always change it if it doesn't work, right?"

She went off to change and I started setting up the travel easel near the windows. From the size of a small suitcase it unfolded into a modest easel large enough to handle anything she would be attempting until much later. The room had an unused feel, so I threw open both windows and looked out over the rim of the hill where a string of white and pastel villas moved off to the southeast. Garden walls were hung with vermilion and fuscia bougainvillea, and the scent of orange and lime blossoms rose on the breeze. Below and to the right I could just see the end of a pergola covered with trumpet vine and wisteria that shaded the tiled length of Barbara's veranda.

I unpacked the supplies and set them on the lamp table. In one corner was a faux marble pedestal, surprisingly light, which I thought must be used for flowers, and I moved it toward the center of the room.

Suddenly she was back wearing a pair of slightly worn jeans in a cut that was probably fashionable three years ago. They looked like they had been used for painting or gardening. The left leg had a short tear on the outside just above her knee. On top she had on an oversize tee shirt with a logo in front mostly covered by an apron that came nearly to her chin. I looked at her for a moment, touched to see her dressed down for once. It must be fun to wake up with her—not the first time I'd thought that.

"What?" she said.

"I like that look," I said. "That's all. You're usually so put together." She came over to me and put her arms around my neck.

"Should I get a STAFF tee shirt?"

"You could never be staff." I looked into her eyes and found myself in a place I had been a number of times before. Her lips were slightly parted and I could see the edges of her perfect teeth. She didn't move, but continued to look back into my eyes. Neither of us blinked.

"Let's find a subject," I said, aware that my lips were about four inches from hers.

"I thought we'd just found one. I believe you know what it is." Her voice held a note of determination.

"A painting subject, I mean."

Reluctantly she pulled away. "I thought I could start with some flowers? I've got two new bouquets downstairs."

"That's what I call a suicide subject; it's guaranteed to frustrate you so much you'll never try to paint again."

"Really?"

"Trust me. You should start with something basic. How about one of the Mayan ceramics? There's a plain one in the shape of a shallow cylinder, some damage along the edge, with several interesting colors in the surface, but no figures. That would be a good start."

"Really? Why do I keep saying that? Shouldn't we start with something beautiful?"

"You only need the painting to be beautiful, and only then if that's your goal. You don't need the subject to be beautiful in itself." She left to get the Mayan piece, wearing flip-flops that slapped against the antique parquet floor salvaged from a Spanish castle.

We set it on the pedestal. "Let's not bump it," she said. "I know it's a fake, but I also know what Perry paid for it."

"Now let's take a close look at it," I said. "What do you see?"

"A pot with three legs. It's nothing more than a two-year-old pot pretending to be an antique. Not very romantic."

"OK. That's the last time we'll give a name to it. Remember when I was painting you nude and I said your body and face were just landscape?"

She nodded. "I thought you were being rude, talking about hills and valleys. But my landscape was a lot more interesting than this, I hope."

"Perhaps, but my point is that everything is just landscape, and since landscape can be about anything, it's easy to imagine that all we care about is the way light and shadow are distributed across it. That's how we know it. That's why we won't need to call it anything. We only care about what the light is doing. You're not painting a thing with a name here; you're painting light."

"But is there anything wrong with calling it something?"

"Yes, the part of your brain that needs names for things is not the same part that paints pictures, but it's too dominant. You need to establish a pathway from your eye to your hand without interference from the naming part. Painting is partly about learning a different way to think. Are you understanding me?"

"I guess so. How do I start?"

"I often start by identifying the darkest parts first. They anchor the picture for you. As you do this you will also be factoring in the colors in the lighter parts, so that when you mix paint for the shadows you don't simply use blacks or grays, you use complements that will emphasize your other colors."

"OK. I can see a long area of dark red, tending toward orange on the lower edge, and as it curves around the back of the...landscape, it darkens further as it disappears."

"Perfect. And the complement of these colors would be?"

"Some shade of green? Maybe more than one?"

"Exactly. So now you'll mix a thin wash of black and green to block that in. These two colors usually mix well together, but you don't want the green jumping out at the viewer; it's just there to pop the reds and oranges, which is closer to what your picture is about."

"When do I put the lines in?"

"Forget the lines. There will only be transitions from one area of color to another."

"This is certainly not what I expected."

"That's good, isn't it?"

I showed her how to mix the colors and thin them, and then I watched as she blocked things in. She didn't feel like she made any mistakes because she had no lines to stay within.

"One thing about starting with washes is that they dry rapidly and you can tweak the colors easily if they're a little off just by going over them again. It's much more forgiving than watercolors, which is where a lot of people start. But watch the light. Get the relative intensity of everything. Think about where you want people to look."

"This is so great! I'm really doing it." She brushed a wisp of hair from her forehead and left a streak of vermilion over one eyebrow. It didn't work well with her hair color.

"Good. You're starting to look the part. I'm going to show you how to clean the brushes now and then

I'll go. Try this several times this week. It's a good idea to paint things upside down if you're having trouble avoiding giving them a name."

I showed her the brush-cleaning routine.

"Do you think you can find your way out? I don't want to leave this, it's so great!" She kissed me on the cheek and I slipped out the door and down the hall. I don't think she heard me go. She was in the Zone.

# Chapter 3

That night I was almost asleep, or perhaps I had been for a while, since it was just after 1:00 A.M., when I thought I heard a noise in the garden. I looked over at Maya, not seeing her well, but I could hear the deep regular breathing that said she was asleep. The bedroom had long windows on two sides, two set back but facing Quebrada, the other two the garden. What I thought I heard was a rake, one that had been leaning against the garden shed along the back wall, falling over and striking the flagstones. There was even a slight bounce. We always kept the garden side windows open at least a crack, even in winter.

I slid the drawer of my night stand open silently and pulled out the .38 Cody had given me, sliding off the safety. Our front door was formidable and opened with a small squeak; I never oiled the hinges for this reason. But I had heard no squeak. I got out of bed without provoking any movement from Maya and crept downstairs. Barefoot, wearing only my boxer shorts and a T-shirt, I canvassed the downstairs. Nothing.

In the kitchen I checked the door to the *loggia*. Still locked. I eased the bolt open and went outside. Moonlight edged the fountain with silver and tipped the bromeliads with a ghostly light, but nothing moved. I started along the wall toward the garden shed and located the rake fallen across the path. Raising the gun, I opened the shed door and found no one inside. The silence was disquieting, but there was no reason to think anyone would want to steal anything from the garden.

I paused and listened intently. Was there the slightest hint of movement in the shrubs? Within the walls no breeze penetrated. I found myself wondering if my hearing was as good as it always been. There was a sudden memory of my father roughly sticking a washcloth into my ears after my nightly bath as a child. "I just want to make sure you can hear me when I tell you to do something," he always said. I always heard him well enough; telling me what to do constantly was one of the things I remembered most about childhood. I knew this was why I'd always be self-employed. I could never take orders from anyone again after I left home.

But this was not about my father. I made a circuit of the walls, my bare feet soundless on the path, thinking about Malcolm Brendel. I could have turned down the portrait commission, but I needed the money. I never knew when I'd hit a dry spell painting, or a show that flopped after what had looked like a productive period. The trick was to maintain my reserves. But there was something about Brendel, something about the entire set-up, that made me uneasy.

Finding no one in the garden, I decided it must have been an animal. But what animal could climb the stucco walls other than a lizard? But there was the bamboo climbing to five- or six feet above the top of the back wall. If something had gotten up from the other side, the bamboo provided a way down.

Eventually I took my uneasiness back toward the house with me, but as I reentered the *loggia* I noticed a pale rectangular form on the table, held down by a candle. I flipped on the lights and looked at it. On a single sheet of letter paper was the word *Asesino* (Murderer) in red felt marker. There was a line under it for emphasis. It was cool night, but I'd experienced no chills until I saw it. Now a wave of goose bumps came over me. I had killed only one man, a federal agent who was holding a gun to Maya's head during our last case. Were his associates now coming after me? When I got upstairs I left the gun out on the night stand. Maya would see it in the morning, and I'd tell her about the noise in the garden, but I planned to say nothing about the note, which I had folded and pushed to the back of the drawer.

"I warmed the chair for you. I didn't want you to freeze your butt again."

"Thank you." Lynn briskly pulled off the nightgown and sat down. It was the following morning, and I had slept fairly well, considering the message in the garden. I helped her resume the pose and then went behind the easel. "Why don't you ever touch me? You're very careful about that," she said. Here we go, I thought.

"I don't touch models, not even Maya when she poses."

"But you touch her later." She smiled as if she now

knew my secret.

"Frequently."

"You're a person of principle."

"No. I hate principle. Not very long ago I killed a man who was acting on principle. He had tortured and then murdered a friend of mine. Someone I respected very much. When I shot him he was holding a gun to Maya's head. That's where principle can take you." It was still on my mind. *Asesino.*

That silenced her for a while as she digested it. The look on her face was perfect, but I had already painted it. Her narrow cheeks and soft mouth with its thin, almost colorless lips, the pale eyes looking straight ahead, curious. The eyebrows nearly invisible. The transition from skin to hair had been difficult. The color change was so subtle I had added shadows that weren't there.

"I guess I'm kind of shocked to hear that, coming from a painter. I guess art is a tough business," she said after a moment.

"It can be, but not because of that."

"Do you want to tell me more?"

"No."

"Do you even want to touch me?"

"I thought you didn't like sex?"

"Maybe it could be better."

"You're sweet, Lynn. But maybe what you're feeling is something I call studio intimacy. Imagine that you are posing nude in a life drawing class at the Bellas Artes. Spread out around you in a half circle are fifteen students of both sexes, each drawing you from a slightly different angle. You wouldn't relate to any of them; your mind would be numbed, and somewhere far away, isolated. But here it's just the two of us, so we have a relationship."

I paused as I worked and looked at her face, but she didn't comment.

"You can't help but connect with me, and me with you; we can't ignore each other. It feels intimate since you trust me. You tell me things about yourself that you might not tell other people, just as you don't appear nude before other people. What's happening up at the great house?" I was working on her thighs.

"Lots of comings and goings with important people. Black Mercedes and Suburbans with chauffeurs. People from México City, I think. Big, pale-skinned, and mostly handsome. Like you see on TV here."

"You can tell where they're from by their license plates."

"Every weekday morning before lunch my father takes the vice president up onto a hill a couple miles outside of town."

"Where he ascends into heaven?"

"No! What an odd thing to say. There's a radio station there and a broadcast tower."

"What happens then?"

"He makes a tape. It's going to be five tapes a week."

"What kind of tape?"

"Dad doesn't know. It happens inside a sealed room with a red light above the door. Dad waits outside in the car. When Mr. Brendel comes out he's all worked up."

"Hard to imagine, but I guess he was a preacher at one time."

"Dad says there's something snaky going on. He doesn't know what."

"You could do something for me."

"I thought I was already. I don't take my clothes off for everybody."

"You are. But I was hoping you could be my eyes and ears up at the house. I think your dad is on to something and I want to know more. Specifically, I want to know why Malcolm Brendel settled in San Miguel. I have a feeling there's something going on beyond just another expatriate coming down here. It's got my detective juices flowing."

"I can do that. Did you know there's a woman with him?"

"No, is that unusual?"

"Well, Dad said Mr. Brendel was divorced. And the woman is local, I think, just from the way she talks."

"What's her name?"

"Juana Cardenas. She and the vice president are constantly doing it. My bedroom is right over his, and I can hear them. She's a screamer."

"Really." I paused, brush in hand. I was trying to picture Brendel unbending that much.

"I have my own name for her. It's kind of crude."

"What's that?"

"Juana Fuck."

This caught me by surprise.

"What's she like?"

"About thirty-five, medium height; attractive, I guess, maybe well used and a little bit fleshy in the middle. I think she's been around the block a few times."

"Fleshy compared to you?"

"Yes. Of course, most women would be. And I think she's a phony."

"You're not just feeling protective of Brendel?"

"No, it's because of the way she acts. She sucks up to him a lot, as if everything is about pleasing him."

"Maybe it is. He's awfully demanding, and full of himself. It sounds like she's perfect for him."

"Maybe." She was biting her lip.

"Did your dad tell you I made a deal to do Brendel's portrait?"

"No. Really?"

"Yes. It's because of your input, so thank you. Now we're probably done for today."

I went over to the platform. "I think I'm going to touch you now," I said, and held out my hand. She put her palm in mine with a ladylike gesture and pulled herself up. With my other hand I gave her the nightgown. She held it up to her neck for a moment, not lifting it over her head.

"I think you really see me," she said.

"I need to, in order to do this."

"But, differently, somehow."

"Not differently. I only see you. Others don't. I sell vision by the square foot." I watched her bones move as she walked toward the screen. She kept the nightgown on her arm.

"Tell me something," she asked at the door a few minutes later. "Do you ask a lot of girls to pose nude for you?"

"Not a lot. Mainly only when I see something I haven't encountered before that might work on canvas."

"Do they all say yes?"

"Not even half. But even when they say no they're still flattered."

Most of them, anyway. But none of them has ever hit me with her purse.

After dinner we were sitting in the *loggia*. I could see Maya had something on her mind. She was usually chatty while we ate. I thought she was going to ask me about Lynn again. She still didn't understand my reasons for wanting to paint her, although I had tried to explain them. In the fading light she was staring at the young banana tree we had recently planted by the south wall. It was trying to decide whether to grow or die.

"My family is coming," she said, in the same tone she would have used for, "I've been sentenced to death by firing squad by the new revolutionary government."

I don't panic much, so it was easy to keep my voice neutral. "When?"

"I'm not sure. They're on a road trip now. Puebla, Cuernavaca, Querétaro, Guanajuato. San Miguel, of course. When they get here depends on how long they stay in each place. My father likes to be spontaneous when he's not working. They won't stay long; they don't care much for San Miguel because of all the gringos."

"Just your father and your stepmother?"

"And Soledad."

"We knew I'd have to meet them sooner or later. How old is Soledad now?"

"Nineteen."

Maya's mother had died when she was five and Soledad had come early to her father's marriage to Cassandra, a woman who worked for him at Pemex, the Méxican national oil company.

"What are they like?"

"My father works hard, so when he's on vacation he tries equally hard to relax. I think he will make a point of being cordial to you. Cassandra is ten years younger, early forties now. Still attractive, but she and I were never close. Soledad was her pretty baby, the one she always wanted."

"How did she turn out?"

"Soledad is trouble. She went to three different high schools. Now she is at the university in México City and I don't know how it goes, but there are probably still too many boyfriends. When I am home visiting, she and I fight all the time. She likes to think she can outdo me in everything." She shook her head slowly at the absurdity of it.

"So she's going for a Ph.D. in history to beat your master's degree?"

"No, she's going to major in fashion merchandising. I don't think I want them here in the middle of our life right now, but they are family. You know how it is in México."

"Yes."

"There is one bad thing that will make you mad."

"What?"

"You can't be living here when they come." Before I could say anything, she added, "I know it's your house. Don't tell me about that."

"So I should put on my old painting clothes and sit in a doorway down by the *Jardin,* holding out a cup to the tourists?"

"You could do that, or you might go stay with Cody. He has a big sofa." She gave me her best smile.

"Wouldn't it be easier to just tell them we live together? It's been five years. He's probably figured it out already. Besides, no one who looks like you could still be a virgin at twenty-eight."

"Thank you, but I can't do it."

"Maya, he's not even religious. What could be the objection?"

"He's still my father. You don't understand what it's like to be a daughter."

"What about the studio? Are you going to pretend to be a painter?"

"I will say I rent it to you because your place is too small to have one. We'll just have to move out some of your clothes. I know this is not fair, but I'll find a way to make it up to you. Maybe we could use the handcuffs again?"

"It's a deal."

The next morning I went by the condo of our retired Peoria cop friend Cody to see if he needed a roommate for a couple of days. It was an extra gun of his I had taken out to the garden the night of the *asesino* note. The place occupied the third floor of a newer building near Prolongacion Aldama. The builder had decorated it in what realtors called "neutral decor," meaning white walls and beige tile counters. There were the obligatory beams on the ceilings. Rather than get more intense with colors, Cody had chosen mementoes from his past to decorate the walls; a couple of citations for bravery and an award from some civic group for saving a child from drowning. He never talked about that, but the presence of the award indicated he was proud of it.

Facing a substantial TV set, the seating was mostly black leather and over the gas fireplace mantel was a small oil sketch of an Indian boy on a burro I had given him one year for his birthday. On the opposite wall, adjacent to the kitchen, he had hung a framed poster of the pyramids at Chichen Itza. Overall, the place made no statement other than "Here I am for a while." He had just made a fresh pot of coffee, and we sat out on his balcony and watched the traffic snaking through the narrow street beyond his garden wall.

"I heard you've got a new model these days," he said. "One whose charms are not quite fully formed."

"Her name's Lynn Washburn and she's legal. Where did you hear that?"

"I ran into Maya at the English Library yesterday. She was taking out a few crime novels. So tell me about her. Maya thinks you're getting kinky. How old is this girl exactly?"

"Twenty, going on twelve."

"And she weighs only forty pounds?"

"Maybe a hundred."

"Eating disorder?"

"I don't know, but it has occurred to me. Maybe I'll feed her something one of these days and see what she does. But she is definitely not a model that Rubens would have used. If she has an ounce of fat I haven't been able to locate it, and I've tried."

"But you like her."

"I do. She does waif-like innocence better than anyone I've ever seen. It's like she's kept her childhood face. I've taken that quality and made the picture rather provocative. It's working so far. Interestingly, her father is driver and secretary to Malcolm Brendel. And now because of that connection I'm going to do Brendel's portrait."

"No waif-like quality there. You're not old enough to remember him, but he's a piece of work. Rose from the dead, you know." He looked at me over his cup and then picked a couple of dead leaves off a struggling succulent next to the rail. I tried to think what it might be like to have that always be the first thing people said about you.

"It's worked for other people," I said. "Not recently though. I did some research on him. To say he's colorful is like saying Jackson Pollock's drippy. But here's something else; I got a check for the deposit signed by Brendel and drawn on the account of an outfit called Dos Cerros. I talked to Delgado about them and, in so many words, he said run for cover."

"Never heard of them. Delgado would probably know, though. He's always got his ear to the ground."

"I think Brendel's up to something funny. Feel like taking a look at it? It would be *pro bono*."

"I was never any good at Latin, but back in my cop days *pro bono* usually meant up to no good."

"Something like that. Anyway, no one's hired us yet and no one's likely to. It's just ordinary snooping. I can't rationalize it beyond saying that I know that he's up to something and it piques my curiosity. Lynn's going to be my mole in his house."

"And because you're doing his portrait you feel justified in digging further?"

"Just part of getting it right. You have to know your subject. But I was already interested before the portrait offer came up. Delgado also told me that Dos Cerros bought the house for him, for five million."

"Ouch! Not pesos?"

"No, not pesos."

"I see your point. Count me in. I think I can smell something here too."

Then I told him about Maya's family visit and my impending homelessness and he showed me where he kept his extra blankets.

"Maybe we could put each other's hair up and make s'mores," I said.

When I got out of the artmobile back on Quebrada, I was stunned to see Maya dashing in and out of the house dumping suitcases on the sidewalk and piles of my clothes on top of them.

"So it's come to this," I said.

"Come to what? They're going to be here in two hours. Throw this stuff in the van and get rid of that outrageous picture upstairs. And don't bring that *flaca* (skinny girl) over here again until after they leave."

"It's not kinky, it's just a different look." I said over my shoulder, loading the clothes in the van, but she was already back inside. I went up to the studio and carefully slid the Lynn Washburn picture into the storage slots, avoiding any contact with the wet paint. Then I made a quick walkthrough, but there was nothing else incriminating. Lynn had remembered to take the blue flannel nightgown with her.

As Maya pushed me out the front door she said, "Dinner's at seven. You're invited. And don't wear that damned STAFF tee shirt!"

Here in San Miguel the quickest way to indelibly mark yourself as a gringo is to show up on time, even at your own house. If the invitation was for seven., the Sanchez family would probably appear at about seven-thirty, never earlier. I arrived at seven-forty, not wanting to get there before them and have it seem like I was co-hosting the party. As I rang the bell I was staring over my shoulder at a very clean Chevy SUV with México City plates. I knew I had timed it right. Maya came to the door with a not quite genuine look of welcome. "Paul, I'm so glad you could come." She'd never make it on the stage.

"Thanks for inviting me."

She led me into the living room and Ruben Sanchez rose to shake hands. He was a lean, handsome man, nearly as tall as I am, with graying hair and a deep cleft in his square chin. In Maya's face the cleft had migrated northward and divided into a smaller, delicate dimple in each cheek.

Maya introduced me all around. Ruben wore dark, carefully pressed slacks and a tan short-sleeved cotton shirt. "*Mucho gusto,*" he said. "I have heard much about your work from Maya." He gave me a broad smile. Maya stood by with her hands gripping her elbows. Cassandra offered me her hand but did not rise. She had on black linen capris and a hot pink cashmere twin set with the cardigan tied over her shoulders. There were silver hoops in her ears and an antique Méxican silver cuff on her right wrist. She didn't quite look like she was in her early forties. She was not overweight, but her skin looked soft and inviting and the overall impression was of yielding flesh. Where Ruben had Maya's oval face, Cassandra's was round and her lips were full. Her hair was subtly curled and came around the lower edges of her ears to reach her collar. In México, a woman's hair gets shorter as she gets older, and Cassandra's had not yet caught up to her age.

At the other end of the sofa, with her arms folded and looking me directly in the eye, much as a fox looks through a fence at a chicken, was Soledad, and she was a babe. Trouble was stamped all over her, from the tight black leather skirt with a hemline midway between her knees and her hips, to the beige, deeply scooped cami with spaghetti straps. Her cleavage called out to all the men on the block, and perhaps as far away as the *jardín*. Certainly from where I stood I could hear it well. I was reminded of the call of Circe from her enchanted island to the crew of Ulysses' ship in the Odyssey. When they landed they were all turned into pigs. I hoped my nose and ears could retain their shape through dinner, but I wouldn't have bet on it.

Soledad's face was round like her mother's, but she had Maya's dimples. Her eyes were dark and widely spaced and her sensuous mouth seemed ready to start singing something sweet but dangerous. Her black hair held caramel highlights and hung just below her shoulders.

I felt someone working at the fingers of my right hand, and found Maya closing them around the stem of a wine glass. I forced myself to look somewhere else and raised it in a toast.

"Welcome to San Miguel," I said to the group at large.

"We are so happy to finally meet you," Cassandra said. "Maya said that you rent the studio upstairs."

"My own place is too small to have one, unfortunately. Rents can be expensive here." Maya shot me an alarmed look.

"I am so lucky to get this place cheaply," she said quickly.

"So you are with Pemex?" I asked Ruben.

"Yes, I started there as a petroleum engineer and I now run vehicle transport for them. Sometimes as you move up, you move away from your original field."

"So, you're talking about the truck fleet?"

"Exactly." He pulled the crease in his pants legs slightly higher over his knees.

"Ruben coordinates retail deliveries for all of México," said Cassandra with a bright smile, "as well as vehicle acquisition and disposal." Normally in México such a position could be an opportunity for serious personal gain, but Maya had never suggested her father was wealthy. Soledad had not said a word, but continued to stare at me. I tried not to look at her because she was showing so much skin I felt I should have a canvas in front of me and a brush in my hand. I could sense Maya's eyes on me.

"I've just come across a company here that does some independent exploration. Maybe you know them," I said to Ruben. "They're called Dos Cerros."

There was a slight hesitation. "Yes, that is part of their business. Because oil here is a government monopoly, Pemex buys any field Dos Cerros successfully develops and pays them a royalty on production. Dos

Cerros also has resort properties. Do you have some business with them?"

"I have been hired by them to paint a portrait of a man who was once vice president of the United States."

Ruben Sanchez rotated his wine for moment, looking into the glass with a startled expression, as if he had discovered a snail in it.

"That would be Al Gore?" He was actively searching now for any logic in this.

"No, Malcolm Brendel. He served a long time ago." Maya disappeared into the kitchen. I heard the oven door open. "Excuse me a minute," I said, crossed the dining room and stuck my head through the doorway. "Do you need some help?" She shook her head and as I turned to go back to the great room I came face to face with Soledad.

"Some day I will have a house like this," she said, "but much newer. Maybe bigger too. It could have some of your pictures." For the first time she smiled. It was full of shining possibilities. She stood with her weight on one leg and the other knee bent forward. She was an inch or so shorter than Maya.

"That would be great," I said.

"Maybe you could paint me too then?"

"I'd love to. I seem to be doing more portraits lately." I hoped it was a portrait she was thinking of, perhaps with a riding crop in her hand and her foot on some hapless guy's neck. She smiled again as Maya called us for dinner.

I poured more wine all around as we sat down. Soledad seemed to be going through hers quickly and her cheeks glowed with cheer, but her parents didn't say anything so I filled her glass again.

"Are you showing now in a gallery in San Miguel?" asked Cassandra as Maya entered in a skeleton print apron and began serving. She had a businesslike look on her face, as if her parents' visit cast her in the role of staff. Earlier she had refused my offer of help, saying I was a guest and should act like one.

"Yes, Galeria Uno. They're mostly still lifes. A lot of sliced fruits in lush colors, some watermelons, but not in the usual México style." I didn't mention the nudes of Maya adorning two walls of my Yucatan gallery in Mérida. "I can show you some things upstairs later."

"This *molé* is really good," said Soledad. "Whose recipe is it?"

"Rigoberta's. Why?" said Maya, looking up at her. Rigoberta was our cleaning lady, who doubled as a major resource for traditional Méxican recipes. We clearly didn't pay her enough.

"Yours was never this good at home," Soledad said with a broad grin. A ghost of a smile quickly passed over Cassandra's face and was gone. I felt a bare toe creep up my ankle. From the way we were seated at the table it had to belong to either Ruben or Soledad, but neither of them looked at me. Maya swallowed this silently but I realized we wouldn't be able to get rid of them quickly enough to prevent some kind of damage. I had long ago learned that within the fabled closeness of Méxican families there occurred some very nasty infighting.

After dinner Ruben and I went out into the lingering warmth on the *loggia* for a brandy and a cigar. I made a show of asking Maya where the switch was for the garden ground lights. She was cleaning up under the critical supervision of Cassandra and Soledad. I brought out a couple of Cohibas, the favorite brand of Fidel Castro until he quit, and we blew smoke rings into the evening air.

"It's quiet here," he said.

"It's just 75,000 people. Our main source of noise is the firecrackers."

"I meant for crime. Maya told us that sometimes you act as a detective."

"'Act' is probably a good word." This conversation was entirely in Spanish, and the double sense of the word "act" as I used it was not clear to him. "Sometimes I try to help people with confusing situations," I went on. "But mainly I paint."

"Is there such a situation then with Dos Cerros, where a criminal inquiry is in order, or is it simply a portrait for the vice president? If you don't mind that I ask."

"I don't mind. There is something odd about it. It's not clear why the vice president would settle here, even though it is a sweet place for gringos. Even more unclear is why Dos Cerros would spend five million dollars to buy him a house."

"*Madre de Dios*! You can spend that much for a house here?" He stumbled to his feet and coughed on a mouthful of cigar smoke.

"You can blame the gringos for driving the prices up."

"I will! So *Señor* Brendel must be doing something very important for Dos Cerros."

I nodded. "What is the significance of that name?"

He thought for a moment, then something came into his mind.

"I think it must be this: the owners are two brothers named Morales from Veracruz. In that area they have a saying, 'May your success be as high as the hills.' They are the *dos cerros*, the two hills. The ones with the big success."

I looked over my shoulder through the kitchen window. Maya had finished her cleanup and the three women were sitting at the island counter with a newly opened bottle of wine. Maya, now off duty, was laughing, possibly for the first time this evening. Cassandra was explaining something with her hands and Soledad, ignoring them, looked a little tilted. With her index finger she traced the grout lines in the tile.

"Has their success been mostly from petroleum or from resort development?" I asked.

"Initially it was petroleum. Veracruz has still some excellent reserves to be discovered. But in the last fifteen years or so I would have to say the property and resort development is bigger for them. It is like a specialty resort that they do, the way Club Med does for singles, or for families; but with Dos Cerros it is for evangelical Protestants. They provide services from visiting preachers, for example. It is what I think they call a retreat."

"And the brothers Morales are evangelical Protestants too?" I already knew this but I wanted to learn his take on it.

"Yes. In the past one would not usually advertise this in México. But now there are five million of them here. And the number grows all the time. It is becoming a powerful group economically."

At this point Cassandra came out from the kitchen. "I was just telling Maya, it's so much easier if you have staff to clean up. To say nothing of the cooking. We've had Ana for twelve years now and I don't know how we could get along without her." She sat down at the table with us and batted some of the cigar smoke away. "Don't forget, Paul, you were going to show us a few pictures."

"Of course. Let me go up and pull some out." It was always better to show people half a dozen preselected pictures or less; more only causes an overload. I also didn't want them poking around in my storage and pulling out the explicit Lynn Washburn picture, causing a different kind of overload.

Upstairs I put on the studio lights and opened the doors of the inventory cabinets. There were still a couple of fruit pictures that hadn't gone down to Galeria Uno yet. One in particular showed pomegranates sliced in quarters, with well-done highlights on the black seeds. I hadn't decided yet whether we should keep it for ourselves. I was thumbing my way through a few others when the door opened and looked over my shoulder to see Soledad come in. She closed it quietly behind her, then came up to the storage shelves and looked over my shoulder.

"I know what you have been doing with Maya." She stood with her hands on her hips and her lips pursed, rocking slightly from side to side. I paused with my hand on a picture, not sure what this meant. Was she talking about the handcuffs? Maya wouldn't tell her about that. I turned toward her and for the first time I noticed she was wearing high-heeled beaded sandals, with butterflies on the toe. It was not lost on me that they were the kind she could easily slip off under the table if she wanted to cause trouble by running her toes up my leg.

"She told me about your Gods and Goddesses show in the Yucatan. I know I can model better than she can. I'm much younger, you know."

I turned to face her and stood up with a patient smile. "Soledad, in a way, modeling is an art, just like painting is. It's not only about your body type, or your age, or the way you hold yourself." Kindly old uncle Paul explaining art basics to the novice.

"You will see." With a single fluid gesture she whipped off her cami and threw it over her shoulder. Her breasts were full and round and her upper body had a fleshier quality than Maya's. Then she pulled her skirt up over her hips. She was wearing the tiniest of ice blue string bikini panties, the kind with just a triangle of fabric in front and straps going around the sides. Her hands went to the straps and she started to pull them down. I fell forward on my knees and grabbed the waistband in front.

"No no no no no, stop that, stop that. Oh, sweet Jesus, keep them on!"

We wrestled back and forth and then suddenly I heard the studio door close softly behind me. My hands were gripping the front elastic of her panties and I was mightily pulling upward as she tried to pull them down with her thumbs still locked in the sides.

"You're pulling out my hair!"

I turned, half expecting to see Ruben Sanchez

in the studio doorway, but it was Maya. Just as bad. Probably even worse.

"Soledad! Paul! Is my sister to be another Barbara Watt in my face? What are you now, a cheek magnet?"

"Cheek magnet? Cheek magnet? You mean 'chick' magnet?"

I admit that there could be several interpretations of what Maya saw as she came in. The fact that her breasts were thrusting into my face didn't look very good either. At least my mouth was closed when Maya came in.

"OK. Whatever. What is happening here?" Soledad had backed away and crossed her arms over her breasts. She had pulled her hemline back to mid thigh and her left foot struggled to get into one of the high heeled sandals which had escaped in the struggle. Then she stood looking at the ceiling. I glanced around the room as I got to my feet, but I couldn't locate her cami. Suddenly I saw it hanging from the top of the center post of my easel and pulled it down. I tried to draw it over her head and she resisted at first but then gave up and put her arms through as I pulled it down. I didn't trust her to do it herself. She adjusted the support in front and then turned and faced the wall.

"Back in the soup," I said.

"You are between the sword and the wall, *Señor* Gringo."

"Yes, I can see that. Soledad was trying to show me that she could pose as well as you."

"And you asked her this?" Her eyebrows flew up.

"No. She volunteered it."

"It's true." Soledad turned to face her sister. "Because I have nicer *chi-chis* than you."

She tossed her hair.

"Is this true?" She was looking around for something to use as a weapon. Fortunately there are no swords in my prop drawer.

"Not nicer. Just different."

Then Maya relaxed a little and a steely grin came over her face. "You did this," she hissed at Soledad, "because if it was Paul's idea you would be getting undressed behind the screen. I know this. That is how he is. Besides, he would never have you pose with Papa here."

"You never took my side, even with Mama." She folded her arms again.

"I never had a chance. And you will not be posing for Paul, ever." She stuck her chin out. "Besides, those are my panties. Now they are all stretched out. Now they would only fit your mother."

"You left them at home."

"You will stay out of my room. What else have you been wearing? Not the cashmere, I hope?" I was quietly making for the exit as they continued to argue.

Back at Cody's after eleven I slumped down at the dining table. He pulled a brandy bottle out of the cupboard.

"Make it a double," I said. "I can't do this family stuff."

"The father?"

"No. The seester. She had a little too much wine and wanted to show me she could pose better than Maya."

"And could she?"

"She didn't hold still long enough. I was trying to keep her clothes on and she was pulling them off."

"You have an interesting life."

"Way too interesting. I thrive on calm."

"Hard to find sometimes. Chaos follows you."

"Sadly." I finished the double in a gulp and pushed the glass forward. "Maya thought Soledad was becoming the next Barbara."

"How old is she?"

"Nineteen."

"Well." He began to shake and then to laugh so hard he could barely keep in his chair. "She's just immature," he said finally, gasping for breath.

"You wouldn't say that if you'd seen her."

"What happens now?"

"I think I'll just lay low for a while. Stay alert for flying objects; maybe do a little detective work. Anything to stay out of trouble." And count the minutes until the departure of the Sanchez clan. Get started on the Brendel portrait. Suddenly I remembered the paper from the *loggia* table. I had taken it from the night stand before I left for Cody's.

"This is something," I said, pulling it from my pocket, unfolding it on the table and pushing it toward him.

"Fan mail?" he said, holding it up to the light.

"Right. The kind that keeps you awake nights. It came the night before last and I forgot about it with Maya's family coming. I found it on the table in my *loggia*."

"No watermark, but it's not cheap paper. I guess it wasn't wrapped around a rock and tossed over?"

"It was under a candle," I said. "The only thing I

can think of is the *federales*."

"Is it their style?"

"Doesn't seem like it, but who knows?"

"Might be time to start wearing your gun again."

# Chapter 4

When the Sanchez family decamped two days later for the next oasis on their caravan route, I brought my clothes back home. Cody and I were tired of playing gin rummy. I owed him 140 pesos and I was eager to paint again. Malcolm Brendel was scheduled for a two o'clock sitting, which I was not wild about since I preferred to work in the morning, but his taping session needed to be accommodated. When you're dealing with the big fish, painters are definitely staff. I'd seen it before.

But I hadn't seen Maya since the bizarre scene in the studio and we needed to reconnect. She looked stressed out when I came in, but relieved that we were now alone. It seemed, however, that there might be a few issues left to put to bed.

"I really enjoyed meeting your family," I said. It was neutral enough for a beginning; I was hanging up some shirts in my armoire.

"And which one of them did you enjoy most?" She stood behind me with her hands on her hips. I knew now she was still stewing over the studio scene.

"Oh, it's kind of like apples and oranges; they're

each a little different, aren't they?" I smiled hopefully: I know a minefield when I see one. When she didn't respond I went to my fallback position. "Look, Maya, I don't want to be *Señor* Gringo right now. I've spent the last two nights sleeping on a lumpy couch with no access to my stuff. Maybe we could fool around a little bit? I could peel your clothes off with my teeth?" This often worked.

She took a step back. The dimples in her cheeks and the sparkle in her eyes appeared briefly and then fled.

"I will consider your offer carefully. But you also liked her *chi chis*, yes?"

My shoulders sagged. "I barely saw them. My eyes don't focus well that close. Besides, there are other good pairs in town. And I don't want to be responsible if your wild-child sister decides to show me what she's got. It was totally her idea."

"Let me see your hands."

I held them out.

"Turn them over." I turned my palms down. I felt like it was my mother inspecting them before dinner.

"I see you have at least combed her public hair out from under your fingernails."

"I showered. I usually do."

We left it there. Although I didn't feel at all responsible, I wasn't going to win anything and I wanted to get my mind in shape for Malcolm Brendel, who was likely to be another handful.

At ten minutes after two the bell rang and I opened the door. A beefy Méxican guy in a black suit and shirt pushed past me into the house and marched out toward the garden, looking into the other rooms as he went. One hand was inside his jacket. Malcolm Brendel came in behind him and was followed by another Méxican dressed identically and built on the same scale as the first, carrying a suit bag. I wondered for a moment if these were the two hills guys in the flesh. There was enough of it.

Brendel paused in the entry and surveyed the interior, while he kept one hand held stiffly in the pocket of his jacket, as if he had been spending too much time with Prince Charles lately.

"I think of this as my Secret Service detail. Burton will stay here by the door," he said without a greeting.

"Burton? His name is Burton?"

"Burton Hernandez. I understand his mother was an admirer of Elizabeth Taylor. Where shall we be?"

I led him upstairs to the studio and the suit bag followed. Brendel stood for a moment and examined the room, taking in the two banks of long windows, one facing north, one south, and the row of storage racks where the half-finished picture of Lynn was hidden. He gestured to the sofa and the other man pulled the cover off the outfit, handed it to Brendel, and sat down.

The vice president had carefully removed his suit jacket and now traded it for a white surplice that he pulled over his head, and then over it a sky blue robe with a wide collar that reached nearly to his shoulders. He passed his fingers over his hair to see that it was undisturbed.

"I thought we might use this chair," I said. "Stephen Washburn said you wished to be seated." He looked at it dubiously. It was Méxican Victorian style upholstered in burgundy brocade. "I can change the color of it in the picture. I think it might not work with that robe."

"I think it will do. It has arms and I had imagined a pose not unlike that of the Lincoln Memorial." He sat down in the chair and arranged the robe so that little of the upholstery was visible. Brendel had a narrow frame, but the robe gave him ample volume. His hands gripped the ends of the chair arms and his feet were flat on the floor. The surplice came over his knees so that his dark trousers barely showed.

I sat behind the easel and fluffed the ends of a couple of brushes, studying the tableau.

"And who are we today, sir?" I asked, trying to lighten the tone a bit.

"Today we are an actor, as we are every day; one to make the Barrymores weep with envy."

"Drew?" I paused hopefully. And was there more than one?

"In point of fact, I refer to Lionel, Ethel, and John. The young woman you make reference to is John's granddaughter." He looked at me gravely.

I shrugged, not sure what to make of this. "Would you like to have music? I have Coltrane, Chet Baker, Bill Evans, Miles..."

"Do you have Richard Wagner?"

"No. Sorry."

"Anything less would be too pale."

"Could you characterize your mood for me? I mean the one you wish to convey. I'm not sure how this picture will be used."

"This should in no way tax your abilities. Simply paint what you see; dignity, strength of character, integrity, and, of course, resilience. Little or no invention will be required for this." I was to be simply a camera; the subject would express itself unaided.

"I see," I said, wondering which brushes would do that. Probably the much more expensive sables, not the hog bristle brushes I usually bought, which required effort on my part to achieve a result.

"Its use would be for only the highest purposes." In other words, he wasn't going to tell me.

"Are you committed to the color of that robe?" It didn't do anything for the tones of his skin or hair.

"It is the color of God's own heaven. Certainly there could be no color more suitable?"

"All right." To me it recalled the color of the bridesmaids' dresses in a small town wedding, something to be discarded after a single use because there was nothing else you could ever use it for. "Would you like to be facing me directly, or slightly to the side?"

"Directly."

Brendel's face was narrow and aristocratic, with a slender nose and vigorous brown eyes full of movement. His hairline receded only at the corners of his forehead. Over a firm chin, his lips were thin and nearly the same color as the surrounding skin, which was pale, but interrupted on the cheekbones and nose by a slight flush. His face looked all of his seventy-three years, but his overall vigor suggested someone younger. While there was much to generate character, I was seeing nothing that was going to work with the robe. With a different client I would have radically altered it, but now I knew that wouldn't fly with Brendel.

On impulse I got up and closed the shades on the north end of the studio and then I saw how it would be. I'd paint the shadows, which were now deeply articulated on one side of his face and among the rolling folds of his gown, and within those darker areas I would create the complementary tones that would make his face and body read properly. The color in the shadows would anchor the picture and hold it together. This was a backwards way to do it, but there was nothing in the lighter tones that worked otherwise.

Instead of thinly locating the forms and then starting his face, I began by mixing small batches of color and locating them next to lighter areas until I had a workable color design that included his skin tones and the offensive robe. This took a while, and when I was starting to get into his eyes and nose, he abruptly looked at his watch and stood up.

"I believe that is all the time I can devote to this today," he said.

Suit Bag leaped off the sofa to receive the surplice and robe and then held Brendel's jacket as he slid into it.

"Washburn will contact you to arrange our next session." He didn't ask to look at the picture, which was OK, since I don't like to show a portrait until it's finished.

Burton, the front entry guard, went out to start the car as we came down the stairs. I was the last of the four of us coming out onto the sidewalk when I heard a gunshot which must have gone wild because no one fell, although we all ducked. Burton slid back out of the Town Car on the passenger side and leveled his gun at an older black Chevy sedan that was spinning away from the curb. He fired and then the man in the Chevy fired again and Burton fell straight back onto the narrow sidewalk, hitting his head on the wall of the house. Suit bag was firing at the Chevy and trying to shield Brendel with his body, whom he had forced down on the sidewalk. At the same time I retrieved Burton's gun and jumped into the Town Car. The tires squealed on the cobblestones as the powerful engine came to life. I hoped Suit Bag was aiming over my head.

The old Chevy flew down Quebrada, dodging traffic and fishtailing on the cobblestones, then spun around the corner onto Pila Seca, and I was right behind him. The engine in the Lincoln was huge and powerful, but the car handled like an antique cabin cruiser, nicely detailed, but wallowing on the turns like it was moving sideways through heavy swells. The Chevy pulled out onto Zacateros, narrowly avoiding two taxis, and headed for the edge of town. I speeded up and rammed his bumper on the driver's side, hoping to turn him sideways. The impact only shifted him slightly toward the right and his passenger side tires went up the scooped edge of a driveway and he shot down the street with two of his tires on the sidewalk. As he came off the curb his front bumper caught the back wheel of a row of pizza delivery motor scooters and they went down like a wave of dominos. Past the wreckage I wheeled into the curb after him, trying to get around the cars ahead of me, but hitting the sharp edge of the stone, my front passenger side tire exploded into a pinwheel of rags. As I came to a stop I fired a single shot and saw a puff of vaporized glass stream away from a round dark hole in his back window. He kept on going. It occurred to me that I hadn't really wanted to hit the driver in the back of the head, but I had never had any target practice. Shooting from one moving vehicle to another requires some finesse.

Locking the door of the Town Car at the curb I noticed a small stylized logo under the door handle. It showed a wavy line with two humps over a straight line. Dos Cerros. They could bill me for the tire. I walked the mile-and-a-half back to Quebrada, with the gun stuck in my belt. No one approached me and my knees continued to shake the entire way.

Coming up Quebrada I saw an ambulance pull away from my entry. Standing by the door were Cody and Maya in one group, and further up the sidewalk, Malcolm Brendel and Suit Bag, with a San Miguel police officer writing rapidly in his notebook. As I came up closer I could see an irregular-shaped star blown out of the peach-colored stucco to the right of my stone door casing, exposing the rough stone beneath. Below it, Burton Hernandez's blood darkened the wall and the sidewalk. I started to run.

"How is he?" I asked Maya.

"They would not say, but he was conscious. The wound was higher in the chest, and there was no blood coming from his mouth or his nose. I called Cody. You didn't catch him?"

"No. This is not a town for chase scenes."

"Delgado was here," said Cody. "He's out looking for you."

I walked over to Brendel and handed the gun and the car keys to Suit Bag. "Your car is down on Ancha de San Antonio with a front tire blown out. It's in front of number 61. Sorry. I can give you a ride back to Cuadrante, if you want."

Suit Bag waited for Brendel's reaction.

"I think I would like to continue these sessions in my home, Mr. Zacher. This seems like an unduly rough part of town. We have called another car. Thank you." He seemed undisturbed that someone had tried to kill him. Maybe it wasn't the first time.

A few minutes later an identical Dos Cerros Town Car, driven by Stephen Washburn, pulled up and they sat inside while the cop finished his interview. Then Washburn whisked Suit Bag and Brendel back to what they were now probably thinking was the good part of town, even though it was just a few blocks away. Maya went back inside, shaking her head, and Cody and I crossed the street to where the Chevy had waited for the vice president. Almost immediately I found a fragment of cellophane wrapper, possibly from a cigarette package. I trapped it between a credit card and my driver's license and brought it into the house. I didn't want to wait for the police to return from looking for me and take a chance that it would blow away. Keeping the chain of custody on evidence doesn't mean that much in México.

Cody and I sat down in the living room and Maya retrieved the brandy and a bucket of ice from the kitchen. "I hope this detective business is not starting up again, because now we are in the soup again, aren't we?" she said.

"Brendel is, apparently," I said. "I hope that's all. The shooter didn't seem to care about the rest of us."

She poured out three glasses and stood by her chair with her arms folded over her chest.

"It's not unusual for a man in public life to leave a

string of enemies in his wake, even someone of flawless ethics, which I gather is not what we have here," said Cody, taking a long sip of his brandy.

Maya's cell phone beeped. It was Delgado, wondering if I had returned.

"Delgado's on his way back now. They didn't find the shooter," she said.

"So what have we got?" asked Cody.

"Not a lot. When the first shot went off we all ducked behind the Town Car. Then Burton and Suit Bag came back up and started firing back. I was down lower with Brendel and I didn't get a look at the shooter."

"Suit Bag?" asked Maya. "Surely not a México name?"

"I couldn't say if he was Méxican or not. But the car was an older black Chevy full-size sedan. You know that design from either the late eighties or maybe the early nineties where they were all bulbous and silly looking? Anyway, I was too busy driving and dodging pedestrians to even get the license number."

"It's probably stolen anyway," said Cody. "Would you use your own car for a drive-by shooting?"

"Not even a gringo would do that," said Maya.

The doorbell rang and I went to let *Licenciado* Delgado in. "Welcome back to the hot spot, *Licenciado.* Please come on in and sit down. You know Maya and Cody. How about a brandy?"

"Thank you. I am very happy to see you are back safely. As for the brandy, it is not my favorite, but if you have a tequila? It is nearly the end of my shift. Of course, normally I wouldn't..."

"This is your lucky crime scene, *Licenciado.* I have

only Don Eduardo Anejo." I really had Cuervo too, but we only used it for toasts with the staff, birthdays and so on. On this occasion I wanted to cultivate Delgado's goodwill.

"You honor me, *Señor* Zacher."

"You have been very helpful to me, and because of all the trouble we have had this year, I feel that I am now the gringo liaison with the San Miguel police." I poured him a shooter of the tequila in one of those glasses shaped like a tall thimble. "So let me tell you what hap—"

Delgado's hand went up like an emergency stop at a school crossing. I paused as he downed the tequila and tears came to his eyes.

*"Madre de Dios,"* he said. "You are a man of honor and integrity after all. Are you quite certain that you have no Méxican blood?" I reloaded his glass. But then Maya came over and sat next to him on the sofa.

"Possibly just a little," I said.

*"Señor* Delgado," she said, "Paul needs to tell you about the car with the shooter before he forgets." She shot me a look and took his hand between hers. He regarded her solemnly, nodding his head. "It is because he sees things differently that this information may be important."

"Of course. Please proceed."

I told him what I had told the others, realizing how inadequate my report was. "There are probably some bullet holes in the side of the car from Malcolm Brendel's guards, and there is one in the back window from me. But the shooter kept driving down Ancha de San Antonio, so I doubt that I hit him."

"Well, now we are in very grave territory, because *Señor* Brendel is of international significance, being both a formerly high official of your country and a newly arrived guest in ours. My crew is examining the street before your house for shell casings or any other clues he may have left behind."

"I have something, then, *Licenciado*." I recovered the cellophane from our key tray by the front door. "This was in the space the car occupied. It could be from anyone, but perhaps from the shooter. It was on the pavement near where the driver's door would have been." Delgado called one of his crew in from the street, and without touching it with my fingers I dropped the cellophane into an evidence bag he produced.

"And as for the man himself? My people have already interviewed the vice president and his aides," said Delgado. "But we know only that the man was Méxican and from his height in the window of the car, probably not very tall."

"I wasn't even sure of that much," I said.

"Why would someone wish to kill *Señor* Brendel? Do you have any thoughts about this? Because he has not been in power for many years. He is not the leader of some faction that may yet regain power, isn't this true?"

"Yes," said Cody, "his career was finished more than twenty years ago."

"So then please explain me why? Because here in México we often shoot people in power or if they seem about to gain power, but not after they leave office, usually. We just allow them to go away to retire to their impressive ranchos and haciendas. You will excuse me if I say I think this is the more civilized way."

"Of course it is, but I can't explain this yet," I said. "I know something is going on with Dos Cerros, as we spoke about before. Could it be that there are enemies of Dos Cerros that are now coming after Malcolm Brendel? This is where I would look if I were an investigator."

"I can look at this as you say, but in truth, few would choose knowingly to oppose Dos Cerros."

"Well, in any case, could you keep me informed as the investigation develops? I feel like I have a personal stake in this since the shooting occurred on my doorstep, practically in my *zaguán*. I knew this would violate the policy of La Agencia del Ministerio Publico, which was to guard all information about a crime the way you would hide grain during a four-year famine, but I was counting on some residual goodwill from him. We were not quite good friends, but we were probably as close as a gringo and a Méxican cop could get.

"Of course this would not normally be our practice, but for you some flexibility is possible." He shook his head thoughtfully. "I never dreamed I would be saying that, but the life, it is a school sometimes."

Nodding, Maya picked up his hand again between hers. I thought for a moment she was going to press it to her breast, but instead she gave him her high voltage smile. He looked into her eyes for an instant and then rose from the sofa.

"I must return then," he said. "Many thanks for the superb tequila."

Maya and I had just finished lunch the following day, Tuesday, when I received a call from Delgado saying that the police had recovered the stolen Chevy sedan abandoned off the Celaya road. In addition to several excellent fingerprints, they had also found two shell casings on the floor under the driver's seat. No trace of blood was found in the car. Based on the prints, Delgado had pulled a set of mug shots from the computer and wondered if I could come down and try to identify the man. Privately, I had little hope that his picture would mean anything to me. Everything at the moment of the shoot-out had been moving at the speed of light and I had no recollection of the driver. So much for the visual acuity of painters.

Delgado's office was on the second floor of one of the grand arcaded buildings facing the *jardín*. This was not my first visit. I climbed the wide marble staircase to the upper level. The floor was eighteenth-century tile and the desks were K-Mart. The fluttering fluorescent lights on the ceiling gave his brown suit a greenish cast. Directly above his desk a fan emitted a frustrated hum, but the blades did not turn. He rose to shake my hand.

"You are so prompt today," he said. I was fifteen minutes late. "Please have a seat. I must thank you again for the wonderful hospitality of yesterday afternoon. Rarely have I been received with such style on judicial business."

*"No hay problema,"* I said.

He sorted through some files and pulled out a slender one. At his right, on a battered green metal cart, was a small TV set with a VCR tape slot in the bottom.

Behind it, a long extension cord snaked off among the desks. He opened the file folder and placed a sheet of paper in front of me. At the top were full-face and profile views of a young Méxican man. Below, in a smaller format, were four close shots from differing angles. Below this were two rows of fingerprints. Across the top I read, FLORES, ANGEL. I studied the pictures, but I couldn't say whether this was the man in the Chevy.

"I just don't know," I said, shaking my head. "As I told you yesterday, there was no opportunity to get a good look at him. You know how it is when things are happening so fast, you don't focus on any single thing."

He nodded. "And the name Angel Flores is not known to you either?"

"No. I take it he must have a criminal record?"

"Yes. A variety of things: assault, extortion, robbery. He is also wanted for questioning in some open cases."

"I'm sorry, *Licenciado*, I wish I could be more helpful." I leaned back in my chair and slid the sheet back to him. I thought I was finished.

"Perhaps you could take a look at this, then." He swung around to turn on the TV set and when the picture filled in, hit the play button on the VCR portion.

To my surprise, in the grainy image that came on, Barbara's head appeared, facing the camera, but looking somewhat downward. Over her shoulder was my face, and I was talking to a smaller man who looked away from the camera and was mostly hidden behind Barbara. There was no sound, and I realized this had to be the security camera at the ATM machine where we had stopped for cash on our way for art supplies. The sequence lasted only about thirty seconds and then the man turned and faced the camera for the first time. Delgado hit the pause control and froze the face. It was Angel Flores, unmistakably the man in the mug shots.

It was several seconds before I realized that my mouth was open in utter surprise. I'm sure my tongue was collecting dust. What had Flores been up to? I couldn't think of any explanation for this, except that Flores had wanted to get a look at me, but how would he have known who I was?

"I'm shocked," I said. "I paid no attention to this man at the time. I mean, I remember him asking for directions, which I thought was odd, but I was standing behind *Señora* Watt and I was looking at her neck. I remember that. Surely if you could read my lips you could see that I was giving him directions. I didn't know the man."

"Actually, *Señor* Zacher, we have had visiting here this morning our retired officer Fonseca, who sadly has little hearing anymore, and he read for us your lips. To make no mistake, I have written it down here." He reached into the file again and pulled out a half-sheet of paper, on which he had written in pencil in Spanish:

Of course. You won't need the map. Go straight along under the arches to the corner, turn left, and it is two blocks up.

"Well, there you are," I said, relieved. "I think that's exactly what I must have said. I remember now that Flores had asked me for directions to the post office."

"Most likely," said Delgado, nodding reassuringly. He pulled out another sheet from the file. On it was a hand-drawn map of the *Jardín* and the surrounding blocks. The location of the ATM machine under the arches in the front wall of the bank was marked with an X.

"You see," I said, and picking up a pencil, I traced a line from the ATM along the arches to the corner, and then left for two blocks to the post office. "Here is the route. It's what I told him."

"This is true," said Delgado. "But if the man, whom we now know was Angel Flores, goes the other way through the arches and then turns left and goes two blocks," his pencil was tracing a different route and I had a sick feeling as I watched it move along the paper, "he goes to your house, or rather, to the street in front of your house, where he attempted to kill the vice president."

"Yes, I can see that now, but that wasn't the way he went when I saw him."

"But still, a few days later, when the vice president is visiting for his portrait, Flores returns and shoots at him. Outside your house. You can see how this must look. It is something we cannot ignore."

"Can I ask how you have this tape?"

"Of course, but for any other, we would not be as willing to tell this." He raised both hands in the air, palms upward. "It was left at our reception desk this morning. No one was observed to bring it at that time."

"But the tape must have come from someone at the bank."

"I agree, but from our call to their security desk, no one acknowledges copying this from their system. And the manager, after speaking to various employees, has called me back to say that no one admits to delivering the tape to us either. The thing I find most troubling myself is that if I were to believe that in this film you are giving Flores instructions on how to find your house and shoot at the vice president, then why would you do it when you are with another person, and why in view of a security camera? Not even a gringo..."

"You don't need to finish that statement," I said.

"Indeed. I have been thinking again today of your comment about the turnip truck from some months ago."

"You mean?"

"Yes, exactly. We of the judicial police have not just fallen off, as you correctly observed. My command of English is less than adequate, but I think I know the word of this."

"Right. You've been set up, and so have I."

# Chapter 5

On Saturday Maya and I headed up the hill toward the Los Balcones neighborhood for Barbara's party. Maya had spent considerable time agonizing about what to wear, even though I told her it wasn't formal. We weren't equipped to do formal all that well, which wasn't unusual in San Miguel. Casual we had down perfectly, from long practice. The things I had told Maya about Malcolm Brendel had not warmed her to him, and this didn't make her feel any more at ease either.

She settled finally on the *tejuana* outfit we had used when I painted her as Frida Kahlo some months before. It was white cotton and covered with floral embroidery in lime and rose and ochre. She put her hair up with an orange hibiscus blossom from the garden; her teardrop earrings of a greenish turquoise set in old Méxican silver set off the flower beautifully. I think she believed she would be the only Méxican guest there. If she was right, it would at least set her off from the serving help.

When we drove up, Casa Watt was already top-heavy with staff. As the valets opened the car doors for us I could see others in uniform through the bow window, hustling about in the great room. As I handed the valet the keys to the artmobile, my old Chevy van with the mismatched front seats and the bullet hole in the windshield, I saw a slight smile cross his face. Maybe I was supposed to apologize because it wasn't a Mercedes, but instead I wanted to ask him what he drove. Not everyone has oil money here. Maybe I was a little nervous too.

Inside, the garden had been extended indoors on the main floor. There were vases of cut flowers everywhere and tall potted calla lilies lined the walls under portraits of conquistadores in armor and the Gods and Goddesses picture of mine from the June show in the Yucatan. I felt like I was in old México. The three pairs of French doors facing the veranda were all open to the warm evening, and framed by the center pair was a string quartet playing the gentle romantic music of the Méxican heartland we lived in, the *bajio*.

Barbara met us just inside. Her hair was up, and she was wearing black fitted silk pants, with a teal blue velvet jacket above. Her open-toe spike heels were topped by a filigree of delicate straps, and seemed to say, "Meet me upstairs after the guests leave."

"CFM shoes," Maya whispered in my ear.

"What's that? I've heard of Jimmy Choo and Manolo Blahnik."

"I'll tell you later.'

"Tell me now."

"It stands for Come Fuck Me."

"How lovely that you could come," Barbara said, taking one of our hands in each of hers. "The vice president isn't here yet, but I expect him shortly. Isn't this exciting? I understand he's a little skittish, though, after someone took that shot at him at your place. I guess I don't blame him. I offered to put on some security here, but Stephen Washburn, his driver, said he'd bring his own. Have they caught that man?"

"No, but they know who he is. He's a career criminal named Angel Flores. He was the one standing behind us who asked for directions as we were getting cash at the *jardín*."

A look of consternation came over her face. "What? You mean we were that close to him?" Her right hand went to her neck and touched the chain which held a single diamond the size of her finger tip, as if to see whether it was still there. Her left hand was still burdened by the weight of her engagement ring with its enormous emerald cut diamond, but her wedding band had been retired. Maya nudged me in the ribs, but in a refined sort of way.

"We can talk about it later," she said. "Let's not spoil the party. I want to have fun."

There was suddenly a flurry of activity out on the horseshoe drive and Suit Bag and a similarly constructed Méxican came through the door, but not at the same time. Burton had been easily replaced. They were both wearing the standard black suit and black shirt, and both had an impressive bulge in their left armpit. Suit Bag went through the house and took up a position on the veranda near the quartet and the other man remained by the entry. Outside I could see Stephen Washburn refusing to turn the Town Car over to the valet as Malcolm Brendel came up the steps with

Mayor José Martin, whose portrait I had painted two years before, and the American Consul Dr. Harry Weingard, whom I knew slightly as well. Weingard was a former ear, nose and throat specialist from Maryland who had retired early and picked up the undemanding Consul job in the last year of the Clinton administration. Behind them were two carefully dressed women whom I guessed must be Rachel Weingard and *Señor*a Martin. Rachel Weingard wore a floor-length red silk dress, covered to the neck in front, but bare in back, that I thought was a bit too much.

Maya and I stepped back in the foyer to make room, but Barbara waved us forward again and introduced us. Brendel's eye lingered for a moment on Maya, taking in the curve of her bust, and then moved back to Barbara. He didn't appear to remember me. I guess bad associations can do that. The shoot-out in front of my house had probably sent my stock down. He was wearing a suit that would have cost millions of lire in Milan, in the days before euros.

A dozen or more guests were already in the great room, and two servers in white jackets were circulating with glasses of champagne. Cody was standing at the grand piano and turned as we came in. He was elegant as only a walrus in pinstripes and silk tie can be. Maya went up to him and he bent over as she kissed his cheek.

"You are very handsome now," she said. A server stopped with champagne and Maya and I each took one but Cody declined.

"On duty?" I asked.

"Not really, but I feel responsible, being co-host

and all. I don't do things on this scale at my place." His eyes were surveying the crowd. "Did you know that Perry's kids are coming?"

"No!" said Maya.

"Barbara didn't say anything to me," I said.

Barbara's husband, Perry, had died earlier this year as a result of his involvement with some counterfeit Mayan ceramics. It was possible that his children, whose mother was Perry's first wife, might have thought us in some way responsible, since we had worked on the case. At the end, Maya had killed him after he shot Cody and was about to shoot me. Then he would have killed Maya. If they felt that way, I could see their point, but they were probably missing some of the more critical nuances of the event. Like self-defense.

"I think Barbara felt that it was a goodwill gesture to invite them down from Houston," said Cody, "maybe as a way of normalizing things, or perhaps the Consul suggested it, I'm not sure which. I've been here a good part of the day helping her get things ready. She's really pumped about this; it's her reentry into society."

"What do we know about them?" I said. "Barbara never told me much, except that she thought James blamed her for the divorce. Maybe they both did. But I don't really know anything about the other one, other than that they both split the inheritance with Barbara."

"Right. They each got forty million as well. The second child is a girl named Rebecca. She's in graduate school at Texas A&M. James is helping to run Watt Industries. He's twenty-five and Rebecca's twenty-three."

"So Barbara has two stepchildren within five years of her own age?" asked Maya.

"You could say that. It's probably not that unusual when you think that Barbara was the trophy wife," said Cody. "What I didn't find out until today was that when Barbara and Perry got married, his father was still alive, and Perry hadn't come into the family money yet. The first wife got only about five hundred thousand in the settlement."

"So she's bitter," I said. "Barbara must have been chatty today, despite all the preparations."

"She likes having a man around."

"Tell me about it," I said. Maya shot me a look.

"Paul has started giving Barbara painting lessons," she said to Cody, forcing a smile.

Malcolm Brendel entered the room with his entourage of Mayor Martin and Consul Weingard and their wives, and behind him came a tall, handsome Méxican man in a double-breasted suit. He looked to be about forty and there was no woman on his arm. Maya's antenna went up. Cody leaned over to us and said in a low tone of voice, "I think this must be Antonio Trujillo of Dos Cerros. Barbara told me about him, at least what little she knows. She and the mayor and Harry Weingard all had input on the guest list. Apparently Brendel did too. This guy Trujillo was his pick."

"He doesn't look at all evil," said Maya. She did understatement well.

"Neither did Perry Watt," Cody said.

The room began to fill and I could pick out a number of expatriates that we knew fairly well. Bill Frost, the retired investment underwriter from Toronto whom I had last seen at the Cuadrante house sale was there with his wife, Brynn. I saw Julian Soames at the edge of one small group, alone now since his wife had run off with a German tourist appropriately named Wolf. Clare and Sally Mason came over to us and said hello. Clare (for Clarence, a name that he hated) had owned an insurance brokerage in Kansas City.

"Wonderful to see you in person again," he said, largely to Maya. "I keep seeing your pictures all over town."

She beamed at him. She was clearly the most popular model in San Miguel, although there weren't that many to choose from. Sally was studying the *tejuana* dress.

"It's good to see Barbara entertaining again," Clare said to Cody and me. "They did so much of it when Perry was still alive I'm sure she's missed it. I heard you two had a little run-in with the *federales*. Glad you came out on top. You'll have to tell me some time how you stayed out of prison."

"Just blind luck," I said.

"What are you painting now?" asked Sally, rubbing her hands together. She dabbled in watercolor and considered herself my soul mate. I knew I was supposed to ask her the same thing next.

"I'm working on a portrait of tonight's guest of honor, as well as a new nude."

"No! What's he like?"

"Stiff as a board, with all the magnetism of an iguana. I've heard he was once a good preacher, though. I wonder sometimes how he gets it going. Must take a thorough warmup."

"And the nude? Another one of Maya?"

"Not this time. This one's a writer who's taking a symposium at the Bellas Artes. I ran into her at the John Schleicher estate sale."

"You know, I almost went to that. If I had, maybe I'd be posing for you now," she said.

"You never know." Actually, I did know.

Cody touched my elbow just then and gestured to the door. A young couple came in flanking Barbara who guided them over to the Brendel entourage. She had each arm through one of theirs, which looked a little forced.

"This must be James and Rebecca," Cody said. Maya's eyes got bigger and she stepped to the right to get a better look past Sally Mason. James, like his late father, was an immaculate dresser, in a silvery gray shark skin suit with a pale olive shirt and a tie to match. He was taller than Perry, who had stood about five foot six, and I placed him at just under average height, maybe five eight or nine. He had brown wavy hair that ended just above his collar. Rebecca was much shorter, with closely cut dark brown hair and a man's jacket and slacks with no tie. She had a straight mouth with thin lips and a pear-shaped body, thick in the thighs and, when she turned, in the butt. Her haircut suggested a 1950s duck tail. She looked ill at ease, where James was confident and walked with a slight swagger.

"There's someone you probably won't be painting nude," smirked Clare Mason, but I was thinking Rebecca might be an interesting subject if I could make her awkwardness stand up from the canvas.

"Well, that's one, anyway," said Maya.

"But why not?" I said. "Look at Lynn Washburn; seeing her on the street, most people wouldn't think of her as a painter's model. Let's face it," I said, turning to Sally, "Not everyone can model. It's a special skill that requires more than just taking your clothes off." Now I was thinking of Soledad.

"Isn't that the truth," said Sally, the expert. "I wonder sometimes if I could even do it." I hoped that would keep her from trying.

A server refilled our glasses and I excused myself and moved toward the knot of people around Malcolm Brendel because I wanted to try to catch the kinds of things he said when he was off-duty. If he was ever off-duty. His back was toward me but his audience wasn't far from the bar, so I sat down on a stool and faced the bartender, setting my full champagne glass in front of me.

"Double or nothing?" he said with a grin. I recognized him from Harry's New Orleans Bar and he recognized me.

"...a mere pretense of honor, when at the core..." Brendel's resonant voice came from behind me. A pretense of honor might be something he could speak about at length.

"How are you doing, Manuel? Trade you this for a good rum. What are you pouring today?"

"I've got a Bacardi Anejo, best I can do. We've got better down at Harry's. But I don't think *Señor*a Watt drinks rum, so this is what we have."

"Go for it. It's not bad."

"...without regard for the ramifications in the long term. It's unconscionable to think that whatever the implications of..."

Manuel poured a double and set it down in front of me and winked.

"...ignoring any possibility of redemption." He must

be talking about junk bonds now, I thought, or maybe salvation. I wondered if Juana Cardenas, the vice presidential squeeze, had to put up with all this nonsense. Lynn had said she was a screamer; maybe that was why.

"Have you been listening to this?"

Manuel shook his head and grinned. "My English isn't that good, fortunately. You don't need a big vocabulary to take drink orders."

"...ultimately beyond recriminations. It resolves itself into a simple triumph of the will."

Now I knew where we were going. Back to the Nuremberg rallies of the thirties. I turned on my stool to look at his listeners. Barbara stood with her arms folded, an almost unreadable expression on her face, possibly apprehension about what Brendel would be saying next. Her eyes moved past him toward what might have been avenues of escape. Rebecca Watt had her hands in her coat pockets, as if searching for her car keys, which, of course, the valet had kept. I could only see James's broad shoulders and the back of his head, but his weight was shifting from one foot to the other. Trujillo, at least four inches taller than anyone else in the audience—which did not include Cody—had a look of patient tolerance on his face. He had heard it before and was clearly on duty. Mayor Martin had a smile frozen on his lips. I couldn't see Consul Harry Weingard's expression, but my guess was that it was not very comfortable. I wondered if he would have asked Barbara to host this dinner if he had known what a pompous fool Brendel was.

As I picked up the rum I folded a twenty-peso note

and stuffed it in Manuel's tip jar and headed out to the veranda.

"...and is it truly deserving of only a fragmentary response?" asked Brendel to no one in particular in a manner of expression that seemed to romance each word.

Yes, that's probably all it's worth, and just barely that, I thought as I leaned on the rail overlooking the pool and garden. Suit Bag nodded at me and I nodded back. It was easy to tune Brendel out now with the quartet playing next to us, and I was sure Suit Bag had not heard a word. Brendel used too many big words anyway. You're here to support Barbara, I reminded myself.

At one end of the subtly lit pool a polished bronze cluster of calla lilies arched over the edge and spilled a stream of water from each bloom. It seemed to be the theme of tonight's gathering. I couldn't hear the water's sound over the music, but it must have been a nice touch on a quiet afternoon. I felt a hand moving gently over my back. I doubted it was Rebecca Watt. I turned and faced a lovely Méxican girl in a native style of dress with a flower in her hair. Her wide smile lit the evening.

"You're a babe tonight," I said. "But then, you always are." She put her arm through mine. I moved my fingers over the fine skin of her cheek.

"He's a jerk, isn't he? Is that the right word?"

"None closer. Your vocabulary grows all the time."

"I don't know how you can paint him, then."

"It's a living. This time it pays better than most. I charged a little extra for the jerk factor." I was not sure, however, that in this case it paid well enough to get inside his head in the way that was required to do a good portrait. It made me shudder to think about it. There's such a thing as too much intimacy, and the relationship between painter and subject is a peculiar one. I hadn't dwelt on my unease about him to Maya. I knew she was afraid we'd once again find ourselves up to our eyeballs in some wildly out-of-control case, bullets flying. Personally I didn't think there was any chance of that. Brendel had enemies, obviously, but I tended to think that if Angel Flores knew of all the firepower lined up against him, he was still running.

At an unseen signal the music stopped and the quartet rose and began moving their chairs along the veranda to a position opposite the next set of French windows, which opened into the dining room. We went back into the great room and joined the slow movement toward dinner. Malcolm Brendel was leading the way. I don't know whether Barbara had help from the Emily Post guest placement hotline or whether she had figured it out herself, but each seat had its own place card done in an elegant hand. Cody was standing in his place at the foot of the table; Barbara was at the head and on her right was Brendel. He waited for Barbara to be seated and then he followed suit.

On Barbara's left was Consul Weingard, which placed him opposite Brendel. Then came his wife Rachel and after her, Antonio Trujillo. I was next. It was a pretty heady atmosphere and I was glad I hadn't worn my STAFF T-shirt. Next to me were Brynn Frost and then Rebecca Watt. Across the table, the mayor sat next to Brendel, and then his wife, followed by Maya. After that it was pretty much the boy-girl, boy-girl thing, with husbands across from wives. Between each pair of guests was a bowl of yellow orchids.

Up this close, Trujillo was carefully detailed and immaculate, and smelled good too. He was the kind of guy you saw a lot of on Méxican TV, but rarely on the street in San Miguel, where the natives were considerably shorter and more darkened by exposure to the sun. Maya had already started subtly flirting with him from across the table. It appeared that we had about six servers for twenty-six people, so for tonight, at least, including the musicians and security, the unemployment rate in San Miguel had dropped a notch or two.

A round of champagne came first and somehow the servers knew which of the five glasses to pour it in, and then Mayor Martin rose for a toast. The table fell silent as he spoke in English.

"Some of you may know, indeed I hope all of you know, that it has been my objective to make San Miguel de Allende the number one tourist destination in all of México." He smiled modestly. "Because what we understand here, above all, is hospitality. The simple, but legendary, Méxican art of 'welcome.' We are most amply rewarded tonight because our guest of honor, the former vice president of the United States, Malcolm Brendel, has chosen to make his home among us. There can be no greater confirmation that our efforts have paid off. Welcome, Mr. Vice President!" He raised his glass and everyone at the table followed suit. A little self-congratulatory, I thought, wondering who had written it for him.

Then Dr. Weingard rose. "We have all heard the welcome from Mayor Martin. Tonight in my function as American consul I take pride in extending the welcome of the expatriate community in particular, and to express our sense of honor that the vice president has chosen to join us here in México."

I was hoping that Brendel was not about to launch some political stem-winder, or worse, a sermon, but he didn't. He simply smiled and nodded a few times and then Barbara signaled the servers to begin. Antonio Trujillo leaned over to me and extended his hand.

"I don't think we have met," he said. "My name is Antonio Trujillo."

*"Mucho gusto,"* I said. "Paul Zacher. This is my friend Maya Sanchez."

Trujillo smiled at Maya and then turned back to me. "I believe you are the painter of *Señor* Brendel's portrait?"

"Yes. We have just begun work on it. Are you a friend of his?" I wanted to see if he would tell me about Dos Cerros.

"We have a professional relationship." The servers began setting out plates with *tostadas* topped with lettuce, avocado and tomatoes, with a top layer of crab and scallops. Trujillo took a slow sip of champagne and went on. "I am employed by a company called Dos Cerros. Perhaps you have heard of it?"

"I believe so. Is it oil field development?" I tried my best to look like a simple gringo painter, knowing nothing about Méxican business. It wasn't hard.

"Partly that, but also resorts. This is my connection with *Señor* Malcolm Brendel; he assists us with one of the resort projects." I didn't know he had any experience in property development. On the other hand, he had sold off much of the state-owned conservation property in Kansas, so there was a plausible link. Maybe that was his apprenticeship, the way he got the hang of it.

I nibbled at the first course, a classic ceviche, where the shrimp is marinated in lime juice rather than cooked. The recipe books make the case that this is in itself a kind of cooking. It made me a little squeamish, but it was superb. I smiled at Brynn Frost on my left. I had never met her. At the head of the table Brendel was paying a lot of attention to Barbara, who didn't mind. From the bits of conversation I could hear, they were talking about the White House. Barbara was probably looking for a few decorating tips. Mayor Martin and Dr. Weingard were chatting amiably. I looked down at Cody. None of the ex-pats were talking to him and he looked stranded.

The quartet resumed out on the veranda, doing a muted version of something by Mozart. The servers returned with a French Sauterne and filled one of the other glasses. I glanced at James Watt across the table and down from me. He was talking earnestly to Julian Soames, who had a background in property development in Baltimore, but mainly in residential restoration rather than resorts. As far as I had noticed, neither James nor Rebecca Watt had glanced at me or Maya.

"Do you live in México City?" she asked Trujillo.

"In Veracruz. That is where we have our main offices. A wonderful city, by the way, full of flowers. Have you seen it?"

"Never, regrettably," I said.

"I was there a few years ago with my family. My father works for Pemex and we went with him while he did some business there," said Maya. "Perhaps you know him? His name is Ruben Sanchez."

"I am sorry not to have met him, but then I have always worked in the resort division of Dos Cerros."

Bill Frost, sitting next to Maya, turned to her and said something in a low voice. I saw her face light up; it must have been something about one of her pictures. She said something back and he made a broad gesture with his hands.

"Bill says he can help us with our investments if we want," she said.

Great. I'd been taking small positions in tortillas and bananas, corn meal and salad oil, dabbling in limited quantities of gasoline once a week, things like that. The occasional flier on property taxes about once a year. Seemed like I never had anything to show for it. Maybe I needed to change my strategy.

My appetizer plate was whisked away and another server appeared with a bottle of red wine and filled a third glass. I touched his sleeve and he showed me the bottle. An '82 Chateau Margaux. The evening was improving. Another server moved along the table with plates holding a good-sized filet topped with what appeared to be a cream sauce, and red rice.

Trujillo leaned toward me and gestured toward the plate. "*Rajas,*" he said, "and *Señor*a Watt had the steaks flown in from Chicago, in honor, you know, of *Señor* Brendel being from beef country."

"And *rajas* are?" I shook my head.

"Roasted strips of poblano peppers in cream. Perfect with grilled meat."

Twelve years in México have not taught me everything about the cuisine, and although I have become a fairly good cook, don't expect me to open a restaurant. But my first taste told me I needed to add this one to my repertoire. It was set off perfectly by a sliced jicama salad with orange segments and bibb lettuce. I raised my glass to Barbara and winked. Brendel was vigorously rubbing his palms together and looked like he was loosening up. The quartet was loosening up as well, moving into a fluid Cuban number that I thought I recognized from Ry Cooder's Buena Vista Social Club CD.

"I love your painting," said Brynn Frost, leaning slightly into my shoulder. "Bill and I went into Galeria Uno last month. "We saw all your big fruits. I think we might buy one. Bill asked me if I wouldn't rather have one of your nudes, but I told him I didn't want the competition." She giggled. "Now that I see your model, I'm even more certain." Brynn had a slightly horsey look, not something I generally looked for in a two-legged model.

"Fruits are good," I said. "They're kind of noncompetitive. If they're done right, they really evoke the taste of México." I wish I could paint the taste of this wine, I thought, but there are limits to what you can do with a brush.

Things were clearly warming up, and the chilly reserve of Malcolm Brendel seemed to be succumbing to the general good feeling from the dinner and the wine. When I glanced in his direction I even saw him laugh at something the Consul was saying. I couldn't hear what Brendel himself was saying, but I thought it probably didn't require as many big words as earlier. We finished with a coconut flan, served with a different Sauterne in the fourth glass.

As the party began to leave the table and servers circulated with trays of champagne and cognac, some of the other ex-pats were orbiting around Brendel and it appeared possible that he could make some other connections here. I thought he might need to get out more as well, even with the gunfire in the streets. I also wanted Barbara's reentry into the social stratosphere to be successful. Stopping a server on his way back to the kitchen, I got a refill on the Margaux, then caught up with Maya, who had joined Cody on the veranda. Cody had a half-full snifter of the old cognac in his hand.

"Can't find this in Peoria," he said. "I'm going off-duty now."

"Is that why you left Illinois?"

"Pretty much. Can't find any girls like this there, either." He put his arm around Maya and she curled into his side.

About ten minutes had passed when I went back in to find the powder room in the foyer, but it was occupied and Sally Mason was standing outside the door waiting. I didn't want to get into another painting conversation with her as we waited, so I turned around and went up the grand staircase to find another bathroom, but at the top of the stairs I had another idea. At the far end of the hall was Barbara's studio, and since it had been more than a week since her first lesson, I decided to slip down there and see how she was doing. As her teacher I felt it was OK.

The door was closed so I knocked softly. When there was no response, I went in and turned on the light. Her setup on the pedestal consisted of an unpainted china mug containing several upright brushes and three or four tubes of paint next to it. Your typical art school still-life subject. I slipped behind the easel and looked at the canvas. The shape of the mug was not quite right and the paint tubes themselves lacked roundness, but there was an interesting area on the left side of the mug where they were reflected, and a good angular shadow on the other side, under the handle. She had taken a couple of chances and they were not bad. Two things that worked out of about fifty possible. She was making real progress. Four percent success at this point was great.

I knew there was a bathroom nearer the stair landing and as I went back down the hallway I saw the door was open about a foot. I reached in and turned on the light and pushed the door open all the way. I could almost feel my hair stand on end. Face down on the marble floor was Malcolm Brendel, his left hand reaching toward the base of the toilet, his face toward the sink cabinet, and his eyes wide open, at least the one I could see. From his right ear protruded an artist's paint brush, the bristle end angled forward toward his face. A pool of blood slowly widened away from his head and more covered his cheek. As I knelt beside him I saw a wide discolored swelling on his neck immediately below his ear and moving along under his jaw. I glanced at my watch; not more than fifteen minutes had passed since we stood up from dinner.

I didn't pause to touch his neck looking for a pulse; the vacant stare of his eye told me it would be useless. My feet touched only three or four of the marble stairs as I flew down to the great room. I was already scanning for Dr. Weingard as I came around the corner out of the foyer. He was standing at the bar talking to Mayor Martin as I ran up and put my hand on his shoulder.

"It's Brendel upstairs. I think he's dead." I spoke in a low tone, but I couldn't prevent Mayor Martin hearing this.

I led the way back up, Weingard and Martin at my heels. Weingard was probably moving faster than he had in a long time. Cody had caught the exchange and was right behind them. I pointed to the open bathroom door. The light was still on.

"Stay out," warned Weingard, "give me some space."

I stopped at the doorway, Cody immediately behind me. Martin had whipped out his cell phone and was punching something in rapidly. Cody pulled me around to face him.

"What happened?"

"I came up to use this bathroom because the one in the foyer was occupied. I went down the hall and checked Barbara's progress in the studio and came back here. The door was open slightly, and when I pushed it open all the way I saw him."

"What was the door like when you passed on the way to the studio?"

I thought for a second. "It was closed."

Martin was speaking rapidly into his phone calling for an ambulance and as many police as were on duty.

Dr. Weingard was kneeling alongside the body with his hand on the side of Brendel's neck that was not covered with blood, and then stood up slowly.

"He's gone," he said. "This kind of wound bleeds

out immediately." He looked at me. "How long would that brush be? You would know."

I thought a moment. "There's probably about three inches that we're not seeing."

"That's it then," he said. "The brush enters the external auditory meatus, then passes through the internal, and judging from the angle, punctures the internal carotid artery. Death would occur within seconds."

"How much strength would be required to drive the brush into his head that far?" asked Cody, quite calmly, I thought, but that was his training.

"There's a major ridge of bone inside the skull that the auditory nerve passes through. If the killer had the angle right, and it looks like he did, then it's not that difficult. The brush would follow the path of the nerve. If the handle had been sharpened, then it would be even easier."

The parquet floor creaked slightly behind us and I turned to see Barbara coming toward us from the top of the staircase. I moved back a step and she looked into the bathroom and screamed. Dr. Weingard took her arm and led her away from the door.

"Malcolm Brendel is dead," I heard him say quietly into her ear. "Let's find a place for you to sit down." She was shaking now and her hands covered her face. I took her other elbow and led her into the study. Behind us was a flurry of activity on the stairs. I turned to see Suit Bag and the other security man pushing their way through the group of expatriates. They stopped short of the bathroom door where Cody had barred the way.

"He's gone," he said to them. "There's nothing left to do."

They didn't try to force their way in and I could see the stricken look on both their faces. The entire dinner party was now slowly crowding onto the upper landing, some straining to see into the bathroom, summoned by Barbara's scream, others just wringing their hands. One man had a violin under his arm and a sheaf of sheet music in his hand. Some of the women were hugging each other. Maya appeared at my side shaking her head as she placed her hands over her face.

"Poor man. I know you didn't like him much, but what a terrible way to die. Now we are back in the soup, I feel like we are a magnet for this kind of thing," she said, now folding her arms. She knew the condition well. Her tolerance for these adventures was deteriorating.

"Don't say that in this group," I said quietly. "The part about my not liking him."

Behind me I heard Cody telling the security men to take up positions at the front door and the veranda and to not permit anyone to leave. I went into the study where Barbara was sitting on a sofa with José Martin and put my arms around her. Martin was looking back over his shoulder at the mantel, where my large nude of Barbara had been hanging for the past three months.

"Cody and I are with you on this," I said. "Maya too. You're OK. We'll get through it."

She nodded uncertainly and then suddenly Cody was next to us bending over with his hand on her shoulder.

"We need to have a guest list right away. Are you up to it? We need to know if everyone is still here." She straightened up, but she was still shaking.

"In the desk," she said. "Top drawer in the center.

There's a seating chart with everybody on it."

It appeared that Cody and Dr. Weingard were the only ones thinking clearly. Mayor Martin was mumbling to himself about bad news for San Miguel and I slipped away from the crowd and moved down the hall, needing to verify something. No one paid any attention to me. I opened the door to the studio quietly and closed it before I turned on the light. I didn't bother about my fingerprints on the knob; they were already there from my earlier visit, and to stand there and wipe the knob with a crowd down the hall on the landing didn't seem very smart.

The mug on the still life pedestal held three brushes. In the tray on the easel were four more. I had picked out eight for her when Barbara and I were shopping for supplies at Lagundi. The missing one had to be sticking out of Brendel's ear. I scanned the area in detail, not sure what I was looking for. The paint seemed to be in order. The thinner and cleaner fluid bottles held no information; but in the tray, behind the palette knives was a small pocket knife with an ebony handle inlaid with silver. It had an expensive look, but it didn't seem to be Barbara's style. This had not been part of the original equipment and supplies, and not something you would need for the kind of painting she was doing.

Against the wall was a small wicker wastebasket and I went down on one knee and bent over it, but didn't touch it. It was empty except for five or six thin wooden slivers of brush handle, one edge of each covered in red lacquer, the same as the other brushes. Just what you would get if you sharpened an artist's brush on the pointed end of the handle.

How very interesting, I thought, because now on the murder brush the police will find Barbara's fingerprints, and probably mine as well, since I had handled the brushes at Lagundi when we bought them. I closed the door and had just rejoined the crowd when *Licenciado* Diego Delgado and three uniformed cops came up the stairs.

# Chapter 6

The uniformed cops took up positions at the periphery of the crowd, which fell silent immediately, and *Licenciado* Delgado went directly over to Mayor Martin and they spoke briefly. During my numerous encounters with Delgado in the past year I'd gained a certain respect for him, despite his occasional ethical lapse. Cops, like artists, are not always perfect. Probably for different reasons. I also knew from accounts circulating about his adventure at the town reservoir earlier in the year, where he had gone over the dam in the center of a six-foot diameter pipe twenty-five feet long, that he was courageous and tough. Surprisingly, if I'd had to describe the way he looked now, I would have said frightened described it better than anything else. It was not a look I'd ever seen on him.

Cody was still on guard at the bathroom door and no one was arguing with him. I heard a siren in the street outside. The San Miguel cops began moving everyone down the stairs into the great room. Delgado nodded briefly at me and joined Cody at the bathroom with Dr. Weingard in tow. Cody and Delgado put their heads together as Cody handed him the guest list. Delgado knew Cody from our previous encounters. Cops are cops, and they still think like cops after retirement. I think Delgado appreciated that Cody had secured the crime scene. Two ambulance techs came running up the stairs, but there was no reason to rush. Brendel would not be rising from the dead again. Delgado waved them off. One of the cops put a hand on Mayor Martin's shoulder and gestured toward the first floor. Martin bristled, but then went down the stairs. The cop raised his palms in a hands-off gesture and followed him down. A forensic tech took charge of the bathroom.

This was not the end to the evening that Barbara had imagined; only one of us had. It had been a long time since I'd read Agatha Christie, but this was beginning to look like the revelation scene. All the suspects were gathered in one room while the master detective paces back and forth, and ultimately lays it all out. But that was not modern police procedure, and Delgado was not Poirot, although there was a slight resemblance. What was going to happen were individual interviews.

As grand as the room was, there was not enough seating for everyone and some were standing around the piano. Suit Bag and his partner in failure were no longer guarding anything. They stared at the floor. The San Miguel police had taken over for them and secured the exits. Manuel was no longer at the bar. I assumed he was in the kitchen with the rest of the staff. Barbara sat in a large chair near the fireplace, her hands clasped between her knees. Delgado went over to Suit Bag and they had a brief conversation where Suit Bag gestured to first one area of the veranda and then another. Delgado nodded and went over to the musicians and told them they could go. Apparently they had been in place the entire time, unable to see the staircase. They began packing up their instruments.

Maya and I were sitting on the piano bench and Cody was leaning against the wall next to us as Delgado stood by the fireplace and addressed the group.

"My name is *Licenciado* Diego Delgado, of the San Miguel Judicial Police. It is a very sad occasion tonight to see a man of such prominence killed, especially in a group such as this. Unfortunately, now begins the difficult task of discovering which of you might have done it. *Señor*a Watt has furnished me with a guest list and we will begin by reading off all the names. Please raise your hand when I say your name." He switched to English and stumbled through the next sentence. "If any of you cannot to understand me, please raise the hands and *Señor*a Watt can translate to the English."

He was about to go on when the ambulance staff passed the great room door on their way through the foyer with the body of Malcolm Brendel. Delgado waited until they were through the entry door. It reminded me of the tradition in Latin America of businesses closing their doors in respect when a funeral procession passes.

When Delgado resumed he went through the list, making a check mark after each name as the hands went up. I was able to learn the names of a few people toward Cody's end of the table that I didn't know. At the end of the list reading it appeared that no one was missing. Barbara rose and gave him a staff list and they went into the kitchen to take a head count.

"I hope you brought your jammies. This is going to take a while," said Cody. " It's going to be like a sleepover without enough beds."

After a few minutes Delgado and Barbara returned. She still looked stricken, but trying to recover for the sake of appearances.

"I am now going to take a statement from all of you. It may take just a minute, or it may take considerably longer. Please be patient. After I have spoken to each of you, you may leave. I will begin with Mayor José Martin." Barbara translated. Most likely many of the guests spoke little Spanish. It was no challenge to function that way in San Miguel.

Of course. Proprieties must be observed, even on an occasion such as this. Delgado led Martin off in the direction of the kitchen, I assumed to the small service room where the staff took breaks, where the door could be closed to ensure privacy. I could understand why he didn't use one of the larger public rooms; they were the turf of the guests, people of social stature he could never hope to mingle with otherwise. Being questioned in a staff room would throw them off balance and level the field.

Barbara rose and said to the room at large, "Manuel will be returning to the bar. Drinks and coffee are available. Please make yourselves as comfortable as you can. I'm terribly sorry about this." She shook her head, as if the whole thing were incomprehensible.

José Martin returned after a few moments with Delgado at his heels and said a few words bending over to Barbara, holding one of her hands in his. Then he left. Delgado led Dr. Weingard toward the kitchen. Maya leaned over to me. Everybody seemed to be speaking only in whispers.

"How about one of those good cognacs Perry always had?"

"You too?" I asked Cody. He nodded.

I was not the first in line at the bar. When Manuel got to me he said, "We're not moving much coffee tonight. How about you?"

"Three of your oldest cognacs, Manuel. This group could use a little cheer."

He got down a bottle which had every mark of age but cobwebs. "What's the staff saying?" I asked.

"The only guess I've heard is that it's the valet who didn't get to park *Señor* Brendel's car."

"Seems a little thin."

"I'll keep you posted."

We drifted gently through the cognac as Delgado finished with Dr. Weingard and then interviewed Suit Bag and his associate and released them. Dr. Weingard had remained inside to help with translation. Next came James Watt, and then Rebecca, who took a little longer than the others. When they left it was Antonio Trujillo's turn. I thought it was interesting that the Watt children were not staying here with Barbara. From Delgado's reverential manner, I assumed the next interview would take only long enough for him to shine Trujillo's shoes and kiss his hand. I was right, although from where I was sitting when he left, his hand did not appear to be moist, but his shoes looked pretty good. I was getting a little restless and wondering whether I should have another cognac when Cody's name was called.

I knew Cody had been silently watching the crowd for what he called "tells," those little gestures and mannerisms that might suggest anxiety or guilt. Body language was second only to English with him, and probably better than his Spanish. Besides, he had something close to a Ph.D. in psychology. I couldn't read this gathering in the same way. Collectively they looked like a group of air travelers whose plane had been canceled and got lucky by being placed in a high-end waiting room meant for first class only.

When he was gone I said to Maya, "When you get in there, don't let him get off on a tangent about that portrait I started. I don't think that's part of this."

"I think he's got other things to think about."

I felt increasingly uncomfortable about being drawn into this, more for Maya's sake than mine, but it was clear that our presence here was purely chance.

Cody was gone nearly half an hour and I could see that the remaining guests were getting more jittery. Brynn and Bill Frost were talking to Barbara, trying, I assume, to brace her up. When Cody came out he put his hand on Maya's shoulder. "You're next," he said. We watched her disappear toward the kitchen. Not the first time she'd been questioned by the San Miguel police.

Cody sat down next to me on the piano bench and I quickly got up because I heard it creak in protest. "What's he thinking?" I asked.

"Well, he's angry because he doesn't want this. He feels like there are going to be crowds of people looking over his shoulder on this one, and he's right. The U. S. State Department, for one thing. Brendel was a public figure, of a somewhat shady color, I guess, but not someone you could ignore. I'm sure the ambassador in México City will be raising hell. Be a little bit careful in there. You're one of the guests who was closer to the victim than most of the others."

"You're joking, right? I was hardly close to him. You couldn't get close to him." I heard my voice getting louder than it ought to be.

"I know, realistically, but compared to the others, you had spent more time with him than anyone except Trujillo, Stephen Washburn, and that Juana woman."

"And Trujillo will get a walk."

"Bet on it. He's home in bed now, wherever he's staying."

"What did you make of him?"

"Let's talk later. Here comes Maya."

She still had a good spring in her step and a swing to her *tejuana* skirt, so I guess she hadn't been grilled too fiercely, but her face was somber. She leaned on the side of the piano and said to me softly, "You're next. He asked me what you felt about Brendel. I think someone may have said you didn't like him."

"He was like a father to me."

"I wouldn't try to tell him that."

I crossed the room to the kitchen door and caught up with Delgado.

"Busy night," I said.

"I would prefer to be sitting in my office down at the *jardín*, watching the Saturday night crowd and hoping no one sets his clothes on fire with a Roman candle. Please have a seat in here."

I glanced at the disgruntled staff standing around in the kitchen. They knew their turn wouldn't come until the end. Delgado closed the door behind us and turned over a fresh page in his notebook. He filled in my name, address, and phone number without asking for any of it, and then set down his pen.

"What do you think of this? You like to involve yourself in this kind of thing." He folded his hands on the table and leaned back in his chair.

"It makes me think about Angel Flores again, but I'm not certain how he would have gotten in. It also doesn't seem like his weapon of choice. I assume he hasn't been caught?" Delgado shook his head. "Other than that, I haven't formed any opinion. I had begun to paint Brendel's portrait, as I'm sure you know, but I hardly knew him. I can tell you this: it may be connected to the reason why he was in San Miguel. His chauffeur had expressed some concern about what he was doing here." I wasn't sure if Lynn would have wanted me to repeat this, but I needed to give Delgado something to chew on other than my role in Brendel's life.

"You spoke to him about this?" He shuffled through his notebook while I was answering.

"I was told this third hand. Please don't mention where you heard it."

"This would be Stephen Washburn?"

"Yes. He must still be out front if you haven't released him."

"What were your feelings toward Malcolm Brendel?"

"I found him arrogant and difficult. He seemed unconnected to the people around him, almost as if he was always looking over their heads, perhaps at a higher power. He treated me like staff."

"And this made you angry?"

"Not angry, but frustrated. As a painter I've got to find a way to relate to my subject. I couldn't connect with him. I was starting to feel that the portrait wouldn't be any good."

"But you would be paid anyway?"

"It's possible that it would have been rejected. I couldn't have protested if it was. But it didn't get that far, obviously."

"Will you be returning the money now? They would have given you a deposit, is that not correct?"

"Yes."

"So you lose by his death?"

"Yes. Five thousand dollars."

"*Madre de Dios*! You are very expensive, yes?"

"I wish. I had charged him more than usual because I thought it would be difficult to deal with him."

"I see. So one thing I am doing now is to place everyone at what we think is the time of death, more or less at 10:15. Do you know where you were?"

"As for the precise time, no. I'm afraid I didn't look at my watch except when I got up from the table."

"But you went upstairs?"

"I wanted to use the bathroom and the one in the foyer was occupied and there was one person waiting."

"Very good. Who was that person, please?"

"Sally Mason." He wrote this down.

"Do you know who was in the bathroom at that time?"

"No, but she might."

"Did Sally Mason see you?"

"Yes. She saw me approach her and turn around and go up the stairs."

"Did you speak to her?"

"No. I may have made some gesture, if only to acknowledge her, but I'm not sure."

"Do you know how long she had been standing there?"

"No. She was already there when I came into the foyer."

"So it is possible she may have seen someone else go up the stairs, or perhaps gone upstairs herself?"

"I suppose. You would have to ask her, but I'm sure you have also noticed that right next to where we are sitting, there is a staff stairway that leads to the same hallway upstairs."

"Yes, we have seen this; later we will be questioning the staff on that point. So then you went upstairs looking for the other bathroom?"

"I didn't need to look because I knew it was there."

"And then?"

"When I approached the bathroom the door was open about a foot or so. I pushed it in further."

"Was the light on?"

"I...no, I turned it on. Immediately I saw Malcolm Brendel on the floor, just as he was when you came. I knelt by him but I didn't touch him; he appeared to be dead. I ran downstairs and brought Dr. Weingard up to see him."

"*Señor* Zacher, are you leaving something out now? Think carefully before you answer this."

"Leaving something out?" I was thinking carefully now.

"Exactly. I say this because a witness who was also upstairs at this time has told me that when you came up the main staircase you went not to the bathroom, but down the hall to a room which is used by *Señor*a

Watt as an art studio, a room where she keeps her art supplies. Is this not correct?"

I had about one second to think how not to step in this hole. It was no consolation that I'd dug it myself.

"Well, yes, you're right. I didn't go immediately to the bathroom because I had started giving Barbara Watt painting lessons and I wanted to check on her progress. But I have to say I saw no one else on that floor. Can you tell me who said this?"

"Normally I would not, but I am willing to give you some latitude here. The witness was Rebecca Watt, who had gone to the study and was looking at her deceased father's collection of ceramics."

"Then she also would have seen me coming back down the hall to the bathroom where Malcolm Brendel was, or possibly she saw the killer before that."

"Unfortunately she went back downstairs while you were still in the art studio, and she had seen no one earlier."

"She could have been a very good witness had she stayed. There is something more I'd like to share with you. I don't know whether you have searched the studio or not. When the guests came upstairs after the discovery of the body I returned to the room and found that one of the brushes was missing, and that there were shavings in the wastebasket from the end of a brush handle. There is also a pocket knife on the easel tray that wasn't there during our lesson. I think you will find Barbara Watt's and my fingerprints on the murder weapon."

He was silent for a moment as he made some notes. I found it impossible to read his thoughts.

"Well, you are certainly ahead of me here. I believe we already have your fingerprints from an earlier case on file. But I will obtain *Señor*a Watt's tonight before we leave, as well as those of all the guests and staff as they leave. Just a few more questions and we will be finished. In your sessions with the victim, did he indicate any problems he may have had with anyone in San Miguel, aside, of course, from Angel Flores at the front of your house?"

"No. He spoke mainly of lofty things. Of posing like the Lincoln Memorial, of being an actor..."

"An actor? As in the theater?"

"Not literally. What I think he meant was that he was always on stage, always performing because of his public life. He wished to get away from the house on Cuadrante, to be unavailable. To stop working, in other words."

"I don't understand."

"The way people in public life might crave privacy at times. It was as if nothing he did was quite real. It's hard to explain. He had a certain lack of attachment to things. I'm not sure how that would connect to his murder."

"OK, we will leave that for now. Did you speak to him this evening?"

"Not a word. He was mostly with the mayor and the consul and Barbara Watt. Occasionally with Antonio Trujillo. I didn't intrude and he didn't try to speak with me, just as he didn't speak with the kitchen staff or the parking valet, I'm sure."

"Before you went upstairs, did you notice if anyone was missing from the group?"

"Well, everyone had gotten up from the table and was moving around. I wasn't trying to see if anyone was gone. I couldn't even have said whether Brendel was still in the room. Obviously he and several others were missing."

"Is there anything else you wish to add?"

"No, but I'll call you if I think of anything."

"Thank you. You may leave if you wish."

"I know. But don't leave the town, as you would say."

"Exactly."

Back in the great room the atmosphere was grim. People were sick of waiting and there was no end in sight. A lot of them were sitting on the edge of their chairs with their elbows on their knees, much like the studio pose of Lynn Washburn, only dressed. Ties were loosened. One woman was threading a twisted napkin, snakelike, through her fingers. The bar was deserted, but there were still two large containers of coffee available. It was just after one in the morning.

I collected Maya and Cody at the piano and we went to say goodbye to Barbara. We all hugged her, even Maya.

"This will pass," I said. "Try to think of things that are going right. I saw some good work in your painting tonight." She gave me a wan smile as we parted, and we paused to have our fingerprints taken in the foyer. Outside on the horseshoe drive were one cop and a single valet, and the night was as black as Barbara's mood.

# Chapter 7

When Lynn called me early the next morning she reported that Juana Cardenas had packed up her belongings and left the house shortly after Malcolm Brendel's car departed for Barbara's dinner party. She hadn't thought much about it until her father had returned alone at 3:00 A.M. and woke her up to tell her that Brendel had been murdered. He had been more upset than she had ever seen him. Naturally, she had not watched Juana drive off, so we had no car description to work from. That would have been helpful, but Lynn was no more prescient than the rest of us. After speaking with her father, she had immediately (and imprudently) gone down to the second floor and thoroughly searched Juana's room, but came up with only one thing, which she said would probably turn out to be nothing. She always seemed to have low expectations. Behind the phone table on the floor she had found a piece of torn-off notebook paper with a name and phone number scrawled on it in pencil.

When she said the name was Victoria Mendez I didn't react. I told her it might very well be of value, but I didn't elaborate. I said I wasn't able to speculate at that point on who might have killed Brendel, but I did fill her in with some details from the previous evening, and said I would try to locate Juana Cardenas for an explanation. Then I thanked her and hung up.

Victoria (Don't call me Vicky) Mendez and I had known each other for about two weeks some years before. Victoria had come down to San Miguel as a twelve- or thirteen-year-old child when her divorced mother married Raul Mendez, a local car dealer. The girl found her new environment simpatico and changed not only her last name to match her stepfather's, but her first name as well. So Heather Fisk was reinvented as Victoria Mendez. She was a bright, well-read child and particularly fond of the work of Vladimir Nabokov. It didn't take me long to figure out which of his books was her favorite.

By the time I met Victoria some years later, the free-spirited mother had abandoned both her daughter and the new husband, and gone off with someone else on a further adventure, possibly on the advice of her horoscope. Raul Mendez, the abandoned husband, had no idea what to do with Victoria, so his own mother stepped in to help. By that time Victoria was a teenage handful who had just dumped her forty-six-year-old married boy friend who had two daughters older than she was, which I thought at the time presented an interesting geometry. It sent him careening into a midlife crisis that shattered his law career and his marriage simultaneously. But our little Victoria emerged unscathed. She was a survivor.

I was introduced to her at a fiesta on a stunning April day in the Parque Juarez. Seeing her for the first time under the dappled sunlight filtering through the tall trees, what I instantly liked about Victoria was her milky skin and perfect strawberry bob, the pert young body, the green eyes set off by a brilliant smile and a lot of perfectly even teeth. I didn't intend to paint the teeth, but they certainly enhanced the overall effect. Even with her mouth closed, you knew they were there. Truthfully, at that point I didn't intend to paint her at all, but the married boyfriend was already launched on his downward spiral and she was looking for the next big thing.

This was eight years ago, a long time before Maya, and in those days my judgment was not as finely honed as it quickly became two weeks later. She was frank with me regarding her interest in "Humberts," as she called her older boyfriends, and even when she said she would like to pose for me it raised no alarms because I didn't think of myself as being of the Humbert class. I was only twenty-seven then—in my reckoning, much closer to her in age than your average Humbert, who in my mind tended to be well into middle age, feeling youth slipping away, and hunting for a surrogate.

The idea that I might end up in her cross-hairs was not something I considered. I very much liked the painting that came of this encounter, and sent it off to Galeria Uno at the end of that month. This was before I had begun sending my nudes off to Mérida. Not surprisingly, it sold within a few days and I never heard any more about it. Nor had I seen Victoria since, although I'd thought of her now and then over the years.

The last information I had about her was that she inherited a property here in San Miguel that had belonged to the grandmother, that is, Raul's mother. Perhaps it was her way of providing for the young

Victoria. It might have been meant as a dowry. I was mulling this over as I called Diego Delgado. I knew he routinely kept close track of the gringo community, much the same way that pigeons watched the lunch crowd in the *jardín*.

We went through the usual courtesies. "I know you must be swamped with the Brendel investigation," I said. "But the reason I called is to find out if you know where I can find Victoria Mendez. She's not in Juarde, the gringo directory, or in the regular phone book, but I think she might still be in San Miguel."

There was a pause as if he were trying to isolate something in his mouth that shouldn't have been hiding in his salad, then, "Yes, she is here still, I believe. Is this in some way part of the Malcolm Brendel murder, perhaps?"

"Probably not, but I don't know for sure. If it is connected I'll let you know. Do you know where she is?"

"*Señor* Zacher, you already have that *muy bonita chica* Maya Sanchez. Are you sure you wish now to visit Casa Victoria? Not that it is my business, of course." So Victoria was now an entrepreneur. I wasn't surprised at her choice of business.

"I see. I merely wish to speak with her because I think she might know where to find Juana Cardenas."

"Ah! The woman of the unfortunate vice president. I have her name from Stephen Washburn. She is on my list of people to speak with. But since she was not at the dinner, she has not had the same priority as others. Am I to assume you will be giving us some help with this investigation?"

"Of course. I'm getting paranoid now because of

the ATM machine episode and the murder weapon being a paint brush."

"I understand. You will find Casa Victoria on Privada de la Luna. It is a small alley off Calzada la Aurora. On the left as you go toward the Fabrica Aurora, somewhat hard to find. The entrance of the street is next to a shop that sells roasted chickens."

"Thank you again, *Licenciado* Delgado."

"It is nothing. Please do not mention my name to her. Do you understand?"

"Absolutely."

I made a few notes and then gave Cody a call. We had agreed the night before to have a morning conference about the killing when we were fresh.

At about 9:30 we assembled at the dining room table and Cody set out a large notebook and a couple of pens. "Let's start with a timeline," he said. I brought coffee in from the kitchen and poured out three cups, then put on a couple of Bill Evans CDs from the first trio period, mid-sixties. We sat down and pulled out my checkbook and looked at the back page of the register, the one with three years of calendars too small to see, particularly on the morning following a party. Cody sat facing the fireplace, where over the mantel was the portrait of Maya as Frida Kahlo, wearing the *tejuana* outfit she had also worn to the party last night. He was studying it carefully, comparing it to the rather vague Maya of this morning, who had pulled on a pair of jeans below the jersey she always slept in. She was barefoot.

"OK," I began. "My first contact was with Lynn, the chauffeur's daughter, at the Schleicher house sale.

That would have been October 1st. She hadn't moved in yet, but two days later when she came to pose, they all had, and she mentioned that her father was concerned about what Brendel was up to. She couldn't elaborate at that point. So that was October 3rd." Cody was writing rapidly.

"That's how you found her?" asked Maya, perking up.

"She was behind me in line and she said she had seen my photo at Galeria Uno."

"And I think she found you! So the next thing she is posing for you with no clothes? Just like that? You are very smooth." She pulled a few strands of hair out and examined the ends. "Or she is."

I didn't respond to this, although it did look that way. It was not much different from the way Maya and I had met, and she had initiated things too. "So then the next day, the 4th, she came for a second sitting and also told me about the portrait commission. She was very pleased. That was a Tuesday."

"How did your name come up?" asked Cody.

"Brendel, or her father, I'm not sure which, asked her to check at the Bellas Artes because there are so many painters around."

"But why did she choose you?" Maya said.

"She already knew me. That's how business is done here. It's all about connections."

"She catches on too quickly."

I studied the calendar some more. "Two days later, Thursday the 6th, I met first with Stephen Washburn and then Malcolm Brendel to discuss the portrait. That same afternoon Barbara started her painting lessons and it was when we were getting some cash on the *jardín* that Angel Flores asked me for directions. I told you about that."

"And this is the tape from the security camera that made its way to Delgado by means unknown just after the shooting at your house," Cody said

"Right. But the shooting was the day of Brendel's first session, which was four days later. On the Friday before that, Lynn came for her third session and told me about Juana Cardenas, the woman staying with Brendel."

"And the next day my family came," said Maya. "That was a fun visit." She rolled her eyes.

"I'm going to be very surprised if that's part of this," said Cody. "So you stayed with me Saturday and Sunday night, and that brings us to Monday the 10th for the session with Brendel and the shootout. So the tape was held for four days before it went to Delgado. That's interesting. This feels like it's part of larger plan."

"Held by someone who must have known exactly what was going to happen," said Maya.

"Then nothing more until last night, the fifteenth." Cody was tapping his pen quietly on the notebook.

"One more thing," I said. "Lynn called me this morning to say that Juana Cardenas had packed up and departed the house just minutes after Brendel left for the party. I'm not sure if that means anything, but it looks funny just from the timing." I didn't mention that I was going to try to find Juana by visiting Victoria Mendez's brothel. I figured I'd explain that to Maya later if I was successful. I'm fairly good at improvisation.

"Anyone see a trend here?" asked Cody.

"In a New York minute," I said. "I'm being set up."

"It's circumstantial stuff, but people get hanged for less. It's kind of an odd thing that he was killed with a paint brush, don't you think? I never saw that in Peoria. Most people are shot. This was a weapon that carries a message."

"It's the artist framed. This time the target's on your back," said Maya. "Usually it's me. It's a good thing Delgado's not believing it."

I thought for a moment about the note left in our *loggia*. I still had not mentioned it to her. "Well, it was definitely one of the brushes Barbara and I bought for her lesson. And I found shavings in the waste basket in her studio that were left by someone sharpening the end. But what's my motive for killing him? I gain nothing, and I lose the portrait commission, which this time was twice my usual fee because I thought he was going to be a royal pain. It's ten grand down the tubes."

"He offended you," said Maya.

"Yes, but I've had footprints on my back before, I'm not that prickly. If I was, there would be eight or ten other portrait clients lying dead up in the studio by now. My usual revenge is just to charge more."

"Page two," said Cody. "Then who benefits from Malcolm Brendel's death, if not you?"

Complete silence.

Finally I said, "What if Dos Cerros has enemies who are trying to stop whatever Brendel was doing for them? Even though we don't know what that is, other than that he was making some kind of broadcast tapes, according to Lynn."

"But why make it look like you are the one who

killed him?" asked Maya.

"Maybe you're just a handy smokescreen; it draws attention away from them," said Cody. "That's what I always think when I see a set-up like this. It's always an invitation to look somewhere else."

"All right, I don't know where that goes at this point. But since we're not likely to see the autopsy report, unless Delgado gets really liberal, which I doubt, let's go up to the studio and take a look at something."

In addition to the one I carry on my neck, I own another human skull I keep in my prop cabinet. It's prepared for medical school use, which means the top is cut off and reattached with a pair of hooks, and the lower jaw is held on with springs. I got it a few years ago from a doctor whose wife's portrait I had painted. He said that skulls like this were typically gathered in India from bodies left in the rivers, and it had most likely belonged to a woman in her twenties. I used it for a number of still lifes, which didn't sell that well. I don't know why; it had worked for Cezanne. Two of them were still upstairs in my storage racks. I had never hung them in the house, which may have said something.

We gathered in the studio and I pulled the skull out of the cabinet and set it on the work table. Maya loosened the hooks and lifted the top off and we all looked inside. Other than the major opening for the spinal cord to enter at the bottom and connect to the brain, there were numerous smaller passages as well.

"Look at this," said Cody, "I know a little anatomy. Each of these holes is a meatus. I don't know if you heard Dr. Weingard explain this at the party, but you can see that these two here," he pointed to a small opening in the boney ridges at each side within the skull, "goes through to the outside, right where the ear is behind the pivot point of the jaw. That's where the paint brush entered. If you follow the line of the outside opening, the point of the handle would then go right toward the spinal cord."

"This is making me sick," said Maya. She got up and crossed to the south windows.

"But," resumed Cody, "it gets worse. On the way to the spinal cord, if it even went that far, it punctures the internal carotid artery. Brendel bled out in seconds. It wasn't just the blood on the floor of the bathroom, it was also the large discolored area on his neck where blood was collecting internally. I think you saw that."

"Wouldn't you almost have to be a doctor to know this?" I asked.

"Not if you had access to the Internet, and you wanted to ascertain whether such a murder could be done in a way to suggest an artist was the perpetrator. Or owned a skull you kept in your prop cabinet. I wouldn't let Delgado see this, by the way."

# Chapter 8
## Victoria Mendez

Heather Fisk's childhood had come to an abrupt and unwelcome end at the age of ten, when she awakened one night at 3:00 A.M. to find her father's hand over her mouth and his own mouth pressed between her legs. She squirmed violently until her father's hand moved upward and covered her nose as well. When she relaxed, his hand did too. What followed she mercifully did not remember in detail, but when her father was leaving, he paused at the door and said he was sorry. He had done a very bad thing, and if she ever told anyone he would have to go to jail and she would have ruined the family because it was her fault. He added that it would never happen again. This became his mantra, repeated several times a week at the end of each nightly visit until she found the courage to tell her mother about it two years later. Separation and divorce were instantaneous.

During this hellish interlude Heather learned what men wanted and to hate them for their interest. But she also learned that the focus of her power over them, which she now desperately sought, lay between her legs, and that it was older men, particularly, who were most vulnerable to it. Boys in her class at school held no interest for her. This knowledge furnished a format for her revenge. When a girl classmate in seventh grade provided her with a well-worn copy of *Lolita,* her course through life was set. She had never dreamed there was a guidebook.

Her manner became provocative in the presence of her mother's boyfriends. She took pleasure in their discomfort when her glance boldly locked in on theirs. When it came, puberty didn't slow her down. In her secret knowledge, she now treated boys her own age with unveiled contempt.

When she was thirteen her mother moved them to San Miguel de Allende, where she married the Volkswagen dealer whom she had met at a convention in Chicago. Heather not only cheerfully took his last name, but in celebration of her new dominance over a succession of older lovers, she added Victoria. She had triumphed over her past, extracted from it what she needed, and when her mother deserted them both, knowing the direction her daughter had chosen, and feeling both responsible for it and unable to change or deal with it, Victoria settled into her future. Raul Mendez, both baffled and guiltily attracted to her, kept his distance and avoided her gaze.

When Victoria's mother did not resurface and could not be located, Raul's seventy-five-year-old mother stepped in. She was shrewd enough to see what was happening, and although she was unable to find any way to stop it, she sought to reduce Victoria's dependence on the men in her life by altering her will to leave the precocious child a property that might furnish her an independent rental income. When she died just after Victoria's nineteenth birthday, she had no idea that this bequest would open as a brothel six months later. The opening would have taken place earlier but for a three-month marriage to one of Victoria's "Humberts," a forty-something Méxican teacher who was quickly disillusioned by her instant infidelity. When the brothel opened, the young madam's plan was simple; the twisted race of men would provide her with an ample income for the rest of her life and compensation for her truncated childhood, paid in nightly installments.

Today Victoria, now twenty-four years old, was lying on her back in the shallow water of her bathtub, trimming her strawberry pubic hair into a perfect heart shape. It was a symbol of joy, her emblem, one of a pair of emblems, actually, the other being a small scorpion tattooed on her left buttock, tail raised to strike. It was her *Yin* and her *Yang*, the two components taken together expressing her view of life, neither complete without the other. But together, so effective.

She was grooming herself for a meeting later in the day with James Watt, the young heir to part of the Watt Industries fortune, whom she had met in February when he came to San Miguel immediately after the death of his father, Perry Watt. The sad occasion for his visit had not prevented him from visiting Casa Victoria, where he found Victoria herself a delightful distraction from his grief. In turn, she found James full of himself, and easily got him to talk about his prospects in Houston. He was only a year older than Victoria, and though he had accepted the favors of many women with a sense of entitlement, she found he knew little about them, being too self-absorbed to really see them.

James Watt had been, like an understudy in the theater, unexpectedly summoned from the wings to assume the role of star. Having so fortuitously come into a fortune of forty million dollars, he fancied himself now as a captain of industry, a puppet master, a stage director guiding a cast of hundreds at Watt Industries, where the fun was in the game itself, its outcome never in doubt. Money in abundance he was accustomed to; power was his new aphrodisiac. He moved people about within the company like rats in a maze, placing them in unaccustomed positions, taking delight in their struggles to adapt.

At their first encounter, James Watt was not to Victoria's taste. He was only slightly over five foot eight, and lightly built. He was one of those people who foolishly believed the phrase, "Only the best is good enough for me," and so in the process of rarely getting the best of anything, he was overcharged for everything he got. Victoria, who knew the value of a dollar, as well as exactly what it took to get one, thought him a simpleton in this regard.

In five years of operating Casa Victoria she had grown weary of the sex trade and found herself daydreaming about respectability. She owned the Privada de la Luna property and the adjacent house free and clear, and she conceived the idea of making it a bed and breakfast, a perennial favorite in San Miguel. The obstacle was money. The brothel provided a good income, but the facility was run down and drab; conversion to an inn would require a thorough remodel of both properties. She had taken bids from two contractors and discovered the project would cost nearly $200,000. And there were no mortgages in México, except on new developments.

Over the months following Perry Watt's death, Victoria saw more of James. She was careful not to humiliate him as she did so many of her admirers, and he was always left with the impression that she had been waiting for his return. She began to speak to him of her desire for respectability, although always noting that she would continue to be there for him personally once she left the business. One night she showed him the plans for the bed and breakfast remodeling. When he asked what the project would cost, she said nearly $200,000, and he only shrugged as if it was no great matter. While he anticipated that a request for aid was somewhere in place down the road, his focus remained fixed on her flawless milky skin and exquisitely nubile private parts. In Victoria's plan, once she had gotten James aboard as a silent partner, he would be discarded.

During this time her focus was centered on someone more to her taste, the fortyish Veracruz businessman Antonio Trujillo. He had cruised into her presence buoyed by the sure awareness of his own good looks; before she knew his name she felt she should recognize him. At six-foot-three, carrying years of experience in the resort industry and a certain forceful technique in bed, he was a bear more suited to her den. His presence gave off vibrations of power, and when he tied her wrists behind the bars of the headboard and roughly ripped off her clothes, she was reminded of her father's late-stage incursions into her bedroom, when he had become more violent, but without the whiney apologies at the end. Trujillo never apologized for anything, and he was one man she found it difficult to hate.

An hour later, having dried her hair and dressed, she saw through window the houseboy approaching her quarters. She assumed he was coming to tell her that Antonio Trujillo had arrived. He stuck his head inside the door.

"There's a Paul Zacher to see you, ma'am."

She needed no explanation to know he was looking for Juana Cardenas, and she only had to hold him at bay long enough to get Juana away from the property. Or perhaps there was another way, something that would subtly alter his experience of the meeting.

# Chapter 9

When I located Privada de la Luna that evening it turned out to be a dead-end lane too narrow to negotiate with the artmobile, so I parked down on Calzada de la Aurora and walked in. The sun had already edged below the western hills and little of it would ever have penetrated the Privada anyway, providing a comforting anonymity for Victoria's clients. A hint of the comforts that lay inside.

Maya had been increasingly overtaken by gloom as the day wore on. She had initially treated the idea that I might be a suspect in Malcolm Brendel's murder with a light touch, seeing it mainly as a break from having a target on her own back. Like me, she at first didn't believe anyone could take it seriously. It helped that Diego Delgado apparently felt the same way. But like the 800-pound canary in the story, no matter how you rationalized it, it was still there, and you had to wonder what the next move would be from the people behind this situation. Finally, she had gone to her friend Marisol's house to share a bottle of wine, so I left her a note saying I was going out to try to find Juana Cardenas, which was the truth, although it lacked detail. I left out the fact that my inquiries were taking me to a brothel. Maya can get snorky about things like that.

Halfway down the Privada I found a small orange and green neon sign framed within a shallow box so that I didn't see it until I was almost directly in front of it. The main device was simply a V, but a green line moved downward from the apex and bracketed it on both sides so that it might have been a pubic triangle centered on two thighs. At the upper edge was a single dot of light, which I took to be the navel. Or was it a martini glass? A nice touch; I'm always sensitive to good graphics. I rang the bell next to it and after a few seconds a sliding panel opened in the door. I wondered if I was going to need a password.

"Paul Zacher to see Victoria Mendez."

"Please wait." As far as I could see, the face belonged to a young Méxican, not very tall judging from the height in the door. It was not Angel Flores. A moment later he returned and led me in.

As I followed I wondered where the years had taken Victoria Mendez. She seemed to be launched on a big slide the last time I'd seen her, but at the same time she was a proven survivor. I couldn't imagine her coming to grief.

The house was a single story and of no great pretension. This neighborhood had never been aristocratic and therefore not a target for restoration. I had not seen any gringos on the street driving in. The inner courtyard was paved and four or five empty tables clustered around a fountain that was not running. It must have been a slow night. We rounded the corner and he showed me into an office. It was a long room with a high, beamed ceiling. It would have been originally the great room of the house. Surprisingly, on the wall opposite the door hung the picture of the sixteen year-old Victoria that I had not seen since I painted it eight years ago. Entering from the adjoining room, she held her hands out and took both of mine.

"Paul, how great to see you again!"

"It's great to see you too, Victoria, but this isn't a business visit. I'm trying to find Juana Cardenas. I heard she might be working here."

"Please have a seat, Paul. It's been a while. First let's have a little chat. I hear about you now and then from some of my guests. A lot happens in eight years; I guess you've got a México girl now."

I didn't want to address this. "I never see you around, you know, parties and so on." My instinct was to leave Maya as far out of this as possible. I sat down at the table opposite her. Victoria hadn't changed much; a few fine lines at the corners of her eyes, perhaps a firmer set of her mouth. There was also greater assurance in the way she held her head. The pale skin and strawberry bob were the same. She wore three or four rings; two of them looked impressive. A couple of prosperous Humberts, I thought.

"The only parties I go to are here. You wouldn't believe how much fun we have. I see plenty of the gringos, enough really, but this is your first visit, isn't it? Will you have a glass of champagne with me? That's all I drink now."

"I'll have one, thank you. How did you get that painting? I haven't seen it in a long time." She got up and went over to the sideboard.

"I bought it at an estate auction in México City. I

just put it up there a few days ago. What do you think? Does it stand the test of time? Do I still look that good?" She turned around slowly to make her point and then returned to the sideboard to open the champagne. Her dress was in the Chinese style, close-fitting in a dark green and turquoise color, with a slit that came high up her thighs. I didn't comment. She poured out two glasses and brought them over to the table. I couldn't see the label, but the taste and the nose said California.

"Not from the Schleicher estate auction?" I wasn't aware of any other recently.

"Of course."

"I never knew who bought it, but that makes sense. Ramon Rivera at Galeria Uno said the buyer wanted to remain anonymous. Funny, but I never saw it in Schleicher's house."

"You were in there?" Her eyebrows went up.

"A couple of times. He wasn't home."

"You do get around." She gave me a coy smile. "I had pictured you hunkered down in your studio all the time. Anyway, John Schleicher had a room off the garden, in the staff and carriage building along that back wall. Maybe you missed it. Kind of an amusement room, I guess. He had some strange tastes, but I'm used to that. One thing he liked to do was pretend he was Stanford White and I was Evelyn Nesbit. I had never heard of her before. Schleicher said he would be the great architect and pillar of the community and I was the Gibson Girl. It was an odd fantasy; I never really understood what he was talking about until a couple years ago when I did some research and then rented *Ragtime*. He had a swing mounted from the ceiling.

We'd both get toked up on cocaine and I would fly back and forth across the room naked. I spent a lot of time there." She sipped the champagne and gave me a warm smile. Maybe this was what was meant by "swinger." I wondered now whether one of the rings was from John Schleicher.

"He must have had a lot of time on his hands. How did he connect with you?"

"Ramon told him who I was. Schleicher gave him a couple thousand pesos extra for my name when he bought the picture." I guess art dealers have to do what they can to get by.

"He told you that?"

"Of course. Why hide it? He was quite taken with me. Then, when I got a little older, it ended."

"I see. And you were the sweet thing he debauched."

Her face changed in an instant.

"Don't sound so judgmental. You had your fun too on that last day of posing, remember? You came into me like a freight train entering a tunnel, all your whistles blaring."

"Don't remind me; you could at least give me credit for resisting you for two weeks. That was not my best day; I've got better boundaries now. I never touch a model. How old were you?" Of course I already knew.

"Sixteen. It was a lot of fun at the time. I was still deep into my Lolita thing then. I just wanted to do every guy who was older, especially if they were married."

"Victoria, if I remember correctly from the book, Lolita was twelve years old."

"So I got a late start." She paused for a moment and shrugged with one shoulder, as if tossing off my remark, and looked into her glass. When she looked back at me there was firm set to her lips. "Maybe not so late. I never told you all of it. Or anyone, really." She stared at the picture for a moment.

I looked back at it myself. There was a certain nasty energy coming out of it that I may not have been aware of when I painted it. "It was all about power, wasn't it?"

"Yes, it was, and it still is. I loved to get those old guys going and make them come after me. It was always fun to see how they went about it. Sometimes they'd just try to sweet talk me, and others would just slip their hand under my skirt and go for it. It seemed like it was always the ones who didn't have a girl in high school."

"Victoria, I was twenty-seven then. Was that old?"

"It was to me. You probably went to an all-boys high school, too, didn't you?

"Let's talk about Juana Cardenas."

"She's a little old for you, isn't she? Maybe right around your own age now."

"That was unkind. I just want to talk to her."

"She charges the same, talk or no talk. She's in number three, directly opposite." I felt like I'd been dismissed.

I looked back at the picture again as I finished the champagne. It was always like that with paintings I hadn't seen in a while, a way of measuring my progress over time. What jumped out at me now, aside from the strange energy of the sitter, was not how good it was, but how wrong the frame was. Ramon would never have framed it like that down at Galeria Uno. It was simply too massive, the gilt too glaring, and the carving called attention only to itself and competed with the painting. I recalled how restrained the taste was in Schleicher's main house; he must have pulled out all the stops in his "amusement" room. Probably the ropes were velvet and the seat was padded and tufted so it would be warm on Victoria's bare little underage butt. The image of her swinging through the room made me think of a picture by Fragonard or Boucher. I wondered if the vice president and Juana had ever used the swing. The effect wouldn't have been quite the same.

Editing out the frame, the delicate coloring of the young Victoria Mendez was perfectly balanced. The milk-white skin against the red-gold tones of her bobbed hair; the subtle notes of green in the shadows and in her eyes set them off in ways I don't think I could improve on even now. She was seated in a lotus position, back erect and ankles intertwined, hands on her knees with the palms upward. It was the only picture I'd ever done that had an almost pre-Raphaelite sensibility to it. I looked back at her. She had not changed her hair style. Probably everything else was much the same as well. I looked for a loss of innocence in her present face and found none. This had not changed because it was already gone when I painted her. I got up from the table feeling a bit unsteady. Looking into the past so directly can revive some strange feelings.

"Thanks for the drink," I said. "Change that frame when you get a chance. It stifles the picture. It deserves better."

"Come back and see me sometime." She looked at me appraisingly. "I still take a few clients myself. It would be like old times. You could pretend I was still sixteen."

I felt a kind of rush come over me as I crossed between the tables to the opposite side of the courtyard, and it wasn't from her apparent interest, or mine. I tried to orient myself. This had never been a pretentious house—the single story said that—and when it was enlarged by adding its neighbor, the owner had simply opened an arched passage through the wall to the adjoining garden, which was not lit and offered no hint about what it might contain.

Centered in all the arches in the main courtyard hung paper lanterns, one before each door. They shed enough light to prevent tripping, but not enough to identify the customers. There were enough rooms for six or seven girls. Glancing back across the court I could see Victoria still seated with one elbow on the table and her other hand toying with her glass; over her shoulder was the younger, nude Victoria, back straight, small high breasts thrust forward, the seductive party girl staring out from the contemplative pose. At this distance the colors seemed to vibrate slightly. Maybe I should get my eyes checked. The Victoria at the table waved to me with a smile and I waved back. I saw no sign of the doorman.

The door of room number three was open to the interior and a thick woven curtain covered the opening. I moved the edge of it aside and peered in. In the dim light from two small lamps with beaded shades flanking the bed, I could make out a woman sitting in a green silk robe. She gestured gracefully to me to come in. There were magenta highlights on both sides and the top of her henna hair, but her face was in shadow.

"Are you Juana Cardenas?"

"Come in," she said, "come in. I don't think we have met." She made a welcoming gesture and slipped off the robe and lay back on the bed. She had a small belly that she couldn't quite hide, like one of Matisse's odalisque models, and she was made on the pattern of Soledad, but with years more of hard use. Waves of subtly changing light were coming off her face.

"I just want to talk with you, Juana. You can put the robe back on."

She smiled indulgently, as if I had said something naive. Probably I had; I had never been in a brothel in my life. The idea had always seemed demeaning on both sides of the transaction. "That's OK. It's costs the same and you might change your mind."

I didn't want to sit on the bed with her, so I picked up a white plastic drink tray from the seat of a chair next to it and sat down.

"I wanted to ask you a few questions about Malcolm Brendel." Suddenly the name sounded funny, and I almost laughed. Maybe I was nervous.

"I thought that might be why you're here. It was a sad end for a sad man."

She was speaking slowly and the words were coming from a long distance. I leaned forward to hear better, watching her lips form each word.

"Why I'm here," I repeated unsteadily, rocking back and forth as waves of energy rolled through my legs. My head felt off balance on my neck. She didn't seem to respond. "It's why I'm here. I'm here." Something was wrong with my mouth and I spoke loudly the way Americans do here when they have no Spanish, trying to make myself understood. My lips felt loose and rubbery.

She laughed a little, rolling her head back on the pillow, and the light from the beaded lamps reflected from her teeth outward dispersed in all the colors of the spectrum. I leaned forward, my artist's eye trying to record this amazing display of light. As I did the plastic tray in my hands slowly grew soft and melted over my knees and fingers, but without any heat coming from it. I stared down at the tray as holes opened in the surface and lengthened into long oval vents as they stretched toward the floor. Finally, a few last strands of plastic, like cooked linguini, slipped downward through my fingers. Then my arms hung uselessly at my sides, nearly touching the floor. Juana was laughing more now and the sound, still coming from far away, was somehow behind my head.

I jumped up and rubbed my hands over my face. Why was I so tall in the room, with the ceiling only an inch or so above my head and crowding me painfully? I blinked and when I opened my eyes the unadorned walls were covered with pulsating arabesques in a maze of intricate colors, moving from paisley into liquid chaos patterns and back. The single window and the door frame changed into the keystone contours of the Alhambra, draped with magnificent fringed fabrics glowing in the dim light. From somewhere came the scent of incense and exotic music.

Placing my hand against the wall to steady myself caused it to yield to my touch and my fingers and palm penetrated the surface. I yanked my hand away and looked at it, and then at both my palms. They had become hives of small wormlike creatures deeply entwined, rolling around and through each other but keeping the form of my fingers. As I fought my way through the beaded strings in the door frame, hundreds of long fingers clawed at me. Juana Cardenas' cynical laughter followed me out.

In the courtyard I struggled to regain my balance and suddenly found myself against the back wall, which I followed without touching it, apprehensive about what my hands might find, until I reached the archway leading to the neighboring garden. I lunged through it, recovered my balance for a few steps, and then fell on my back on the weedy ground.

As the night sky, rippling with the swirling brushwork of Van Gogh, swung in great arcs over me, I realized I was totally, irrecoverably, insane.

# Chapter 10

I'm sure a lot of people don't fully appreciate dog shit. It had been a warm night at Victoria's place, and as daylight climbed over the wall I found myself lying among fragrant piles of it, now beginning to give off steam in the first heat of the sun, an effect I had never observed before. I lost the content of whatever insights I had about it as I regained full consciousness, but I do know that the subject has rarely been approached with such profundity, and I might even say, sympathy, as well. Apparently this overgrown garden was the scene of an ongoing territorial dispute between two or more local dogs, and claim markers had been placed every few feet. When I was able to stand I was relieved to find that I hadn't reclined on any of them.

Testing my balance by leaning this way and that, I began to regret I hadn't observed the label on the champagne bottle Victoria had used, because I was determined to avoid it at all costs in the future. Probably the same could be said for Victoria herself, although she was harder to label. Maybe this had been payback for the fact that our ten-minute love affair had not led any further. Perhaps she had expected to have a noose around my neck afterward, but I had reacted with shock and a fair amount of regret at what I'd done. It could never have happened a second time.

When I passed unsteadily through the arched opening into Victoria's paved courtyard, I was surprised to see Cody Williams under the shadowed arcade, briskly moving from one covered doorway to another. My tentative shuffling movement must have caught his eye because he stopped and yelled. We met at the fountain.

"You look like you've been rode hard and put away wet."

"In a way."

"Tough night? Maya called me when you didn't come home and I got hold of Delgado. He said you were looking for someone named Victoria Mendez. He knew where to find her."

"Only as a way to get to Juana Cardenas. When Lynn Washburn said Juana packed up and left right after Brendel departed for his last supper, I decided to go out looking for her. I found them both."

"You're quite the detective. So then you got rolled by the best; or from the look of you maybe it turned into a reunion party for the Grateful Dead. Let me see your back." He walked around behind me. "No footprints."

"Anything brown?"

"No. I've been going from room to room, thinking maybe you were curled up with some chippie."

"Find anything?"

"Just this. No one's here." He held out a folded sheet of note paper. Across the top I read *"Grupo Catalina."*

"Doesn't mean anything to me, but then, nothing does right now. I find myself strangely detached."

"I found it in a phonebook in the office; it could have been a bookmark."

"Did you see a champagne bottle?"

"Empty Chandon Blanc de Noirs in the office. Two glasses."

"That's what did it." I gave Cody the details of the evening, omitting only my profound dog shit insights.

"So you got nothing from Juana?"

"I may have. If I did, I didn't save it to disk. It's gone for good."

We searched the remaining rooms. The assortment of liquor bottles, a single well-used peekaboo leather outfit, stained in places, and a half-bushel of condom wrappers told us nothing we didn't already know. There were no personal effects in Juana's room, and the plastic tray was back in its original shape on the chair by her bed. How she managed that I didn't know, but I'm not sure why it surprised me. I found my cell phone and dialed Maya.

"There's a lesson in this," Cody said as we walked back down Privada de la Luna. "Never let a good time impair your interrogation skills."

"I'll remember that."

That afternoon, after a careful shower and a change of clothes, I slid into a chair at a table in the garden at Casa de Sierra Nevada, the delightful boutique hotel and restaurant, just below the hill and down Baeza from Prolongacion Aldama, where Cody had his condo. I felt surprisingly good after my adventure at Casa Victoria, although I didn't plan to repeat it in this lifetime. I looked at my watch; it was five minutes to one and I was early for my meeting with Antonio Trujillo. After twelve years in México, I still operated on gringo time. Under the jacarandas the walls were covered with bougainvillea in shades of brilliant red and orange, freely spilling their petals over the pebbled walks. From somewhere came the scent of jasmine, but I couldn't spot the source. A waiter came over from the arcaded bar area and I ordered a Bacardi Anejo.

My first real taste of normalcy had been when Trujillo called me late in the morning and said he had some additional business for me. Despite what I'd heard about Dos Cerros, my impression of him from the party was not threatening, and I was interested in hearing his proposal. Would it would be portraits of the two big hills themselves, the brothers Morales? I didn't mind some quality portrait work now and then, and I was sure they were well connected. A little word of mouth among the higher echelons of Méxican business couldn't hurt. Maybe I could set up a studio branch in Veracruz. Boardroom portraits to order by Paul Zacher.

The waiter came back with my drink and Trujillo was right behind him, oddly on time. For this meeting he was wearing a crisp pair of bronze linen slacks and an immaculately pressed short sleeve shirt in a pale gray green. It was a good color design, but this was a guy who would look good in just about anything. I stood up to shake his hand.

"I'm very sorry about Malcolm Brendel. I didn't have a chance to talk to you at the party after the police came." I said, after the usual preliminaries. "It must be a blow for your business, to say nothing of your personal relationship with him."

He sat down and nodded sadly. From his shirt pocket he pulled out two Cuban Monte Cristos in the torpedo shape and placed one before me with a cigar cutter. "Dos Cerros will go on," he said, "as we have always gone on. In the meantime we have these. Castro may deny God, but he still makes the best cigars."

"Hard to explain," I said, although I didn't see the connection. Maybe the whole company was required to be evangelical in outlook, or at least to mimic it as a kind of corporate culture. I cut the end from the Monte Cristo and slid the cutter back to him. Trujillo must have ordered as he walked through the bar because the waiter returned with what appeared to be a snifter of old cognac and set it before him.

We puffed on the cigars for a while as he looked around the garden. "I always stay here," he said. "It's a delightful spot at any time of day. Later in the afternoon a fine trio plays, Los Romanticos. But to bring up some business issues, may I ask how far you had gotten on the Brendel portrait?"

"We had only begun, as I think I mentioned at the dinner, so there had been no more than one session. After the vice president was fired upon at my house, he didn't want to return, and we hadn't rescheduled another meeting before the party. So the picture's very rough. It would not be possible to know at this point that it's him. I was mainly blocking in the outlines and developing the color design. Because of the robe he was wearing, I had to approach it somewhat differently."

"I'm not sure I understand."

"The robe was a bad color with his skin tones. He didn't want me to change it. I had to generate colors in the shadow portions that worked better in order for the picture to make any sense."

"And this is not what you normally do?" His look suggested he was genuinely interested in art. Few people ever got into it this far with me.

"No. With most clients I would have more latitude to make changes." I didn't elaborate.

"I see. Let us cancel the contract then and you will keep the deposit to cover your efforts. Please destroy what you have."

"Agreed. But that's a large amount for only a single session. Perhaps you would like to apply it to another picture?" I said, hoping to nudge him along.

He leaned back in his chair and drew on the cigar. The dark green canvas umbrella over our table had a vent in the top and the smoke curled upward through it. A Méxican long-tailed grackle settled on the hedge nearby and watched us with curiosity, first raising one leg and then the other, as if pretending to study his toenails. I wasn't fooled. "I think I would rather have you help us with something else," Trujillo said. "But no offense is meant toward your painting ability."

"None taken." I smiled and waited for more. Trujillo took a long pull at the Monte Cristo and blew a smoke ring that didn't quite work.

"Naturally, when your name was suggested for the portrait, I made some inquiries about you. This is something we would do with anyone whose name is placed before us as a supplier to Dos Cerros." He made an offhand gesture, as if they would have had their garbage collector investigated. "You will understand this, I am sure, because we would only do business with trusted people. This would be the same in your profession, would it not?"

I agreed, blowing a better smoke ring toward the grackle, who cautiously watched it approach. Like I was turning down dozens of jobs every day from people who just didn't measure up. Painters can't be too careful.

"What did you discover?" I asked.

"That, as we had heard, your ability in painting is well thought of here. Even the mayor has spoken of you in the highest terms, and I observed your portrait of him. He told me privately that he would like to look that good. But in some quarters you are also known for your efforts in solving crimes. I am told that even the *federales* are not immune when they are guilty. This is a fact that has impressed all of us in the company. All who are aware of it, that is."

"It was an unfortunate situation. I was lucky they didn't come after me because of it." I remembered again the Asesino note in my *loggia*. Maybe they hadn't forgotten.

"But nonetheless, one that resulted in justice being done, is that not correct?"

"I wouldn't argue with that. But surely you are not thinking of bringing me in on the murder of the vice president?"

"Exactly that. It is a concern of the utmost importance to us."

"*Señor* Trujillo, I confess I am surprised at this." I leaned forward in my chair. "Your company is extremely well-connected in this country. I am sure you have influence with police agencies at every level, and besides, because of the identity of the victim, I would assume that the FBI will be eager to get involved here. I'm not sure what it would take for them to do that, but they'll probably find a way. They're known for that. I'm likely to be just a thorn in everybody's side, a position I've occupied before, and it hasn't earned me many thanks."

As if he were expecting this response, Trujillo didn't miss a beat.

"Nonetheless, it would earn you the thanks of Dos Cerros, something not many thoughtful people would wish to decline." He said this slowly and held up one index finger to make his point as he set the cigar in an ashtray and then folded his hands on the table. The waiter was hovering at the edge of the garden. Trujillo waved him over, but then placed his hand over my empty glass. "If you are drinking rum, my friend, I recommend you change to Plantation this round. As my guest, or course."

When I nodded, the waiter took the order and went back to the bar. I had the feeling there was more going on here than I could see, but on the other hand, I was tempted by the idea of solving this killing. It would be a stretch, but stretching in painting had always taken me to new heights. Besides, I was already in it, although my adventure at Casa Victoria had been a less than brilliant beginning. In any case, the tape of my encounter with Angel Flores strongly suggested I was also connected to this murder in some way I didn't understand. It was a choice of getting paid or not for something I would have to do anyway.

"What I am asking is that you look into this for us in a confidential manner, and that you avoid contact with the San Miguel Judicial Police, or with the American FBI, should they enter the scene. Because we would not wish to offend either of them, or even to appear to lack confidence in the local police, where we are, as you correctly suggest, well connected. I'm sure discretion is part of your service, is it not?"

"It's true that this is how I've worked in the past."

"Then we are agreed? We would like to double your original deposit, since I am sure you will have many expenses." He reached into his pocket and withdrew a folded check, which he placed on the table between us when I didn't immediately take it from his hand.

"I would have just one condition," I said, "before I commit to this. That you explain to me exactly what task Malcolm Brendel was performing for Dos Cerros."

This didn't startle him. He smiled slightly, as if this confirmed, at least in a preliminary way, the confidence they had placed in me. He looked off toward the bar for a moment, where the waiter was seating two attractive young American women. One of them wore a particularly fine straw hat with a violet band. I was reminded of my Women in Hats series of three years before, all of which had sold at the opening. When he had determined there was no one else around us, he went on.

"This is not a problem, nor is it even particularly a secret. I know you are aware of Dos Cerros from its petroleum exploration activities in the state of Veracruz. But in addition, we develop resort properties in other parts of México, and indeed, in Belize and Costa Rica as well. We may have touched on this at *Señora* Watt's dinner. Currently we have in the planning stage a major retreat and resort center for Evangelical Christians, in the State of Oaxaca, near the coast. It overlooks the bay of Huatulco and will be called El Monte Sagrado. It is based on the timeshare principle; a way for like-minded people to come together each year for one or two weeks to be inspired by the finest preachers. It would be a regular renewal of faith.

"Malcolm Brendel," he went on, "was more respected here for his reputation as a preacher than for his term as vice president, which, in a way, was most unfortunate. A misapplication of his talents, shall we say. But few people remember this anymore. He had been preparing a series of taped sermons to be broadcast over radio, and at the end of each, he would include a glowing testimonial to El Monte Sagrado. As a man who had risen from the dead, he had an unequaled credibility, as I'm sure you would agree. As an example of what we all pray for, he is irreplaceable."

"The Sacred Mountain."

"Exactly. In the office we call it Project Sinai." He gave me his charming smile, as if this were something he didn't share with everyone. I didn't doubt it.

"And how did the portrait fit in?"

"It was to be used for promotional purposes, on the brochure, for example. Portraits can have a kind of dignity, a presence you might say, that photographs often lack."

"I agree. It's unfortunate that more people don't understand this. And now?"

"Well, as you know, he did not rise again this time, unfortunately. We have not decided whether to use the few tapes we have. It is a most difficult situation, but we would very much like to see his murderer apprehended. That's what concerns us here."

"And the house on Cuadrante?"

"A ten-year lease of that property was part of his payment. At the end of that period it would revert to us. We had given some thought to using it as an urban retreat center at that point, possibly marketing to people from the U.S. as well. The carriage house could have been easily converted to provide more rooms."

But probably without padded swings, I thought. We sat for a moment blowing smoke into the air. The grackle had given up and left long ago. I reached across the table and opened the folded check. The amount was again $5,000, and under the Dos Cerros name and logo it had the same legend as the first one: Special Projects Account. The signature was Antonio Trujillo; bold, but without the extreme drama of Malcolm Brendel's effort. The Plantation rum was damn good. I decided to switch brands in the future now that I could afford it. I wondered if at some point I might make more as a detective than as a painter.

"I'll take the job," I said. I picked up the check and put it in my pocket. Antonio Trujillo picked up the bill.

When I got home Maya met me at the door with a seductive look, one she needed no practice at, which quickly turned to distaste as she got close to me. She wrinkled her nose.

"What?" I asked.

"It's a beautiful day and I was going to see if you wanted to go up onto the roof garden and we could take our clothes off, but you stink like a cigar."

"Thank you."

"How was Antonio Trujillo? Was he as nice as he

looks?" Brightening with this.

"Pretty nice. I didn't find anything sinister about him. He offered me another job; Dos Cerros wants me to look into Brendel's death."

"But you could have told him no, right? Or did he make it irresistible when he told you that as a painter he knew you saw things differently?" She raised her eyebrows and gave me an impudent look.

"He didn't say that. I'm not sure why, and I didn't go into his motives with him."

"Why not?"

"Do you really think he'd share that with me. I think he wants a source of information outside the police, although I'm certain they can get the police to tell them everything about the case. Maybe it's nothing more than backup, should Delgado miss something. Trujillo knows about my adventure with the *federales*, and apparently he thinks I might turn something up. I don't think he told me everything he knows, though, aside from not sharing his motives. Just a feeling."

"What are you going to do?"

"I'm going to take it. He gave me another five thousand dollars, so that makes ten. The first call I'm going to make is to the FBI."

"Are you thinking they would come down here? Or even that they can?" Her voice rose a notch. This idea appeared to make her indignant.

"I don't know. Surely not for the average murdered gringo, but Brendel was hardly average."

I borrowed her laptop and booted the Internet. Once it came up it took only a few seconds to locate the number for the FBI office in Houston. When I dialed, the receptionist transferred me to an agent named Mercy Collins.

"My name is Paul Zacher and I'm a private investigator in San Miguel de Allende, México," I said. "I've been asked to look into the murder of former Vice President Malcolm Brendel."

"Very interesting," she said. "Are you sure it's him? Because this is the first I've heard about it. I think I would know."

"Of course it's him. And that goes to the heart of my question. Now that you've heard about it, is the FBI going to look into it?"

"Not a chance. Our mandate wouldn't allow it. Anyway, Mr. Brendel is on a short list of embarrassments to the government. Everyone in Washington would prefer that he fade into the woodwork. About the only time we would go abroad is to escort a prisoner back to the States after a court hearing approves the transfer from countries where we have an extradition treaty. And that would only happen if there are no federal marshals available, so it's pretty rare. It does happen a little more often lately, though, because so many marshals are tied up with the homeland security thing. I hope that helps you." I thought back over all the movies I'd seen where the FBI is running a clandestine operation abroad. She must think I was a sap, but I didn't expect to get much out of her anyway.

"It helps a great deal. I just wanted to know whose toes I might be stepping on."

"It won't be ours, Mr. Zacher, we're kind of busy with the Al Qaeda thing anyway. Good luck."

That made me feel better. I could believe Osama

Bin Laden had them tied up, but it was also odd that no news had gone out about Brendel's death. It was possible that the police here had clamped down on the media for some reason I didn't know. Government secrecy in México was a dependable reflex, even when there seemed no obvious reason for it. Were the local authorities under pressure from Dos Cerros while they figured out the correct spin for it?

I went up into the studio, stripped the Brendel canvas off the stretchers, popping the staples off one by one with a screw driver, and threw it in the big paper drum I keep for larger trash. This left me with nothing going on except Lynn, but with the other ideas I had for her, maybe that would last for a while. The Brendel portrait had never looked promising to me anyway.

I pulled the number for Maya's father's office out of the Rolodex and dialed. After I went through the receptionist and Ruben's administrative assistant, he picked up the phone.

"*Señor* Zacher, how nice to hear from you. I hope you and Maya are well?"

"Very well, thank you. And you and your family?"

"Quite well. We all enjoyed our visit to San Miguel. Especially Soledad had a wonderful time."

"I noticed that. She could barely contain herself. But I have a question that has come up since your visit. I came across a company called Grupo Catalina and I can't find out anything about them. I drew a blank on the Internet. I wonder if you could help me?" This was the name Cody had found marking a page in the phone book at Casa Victoria.

"Well, what I know just from the name is that they

are a private security provider. I have seen their trucks on some of the drilling sites we have been involved with as acquisitions. Other than that, I would have to make some inquiries. Do you wish me to do that?"

"If it's not too much trouble."

"Not at all. We feel that you are like family now." I wondered if he knew about Maya and me living together after all. "I will call you right back." I gave him my cell phone number.

About ten minutes later I was studying the Lynn picture, making a mental note about a couple of things I wanted to change the next time I worked on it, when my phone rang.

"Ruben Sanchez again. Here is something that might interest you. Grupo Catalina is a subsidiary of Dos Cerros. The directors are the same. The president is a former army officer from Veracruz. I hope this helps you."

It helped a lot. I thanked him, expressed the hope that we would soon meet again, and hung up.

It seemed like I couldn't go around the block without running into Dos Cerros, my newest employer.

On Tuesday morning Maya brought Lynn up to the studio for her final session on the first picture. Privately, I had my doubts there would be a second picture because there was nothing to keep Stephen Washburn here now. I was frustrated because I wanted to do the side view pose I'd discussed with her as well. I also had some ideas germinating about painting her as San Sebastian, nude, hands tied behind a column, head tilted to one side, and shot full of arrows. I could fake the arrows. One knee would be covering the other. I liked these Renaissance and medieval references. I knew what Maya's response would be; she would think it was beyond kinky. Painters are so rarely understood in their own time. Or even later.

Maya was actually being kind to Lynn this morning. Possibly Brendel's murder had made Maya think we all should pull together, or maybe she suspected that Lynn would be departing shortly. Probably the latter. Anyway, she brought Lynn into the studio with a smile.

"Here she is, *Señor* Pintor. All ready for you."

This sounded a little too much like "*Señor* Gringo" for me to believe there was a genuine change afoot. Lynn didn't know what to make of it and she was somewhat intimidated as she gripped the flannel nightgown as if protecting her meager chest. Maya can be rather formidable, and this is one of the things I like about her. I don't usually like skim milk women, but Lynn had virtues as a model that easily compensated for her pale persona. I think it may have been, that behind her vulnerability and low expectations, there was a layer of toughness and resilience. I hadn't seen it, but I sensed it.

She was shuffling around behind the screen and I started to pull out some tubes of paint. The end was close; I had only her feet to do and her ankles. Feet and toes are much like hands and fingers; demanding in the detail. If they're off even a bit, they look clumsy. Not realizing this, some painters try to skimp on them because the viewer doesn't look at them as closely, but

I don't. Then on to the background, which I still wasn't sure about, but it didn't require her to be there, either. There were some things I needed to refine about her hair. Lynn came out from the screen and pulled the nightgown over her head.

"Ta dah," she said, in a forlorn voice.

"Lynn, come on. This is immortality. Give me a little spark. People will be lusting after you for generations because of this picture."

"Great." Her tone was as flat as her hair.

"What is it?"

"We have to leave."

"Why?"

"Well, because Mr. Brendel's dead. It turns out the house was his on a lease deal. He didn't own it. Now the lease goes to the heir."

"And who is that?" This information might be genuinely helpful.

"We don't know. My dad's upset. Eighteen years with Mr. Brendel and he doesn't know what he's going to do now."

"Bring your knees together about an inch and spread your feet out about half an inch apiece."

"You're pretty cool today."

"Do you think I could do this if I wasn't cool? Do you think I could spend every day with stunning women like you in front of me if I wasn't cool?"

"Thanks, I think I get it. You're just full of it, that's all."

"Lynn, I'm only trying to cheer you up so your feet don't look all droopy. I need them fresh and perky today. Think of your toes as dancing, but without moving. What are you planning to do?"

"I'd like to stay and finish the current session of the writing seminar at the Bellas Artes, but I don't know how. If we don't have a place to live and Dad doesn't have his job, it's hard to see how that could happen."

"What's going on at the house?"

"Well, the security guys are gone. There's been no sign of Juana, of course. It's mainly Dad and me. That Trujillo guy came by and picked up some papers on Sunday evening. He's the good looking one. Dad asked him what was happening. He said that the 'company,' that's Dos Cerros, I guess, would continue Dad's salary for thirty days, but that he wasn't sure how long we could stay in the house, and we'd have to settle that with the heir. It's kind of lonely."

"It must have been a lot more fun with Brendel and Juana there; he was such a party animal."

"You shouldn't say things like that about him now. At least there was a focus then. There was some reason to be there, something to do. He always was making some new set of demands. Now we just sit around and watch TV, and I don't understand most of it. Dad didn't really like Mr. Brendel that much for the past few years, but now he misses him."

I was working on the shadows and braces under the folding chair. All the linear parts made an interesting contrast with the patchy small planes of her legs and feet. I made the platform look like an airy stretch of floor, with hardly anything to support her. The legs of the chair became vague where they touched it. She might fall through it, or be absorbed by it. Ambiguous, ethereal. Much like this case.

"You're wiggling your toes," I said. "I only wanted them dancing spiritually."

"Sorry."

"Heard anything about the funeral?"

"Only that the instructions are with the will, which was with the things Trujillo collected from the house. I guess the authorities in Guanajuato haven't released the body yet."

"It can take a while. If it wasn't a murder, he would have to be buried or cremated with twenty-four hours. Who is the next of kin?"

"I don't know. I guess there are no kids, and he was divorced years ago."

"You know, this is our last session on this picture. Whatever remains for the background can be done without you."

"I know. It's another thing coming to an end. I've gotten to like posing and I think I'll miss it."

"If you end up staying, would you pose for the other picture we talked about? The side view, with your chin on your shoulder?"

"I'd love to, but I don't think it will happen."

# Chapter 11

I finished the background on Lynn's picture over the following two days, then sat and looked at it for a while. I was glad to have it, because the investigation had come to a dead end just as my role in it had become official. With mixed feelings I stopped back twice at Casa Victoria but the house was closed up and the pubic triangle neon sign was unlit. I tried to call Barbara three times without reaching her, but I knew Cody had spent at least one morning with her and she was recovering her equilibrium. He also said Delgado had not called her for anything more.

But here was Lynn, the frail waif child, turned into a disconcerting painting that pleased me as much as anything I'd done in a long time. I thought of it as in-your-face innocence, but I didn't plan to use that as the title. The cool, detached tone of her expression worked especially well. Maya still didn't understand it, and I didn't think she ever would. She's committed to the idea of beauty in pictures, and I generally work with that goal too, but Lynn offered the opportunity for something different. I was excited to try the side view picture of her, thinking of the long hollows on her thighs. Maybe it would happen. Maybe Barbara would decide she needed a driver and they could stay.

As I was thinking about this the phone rang. The caller identified himself as Alberto Gomez, an attorney working on the estate of Malcolm Brendel. After the usual courtesies he wondered whether I might find a moment to stop in at his office. Perhaps he had something to contribute to the investigation, although I couldn't think how he knew to call me. Maybe he had my name from Trujillo. He didn't want to be more specific on the phone. Since the timing was right I suggested I could come in that afternoon. He agreed.

Gomez' office was in a small commercial building not far from Casa Victoria, a block farther down Calzada de la Aurora from Privada de la Luna. It had a yellow facade and a large barred window open to the street. From the outside, it could have been anything. The structure itself might have been from the thirties or forties; it could have been a toy store or a meat market on a long street of small businesses. A few doors down was a larger building that housed the Michoacan state outlet for folk art. Over Gomez' door in black letters on a gray background was the word *Notario.*

Inside, however, a different taste prevailed. The decor was crisp and hard-edged, with black lacquered furniture and brushed chrome and frosted glass lighting. The receptionist was dressed in black and white; crisp also, but softer around the edges.

"Paul Zacher to see *Señor* Gomez," I said. She led me in immediately.

Gomez's office had walls of lacquered eggplant, that dark, warmish violet that popped the greens in the line of potted calla lilies gathered at his window. The trim at the doors and windows was a pale putty color with subtle greenish overtones. Again the black lacquered desk and seating. The brick red and pumpkin-colored *barro* tile on the floors. Lighting with greenish frosted glass shades to match the reception area, with a hint of Art Deco. The person who had put this together knew his stuff. My only problem with it was the lack of art on the walls. "Clean lines," that favorite phrase of architects and designers, often means no pictures. Gomez stepped forward and put out his hand.

"*Señor* Zacher, I am very pleased to meet you."

He was a year or two older than I am, wearing a pressed black shirt and straw colored linen slacks.

"Please have a seat."

"I love your decor. Were you an architect before law school?"

"Actually, it is my wife who is the architect. This is her work."

"Is she in practice here in San Miguel?"

"Yes, she mostly does the designs for colonial-style renovations in the gringo community, but this is her normal taste."

"Very effective. I mean it. It's an inviting work place."

"Thank you. I have been working, as I said on the phone, on the estate of Malcolm Brendel, the unfortunate victim of the homicide last weekend. Were you there when it happened?"

"Yes. It was tragic and quite upsetting to all the guests. They were there to meet him and help him get established in San Miguel." I began to wonder if he were looking for information from me, and if so, what position did this put me in with regard to Dos

Cerros, my new employer?

"Did you know him well?"

"Hardly at all."

"You must have shared some bond, then. Perhaps you were members of the same church community? You are an evangelical Christian?"

"No."

"Fraternal organization?"

"Not my style."

"He was an art lover?"

"He didn't appear to be. I'm fairly certain he knew little about it." A moment of silence followed this. I couldn't see where he was going with it.

"Well, in any case, it is often difficult to see the thinking behind people's actions, but that is not our purpose today. I believe he had no surviving family, and he and his wife were divorced many years ago, about the same time he left office. Of course, you are aware that he left his entire estate to you? Aside from some minor bequests to his aides."

Before he had finished the sentence my vision had already narrowed to almost nothing. It was like looking at Gomez through the wrong end of a telescope. This was nearly the worst news I'd ever received. I couldn't think for a moment; my head echoed with random noise.

"I can't believe that," I managed to say after an embarrassing pause. "Are you quite sure? It really says Paul Zacher?"

"Absolutely. The will is less than a month old."

"Less than a month old," I repeated stupidly. That certainly didn't sound good. "Did you draft the will?"

"No. It is an American will, not Méxican, and executed in Kansas City, Kansas. But all the property is in the U.S., so that's not a problem. That's all I know. You seem to be upset?"

"I, no. I'm just surprised and deeply moved." This was a stretch but I had to respond.

"I can give you a moment, if you wish. Do you need a tissue?" He moved a box toward me. "Otherwise we can review the terms of it."

"No, I'm all right."

"It is a simple estate," he said, opening a slender file, "unencumbered by debt or complicated by real estate freeholds. The bulk of it is in securities invested in your American firm...let me see, Fidelity. Then there is a ten-year leasehold on the property at Cuadrante 13A. This is net of maintenance and property taxes. There is a cash balance in the checking account at Banamex of about 22,000 pesos. That would be subject to change pending any fees or further checks clearing, and finally, there are the personal effects; clothing, furniture, books, mementoes."

"And the value of the holdings at Fidelity?"

He ran a finger down the page. "At the close of business yesterday, the total was $645,330. That's in American dollars, of course. The transfer will require just the formality of removing the deceased's name from the account, since the funds are held jointly in your name and his. The minor bequests have been deducted already from the checking account."

"I see," I said, but I didn't really see at all. I still felt a major chill gripping my body, as if all my blood had gone off somewhere and couldn't be located.

"I don't know if you are aware of this, but there is no estate tax in México. And this is below the taxable threshold in the United States, so there is no taxable event here in either country. Since the Fidelity account was structured with you as joint owner, it would not be part of any probate process."

"Joint owner?" As numb as my lips were, I was surprised that Gomez understood me.

"Exactly. Mr. Brendel must have been fond of you, and to structure it this way implies a great deal of trust. I have taken the liberty of forwarding the death certificate to Fidelity Investments, along with a copy of the will. But the funds should be available to you within a day or two because it is merely a technicality. *Señor* Brendel's final expenses will be taken care of by a company called Dos Cerros. Do you know of them?"

"Yes. I've heard the name."

"They are very nice people," he said.

I nodded. "The best."

He opened the center drawer of his desk and pulled out a set of keys with a metal tag on the ring. Then he slid them across the desk pad. "Here are your keys to the Cuadrante 13A property. The contact number for Fidelity is with the copy of the will. *Señor* Trujillo has already removed the burial instructions and he will arrange the removal of the body from the morgue in Guanajuato once it's released. A simple phone call should take care of your end of it. Congratulations, *Señor* Zacher."

"Thank you."

"And these are your documents. You have a copy of the will, the statements from Fidelity, a copy of the lease on the Cuadrante house." He slid them into a black vinyl document case and zipped it shut. I put the keys in my pocket. "There are also two additional copies of the death certificate here, in case you have anything else come up. I think that's everything. If you have any questions, or if you have need of legal services yourself, please call me."

"Thank you." I had become a person of few words as I stumbled out into the street. The words I was mainly thinking were means and opportunity, which, by themselves were not so terrible; they also applied to everyone else at Barbara's dinner. The addition of the third word, motive, however, was one that, as far as I could see, now applied only to me.

"It's really true?" asked Maya, when I got home and told her about the will.

"Yes, unfortunately. But nothing will change; I would never allow money to get in the way of what I want to do. I'm just going to leave it in place for emergencies, such as legal defense. We'll still live off painting and your income from research."

"So now we are *ricos*," she said thoughtfully, "but it will make no difference?"

"Well, in the States it wouldn't make us rich, just more comfortable. However, here it's not too bad, since we already have this house, and it's paid for. But now we have another house as well, possibly the finest restoration in San Miguel, for our exclusive use for ten years. Minus the month or so that Brendel was there. Plus we have all his stuff. I could have pictures of Sammy Davis Jr. and Peter Lawford on my walls, all autographed. Gerald Ford, even. That would be different."

"And who are they?"

"Just people Brendel hung out with, mostly dead now."

"Like him."

"Yes, like him." I didn't get into the subtler ramifications of the whole will thing because I wanted some time to sort them out myself. Why, for example, was the will made in Kansas City just before he came down? He didn't even know me then. He couldn't have anticipated that I would be painting his portrait, or could he? And how could he? And why leave anything to me at all? At the party he barely acknowledged me. It was as if he didn't know I was his heir. If I'd had to characterize our relationship I would have used the word "frosty." I waited for Maya to go off to the market and then called the number on the Fidelity forms.

"How may I help you?"

I gave the woman my name and the account number and Brendel's Social Security number, which had been on the documents from Gomez.

"And you are the co-owner?"

"Yes. I believe you've been notified of Mr. Brendel's death."

"Yes, but we have not received the necessary documents for transfer, or if we have they haven't been recorded yet. The account is still frozen. In this case, because your name is also on the account, it will be simply a matter of checking the documents and removing Mr. Brendel's name."

"Frozen?"

"When we receive notice of a death, all the assets in the account are frozen until the transfer is complete.

It means that no transactions are permitted."

"That's fine. I'm not looking to make a transaction, but I would like to know when this account was set up. Can you tell me that?"

"I think so. Let me see.....yes, the account was opened on September 16." Just over a month ago.

"Can you tell me if it was a transfer in, or what form it took?"

"It was a transfer of funds from Haverford Bank & Trust, in St. Louis."

"You wouldn't have that number among the documents, would you? I'm calling from México."

She gave me the number and I thanked her and hung up. I checked the will from the document folder. It was dated September 16, as well. I dialed Haverford, and the receptionist transferred me to a hold line, where I sat for ten minutes listening to Vivaldi while I waited for someone to notice me. This at Telmex long distance rates—but wait, I was now rich! And I was not going to be able to spend it easily from prison. Mainly it could go for meals and toilet paper, since the Méxican authorities didn't provide them.

I finally explained my problem to someone named Ms. Nelson. I was simply looking for the source of the money transferred to Malcolm Brendel's Fidelity account.

"I'm sorry sir, I can't release that information. But I can tell you that the source of the funds was not Mr. Brendel. He has never had an account here."

"So," I was saying to Cody and Maya on October 21—the next day—at lunch. "The money leaves Haverford on September 16 as belonging to someone unknown, to us at least, and appears at Fidelity belonging to Malcolm Brendel, with Paul Zacher as co-owner should Malcolm be cut off in his prime. The same day, a will is executed in Kansas City naming the said Zacher as heir to the entire Brendel estate, excluding $20,000 to Stephen Washburn and $5,000 each to Burton Hernandez and Gaspar Frutos, who I guess must be the one I knew only as Suit Bag."

"And something tells me that even if you bribed someone inside Haverford to tell you the name of the person who owned the money before it went to Brendel, it would be another blind alley," said Cody. "There would be layers within layers."

"So now you are the target again," said Maya, "There is something sinister going on here, even though the money looks good on the surface. Maybe you should start carrying your gun." She was usually the one who ended up wearing the target, but I could see no satisfaction on her face that now our roles had switched. There may have been anger in her eyes, but she wasn't looking at me much. We were seated in the courtyard of the Santa Monica, the mellowest place in San Miguel for lunch. The scent of jasmine was all around us; consternation has no odor.

"You know," said Cody, "the way this is coming together reminds me a lot of the scene in Frankenstein, where the jig is up and the villagers have figured out where the monster is hiding and they all gather in front of the castle at night with torches lit. There's always some old ignorant rabble-rouser peasant guy yelling for blood. And the ancient gypsy woman, wise in her obscure lore, who knows all the secrets. All around them the crowd is closing in. And now you're the good doctor. Tough break for you."

"Which Frankenstein movie is this in?" asked Maya.

"I think it's in every damned one of them. It always comes down to the villagers gathering outside with torches. Except now it's going to be the police, with guns," I said.

"You know what?" said Cody, poking me in the ribs with his index finger. "I'm outside the castle yelling with the crowd on this one. I think you did it. I'm a cop, and cops know these things."

"Thanks for your support."

After lunch it was time to check on the condition of my newest castle, and since the villagers hadn't gathered yet outside it, access was easy. The three of us headed off on foot to Cuadrante 13A to take possession. We were met at the door by Stephen Washburn.

"How are you doing?" I asked. I could see from the way he looked at me his attitude had subtly changed. He was a little more deferential, even though he no longer had a job or wore his livery.

"We're OK here, but more or less in a holding pattern, Mr. Zacher. It's just Lynn and me. I guess this all belongs to you now."

"For a while, anyway. I want you and Lynn to stay here as long as you like. I have no plans to move in, and you'd be doing me a favor if you kept an eye on it. I assume you've heard about the money left to you in the will." He nodded. "Have you talked to Antonio Trujillo?"

"Yes. He said you would be acting for the company in looking into the circumstances of Mr. Brendel's death, and that I should cooperate."

"Good. These are my friends, Maya Sanchez and Cody Williams, and they're going to help me look through the vice president's things. Has anything been moved or taken away other than the papers?"

"No. I stripped the bed, but kept his bedroom and the library locked. You probably have your own keys now, but if you don't. I can open them for you."

"I think we'll be all right."

"Call me if you need anything. My room is right at the top of the stairs on the third floor." He smiled sadly. We followed him up, but stopped at Brendel's room on the second floor. I found a key that fit, and opened the door. It smelled a little musty, so I opened both the tall casement windows, which began at the floor and faced Cuadrante. Aside from the bed, everything else looked undisturbed.

"I'll take the bathroom," Maya said.

Cody opened the armoire and began going through the clothes. "Pricey stuff," he said after a while, "but not very much of it. How much would he need, do you think?"

"Who knows? How much work was he getting these days that he had to be well dressed for?" I sat at a small writing desk and started emptying the drawers. It was an odd feeling that everything I touched belonged to me and yet I had never seen any of it before. Most of the contents were routine things, the pens and pencils and notepads you would expect to see in any desk. I found business cards from Antonio Trujillo and one other Dos Cerros executive. Further back in the top drawer was a plain gold man's wedding band in a small gray velvet bag with a drawstring at the top. Inside, the inscription read GB*LOVE*LH. There was no date. I wondered if GB had been Brendel's father. The style was too plain to be able to date it. I put it in my pocket.

"Come and look at this," said Cody, waving at me. He was at the dresser. Check out the underwear." He handed me a cotton tee shirt. The neck band was frayed and the shirt was neatly mended under both arms.

"Who mends underwear anymore?" I asked.

"I guess he hadn't had a gig in a while."

"But this was a guy with nearly $650,000 in investments. I don't get it."

"And look at the shoes," he said. We went back to the armoire. At the bottom were six pairs of shoes; two were Italian and quite new, stylish and pricey-looking, one brown and one black; and then four more that were well worn, but carefully maintained. Cody held one up sideways to me. "Look, it's been resoled and reheeled."

"I don't get it," I said.

Maya came out of the bathroom. "Nothing much. Some expensive colognes and after-shaves, but then a cheap toothbrush and razor. Two pairs of dark blue socks drying on the shower bar. There's some kind of message here, but I can't read it. The toothbrush has been used so long the bristles were bent over the sides."

"You'd think the staff would have done his laundry. Maybe he'd pissed them off too and that's the message."

"Everything is pretty clean." She moved on to check his night stand. She pulled out the drawer and set it on the mattress and began lifting out each item separately as I watched.

"What are those pills?" I asked.

"Viagra. And this," she held up a small container that looked like it could be Binaca, "is nitroglycerin spray."

"So he had a heart condition."

"Right. Also condoms, lubricant, vibrator, lip balm, and a nail clipper. There was another one in the bathroom."

Cody was working through some books in a small stand on the other side of the bed. "This stuff is not what I would have predicted. Look at this." He held up a worn volume and flipped through the pages as if to let something out. *The Elizabethan Dramatists, Vol. II.* He held up another one and similarly fanned the pages. "Eugene O'Neill. And this, *Set Decoration* by Herbert Cromer." Nothing flew out of that one either. The rest were similar.

"Any names in them?"

"No. Just a few book marks and marginal notes here and there."

"Not much distance between being a preacher and being a playwright, I suppose. Or a politician."

I turned back to the desk and found one more thing. In the bottom left drawer was an old black-and-white photograph of a wedding couple, yellowed with time. The man appeared to be a young Brendel in a thick suit, a grin as wide as his mid-century lapels, and next to him a slender woman with a shy smile. Her wedding dress had a satiny sheen with a smooth fitted bodice and a wider skirt, and in the breeze, she held her veil with one hand and the other was linked through his arm. I flipped it over. In pencil it said only, Feb. 21,

1953. I slipped it into my shirt pocket. She must be LH, I thought, but then Brendel would have to be GB. Possibly Malcolm was his middle name and he didn't use his first name. I made a mental note to look into that.

Maya had finished the night stand drawer and turned it over to examine the back, but there was nothing unusual about it. Cody and I replaced the items and put it back. When we turned the mattress and box spring over we found nothing. We looked under the bed and behind the other pieces of furniture as well.

"OK," said Cody. "What I always ask at this point is, what didn't we find?" He held his hand out as if waiting for something to drop into it. "Sometimes that tells you more than what you did find."

"Dental floss," said Maya instantly, "and he didn't have false teeth." She didn't miss much.

"I have something," I said, "although it might easily be in the library. There's no address book or Rolodex, although we do have writing materials. Of course, there's no phone here, either. Let's just keep it in mind for now."

When we went downstairs and reassembled in the library, Lynn joined us and I introduced her to Cody.

"I think you already know Maya."

"Can I help?" Lynn said.

"I'm going to take these framed photos back with me for study." So who's to say I shouldn't have all these celebrity photographs on my walls too? Even Margaret Thatcher. Not many people had one of her. So what if they all had Brendel in them? Add some interest to the studio. Wasn't he a historical figure too, in his own flamboyantly tainted way? Not everyone can be Jimmy

Carter. Not everyone wants to be. Now, with all these celebrities hanging in my studio, I'd have to be on the house tour for sure. I could put them up next to my two framed twenty-centavo pieces, the earnings from my first case. "Do you think there's a box around that would hold them?"

Lynn skipped out and returned in a moment with a large, stout box. "This was part of the vice president's move-in supply."

"How many more are there?" I asked.

"Just two, besides the suitcase."

"Now that's interesting, and it suggests the same thing I was seeing upstairs," said Cody. "This guy was traveling light."

"Does that suggest something to you?" asked Maya.

"It might. I'm thinking of the ten-year lease. Wouldn't that invite settling in?"

Lynn was hanging about at the doorway, not sure whether to leave or stay. Clearly she had never been invited into the room. I beckoned her over as I was pulling the pictures out of the bookcases and packing them in the box.

"How well did you know him?" I asked her.

"Mr. Brendel? Not at all, really. I mean, he never even spoke to me. I don't think he knew I existed."

"I thought your father drove for him for eighteen years?"

"He did, but I was never around, I lived with my mother in Emporia. I had never even seen Mr. Brendel until I got here."

"But how did you end up in San Miguel?"

"My dad told me he was coming down here. I already knew about the writing seminar, and I begged him to let me come along so I could take it. If I hadn't been able to stay with him, I couldn't have afforded it. I mean, it was Chile Colorado teaching; I couldn't pass it up. Like, when would there ever be another chance to work with her?"

"Chile Colorado?"

"The western mystery writer? You don't know her?"

I knew about western writing about as much as I knew about northern, southern, and eastern writing. The books I read tended to ignore geography, aside from occasional scans of the México road atlas, which usually did too.

"OK, remember when you were the spy in the house for me?"

"You mean until he died?"

"Exactly. Now I want something subtler. Are you up for it?"

"Of course. I heard you said we could stay here too." She gave me a big smile and came over and hugged me until Maya started making snorky noises at the end of the sofa.

"Here's what I need. The name of Brendel's father and mother, and the name of his wife, now divorced, OK? I realize this will have to come from your father."

"You got it."

I could have gotten this from the Internet, but I was hoping for the personal kind of collateral information her father might drop into his narrative. I also wanted her to continue keeping her eyes open for me.

"Lynn, be subtle. Get him to reminisce a little about Brendel in the old days. I don't want him to know what you're doing. If he doesn't want to talk about it, I can still probably get it somewhere else, but I don't want to sift through hundreds of web pages when we have a witness right in the house."

"Is Dad a suspect?"

"Right now I'm the suspect and I'm trying to get myself off the hook. I've heard that the ambient light in México prisons isn't that good for painting. It can be difficult to get a north-facing cell."

"Oh, Paul, you would never have killed him." She put her hand on my shoulder.

"Thank you."

At the end of the sofa, Maya's eyes rolled over until the whites showed. Lynn left for her room upstairs and we started the search of the library. There was a large desk opposite the fireplace that Cody went to work on as I packed the photographs into the box.

"It's funny," I said to no one in particular, "that all the pictures are identically framed." No one said anything. "Or is it?"

"Maybe he gathered up all his autographs and had them re-framed to match before he came down here," said Cody. "The way people hang their diplomas on the wall. It's to establish credibility."

All the photo backs were sealed with brown paper, as a dust guard, and I toyed with the idea of slitting them open. But the man was not a crook, at least not recently, so I decided not to. I could always do it later if I found a reason.

"Here's a copy of the lease," said Cody. "Ten years to Malcolm Brendel, his heirs or assignees. It started October 1. But you've got that already."

"That's us," said Maya, brightening. "The heirs."

"Could you see yourself living here?" I asked her, looking up from the picture box.

"Not with what I know went on here this year." And before, I thought, seeing in my mind the young Victoria Mendez swinging naked through the fun room in the carriage house. "Hello," said Cody. "Here's something. It's a Prudential insurance policy in the amount of $100,000."

"On the life of?"

"You guessed it, Malcolm R. Brendel."

"Don't tell me the beneficiary."

"I won't, but your net worth just jumped a notch."

"Shit! Who was the owner?"

"Brendel himself."

"Sweet guy. No one ever looked out for me like that before. Throw it in the box here with the pictures. But would they normally write a policy on someone that old? I'm assuming it wasn't written twenty years ago."

"Most companies will go up to age eighty."

"What's the date on it?"

He opened the first page. "You don't want to know, but I'll tell you anyway. September 16 of this year. It's getting a familiar ring to it."

"I don't think I want to cash it in."

"You might want to rethink that. Premiums can be fairly fierce at that age, and you'd have to keep paying them to maintain the policy in force until you changed your mind. It's a term policy, there's no cash value to maintain it in force if you stop paying." He pulled open another drawer and placed a stack of bills on the desk top. "Telephone, credit card, propane refill, florist, fountain cleaning, looks like the normal things."

"Let's look at the credit card bill," I said. He pulled it out.

"Looks like he paid his cell phone, two charges for clothing, market stops at La Europa, then five restaurant charges. The usual places, Tio Lucas, Bugambilia, El Campanario, Harry's New Orleans."

"He likes the same places we do," said Maya.

"And below the bills, a Bible. New Testament, I mean." He pulled it out of the drawer and fanned the pages.

"I was wondering when we'd find that," I said. "He was a preacher, after all." A single card fluttered out of the pages and fell to the floor. I bent over and picked it up. It was one of those funeral memorial cards that churches hand out on the day of a burial service.

"Lillian Ballard," I read. "February 2, 1932 to March 15, 1989. The Lord is my shepherd." I put it in my pocket next to the wedding photo.

Cody pulled each drawer out and examined the bottom and then replaced them. The only other storage in the room was a built-in cabinet in one corner, with a pair of doors above and below the chair rail, and a matching panel above that followed the lines of the room's mahogany paneling just below the ceiling. When I pulled the handles they resisted at first, as if they were slightly swollen from humidity, then opened with a protesting noise. Both levels contained books; some were related to the theater, others were novels of an old-fashioned kind. They were all well used, unlike the ribbed and leather-bound matched sets that John Schleicher had owned. I moved them around a bit, but it didn't seem worthwhile to open each one and shake it out. I closed the doors again.

"That's it," said Cody.

"I don't want to take anything back except the photos. I think we're finished," I said. "Tell Washburn we're leaving. Maybe he'll give us a ride back with this box. I want to check something in the carriage house." I went out the back way through the garden, already looking trim and vigorous again after the neglect following John Schleicher's death. The fountain had been cleaned and was flowing. On my chain I found a key that fit the door on the left end and let myself in. The first thing I looked at when I turned on the light was the high ceiling; in the center beam were two stout steel rings, but the swing was no longer hanging from them.

# Chapter 12

The phone rang early the next morning and I reached over Maya's motionless body and picked it up. She was lying on her stomach and I couldn't resist pulling up her jersey just a bit and checking out her flawless butt. It was still good. México has a reassuringly changeless quality to it.

"Paul," said a whispering voice of the other end, "it's Lynn."

"Great. What have you got?" I was whispering too.

"I got my dad to open a couple of bottles of Mr. Brendel's...I mean, your, wine last night. Sorry."

"I'll just expense it to Dos Cerros. Go ahead."

"Anyway, I asked him how he happened to start driving for Mr. Brendel and we talked about the old days for a while. It seemed like the natural thing to do, you know? I mean, since it's over now. I reminded him that most of that time I was living with my mother and so I wasn't there to see it much. He seemed a little—guarded, I guess—and most of what he said doesn't have any bearing on what you asked. But I did learn that Mr. Brendel's wife's name was Helen Stanton. Dad couldn't remember his mother's name, but the father's name was Bradford."

"Bradford Brendel? You're kidding me. Someone

had a sense of humor."

"Long ago."

"What I wanted to do was get the initials and compare them with some things I found in his room. But B. B. doesn't fit, and neither does Helen Stanton. But thanks, Lynn. I hope the wine was good."

"It really was. Are we going to get together for a session again soon? To start that profile picture?"

"I think so, but first I need to sort some things out, like whether I need to flee the country. I'll let you know."

"OK. You're kidding again, right?"

"I hope so."

Maya rolled over as I hung up the phone. " We are taking a trip?" she asked.

"Not unless we have to, but I'm worried about all the evidence building up against me. I'm not sure how long Delgado can let this go on without arresting me."

"Isn't it what Cody would call...circum-something?"

"Circumstantial? Yes, it is. But it also means that somebody is working hard at setting me up. Who hates me that much?"

"Let's make a list. I'll get a big sheet of paper." She smiled sweetly, but I had also seen her earlier look when I said I might be arrested.

I left her in bed and went across to the studio and made some coffee. I opened the box where I had packed Brendel's photographs and a few other things from the big house. First I pulled out the black-and-white wedding picture and studied the background. It had been taken on the front porch of a wood-framed house with white or light-colored trim and siding, and a dark screen door with a mailbox mounted on the siding near the latch edge of it. There was a pale rectangle on the box that must have held a name label, but the lettering was too small to read. A photo lab might enhance it, but there wasn't one in San Miguel.

The camera had been situated at the bottom of the front steps. The screen door and the trim around the entry looked like standard circa 1900 catalog millwork, the kind that was widely used everywhere from California to Maine. The bride was standing with her arm raised to hold onto her veil and I couldn't see the house number except for the right edge of what was possibly a three, but might have been an eight as well. Nothing helpful there.

Brendel had changed over fifty-plus years; who wouldn't? But the long slender nose was the same, and the hairline hadn't changed much. The lips were a bit fuller then. I studied the hands for a while; both were visible. But I had nothing to compare them with since I hadn't progressed past working out the color scheme and blocking in basic shapes before the first portrait session ended. I couldn't remember his hands as he posed.

From the box Lynn had given me I pulled out the photos from the bookcase. The ones with Méxican businessmen, I went through quickly. I recognized Antonio Trujillo now but none of the others. They were similar types; light-skinned, tall, wearing mustaches and expensive suits. I couldn't smell the after shave, but I knew it was there. I put them aside. They all had a lot of teeth and didn't mind showing them.

The next one presented Brendel with President Reagan. It must have been about twenty years old. Brendel was much closer in appearance to the way he looked recently. In a stagey shot, they were shaking hands before a marble fireplace of a design that suggested the same period as the White House; 1800 or so. Both looked at the camera. Next was the one with Margaret Thatcher. As I studied it, I began to feel there was something wrong with it.

Mrs. Thatcher was clearly looking across at Brendel, but he was looking only approximately toward her, even slightly past her. It was difficult to say exactly. Why would they be posing for a camera shot, but with him looking over her shoulder? Perhaps he was noticing an attractive server bending over at the next table? And there was something odd as well about Brendel's neck. I remembered in detail the way he held himself, both from the single session in the studio and from my meeting with him at Cuadrante and then at Barbara's party; I didn't think his neck came out of his collar in this way.

As a painter I'm not a big fan of photography. It seems like cameras record details fairly well, but they also evoke stiff postures and artificial expressions from the people posing. They rarely capture the humanity of a subject (this is the task of the painter) unless the photographer is a Liebowitz or an Avedon or Lord Snowden. But this was not what was bothering me about this photo. There was simply something wrong with the way Brendel's neck fit on his body, and it wasn't from the way he was sitting. I slit the brown paper backing the picture and pulled it out of the frame. Under a magnifying glass I couldn't find anything else wrong. It didn't appear to be tampered with. The paper was intact and the surface undisturbed. But a more sophisticated alteration wouldn't show up on the paper's surface texture anyway.

I set it aside and pulled out the next one, which showed Frank Sinatra seated at a white grand piano with the lid down, eyes bright and mouth open as if singing or at least talking to Brendel, and the vice president leaning toward him with one arm on the lid, a drink in his left hand. There was again the sense of him looking past Sinatra. Why would Brendel be looking past him as he sang or spoke to him? It seemed rude or, at the least, careless. Of course, I had found his people skills somewhat lacking, but you'd think with Frank Sinatra he'd be on his best behavior, not that Frank always was.

With Gerald Ford they were both standing on the green and looking out along the fairway. Nothing seemed odd or unusual. With Sammy Davis Jr. and Peter Lawford, all three looked into the camera, in a row like a chorus line, but this time it seemed that Brendel's head was just a bit too large for his body. I cut the paper backing on this one too and examined it under the glass, but again, no signs of tampering. I began to feel that I had to check out further this somehow. Lawford and Davis had both died years ago, and I remembered that Sinatra had followed them in 1998. Reagan had died in mid 2004. I had heard that Charlton Heston was vague now. None of the others could help me short of a seance, which were often a little light on specifics. I wasn't sure there was anything wrong with the Gerald Ford shot. It came down to getting hold of Margaret Thatcher to verify her picture. Surely that wouldn't be a problem.

I found the number for the British Embassy in México City. There was a pause from the receptionist when I told her what I wanted, and then she said, "Let me connect you with our Mr. Braithwaite. He deals with requests of this kind." There must be a lot of people in México trying to reach Mrs. Thatcher, I thought.

"Alan Braithwaite. How may I assist you?"

I identified myself. "I'm working on a homicide investigation and I need to send an e-mail to Margaret Thatcher."

"I see. Are you with the police? Because perhaps I'm not the one you should be speaking with; we do have a police liaison on staff."

"This is an unofficial inquiry."

"Mr. Zacher, was it? Surely you don't think I can simply give out Lady Thatcher's e-mail address to any caller, no matter how well-intentioned?"

"You don't know it, do you, Mr. Braithwaite?"

"No, but I can get it."

"All right. Here's what I was really about to propose. I will send you an e-mail addressed to Mrs. Thatcher. You will then read it, decide whether I am a lunatic or not, and subject to your conclusion, forward it to her. She will then respond or not directly to me, at her discretion. Are you willing to do that?"

"As you say, subject to the contents of the e-mail, I can do that."

"OK. You should have it in a few minutes. Thank you."

I fed the photo through my scanner/printer/copier and composed the following e-mail message:

Dear Lady Thatcher;

I am a private investigator presently engaged in the investigation of the murder of former Vice President Malcolm Brendel here in México. The attached photograph—unfortunately not dated—has come up in evidence and we have some reason to believe that it may be fraudulent. I would greatly appreciate it if you could examine this picture and let me know whether you think it can possibly be genuine.

Yours,

Paul Zacher

San Miguel de Allende, México

I attached the scanned photo and hit "send."

Maya had disappeared and I had a solitary lunch on some leftover enchiladas from the refrigerator, washed down with a Negra Modelo. I couldn't assess the likelihood of getting a response, but I felt fairly certain that the embassy would at least forward it to her. The phone rang just as I finished, but it was not Margaret Thatcher. It was Antonio Trujillo wondering how my investigations were coming. I gave him an update, neglecting to mention the contents of Brendel's will, since he had collected it from Cuadrante and must have known what it contained, and he thanked me politely and hung up.

Back upstairs in the studio I examined the photos again and came up with the same opinion. I had to trust my eye here; some things were just not right. I studied each one again and found no additional problems, but none of my earlier discoveries looked any better, either. I made myself some more coffee, studied the Lynn painting for a while, then swept out the studio. Finally I couldn't hold off anymore and checked my e-mail. There, among the usual pharmacy scams, three hot investment ideas (how could anyone know about the inheritance so quickly?) and four urgent messages about penis enlargement, was the Margaret Thatcher response.

It was not, of course, from Lady Thatcher herself, but rather from her executive assistant, Laura McGinty. Lady Thatcher, she said, had examined the photo and was quite certain that it could not be genuine. She was sure as well that she had never sat down to either dinner or lunch with Malcolm Brendel, and indeed, Ronald Reagan had not used him in any foreign assignments as far as she was aware. There was apparently some lack of confidence between the two of them, and naturally, for security reasons, they would not often be present at the same functions.

Furthermore, Lady Thatcher had not been made aware of Malcolm Brendel's murder and, the last she had heard about him, he was off for an extended stay either in Venezuela or Paraguay. Lady Thatcher had asked her to convey to me her hopes for success in my endeavor. (Laura McGinty spelled it "endeavour.")

OK. I guess one Latin American country is like another to some people, but you might think Lady Thatcher would be better able to distinguish among them. This was the information I was looking for, but I was again surprised there had been no news release about Brendel's death. Was Dos Cerros somehow muzzling the local authorities while they figured out what to do next with their planned publicity campaign? It was starting to look like it.

So anyway, a few, possibly all, the celebrity photos were fakes. Was it no more than a bit of legend-building on the part of Brendel? Wasn't being governor of Kansas and then vice president enough for a man who had also risen from the dead? Who was this guy, anyway?

I took the New Testament out of the bottom of the box and thumbed through it. I had not handled it before and now I noticed that the inner cover page was missing, sliced cleanly along the binding. It was the place where the owner might write his name, perhaps including information about family members and dates of births and deaths. How odd. Not many people mutilated Bibles. I checked the inside back cover; it was present and blank.

Looking again at the photos of Brendel with the México business figures I found nothing strange about them; none of the necks were funny and the heads were all the correct size. The men seemed to be genuinely interacting. Maybe he had used the faked photos to sell himself to the Méxican business community. I dialed Cody to bounce it off him.

"Williams."

"I've been spending a little time going over the photos we got from the Cuadrante house."

"Trying to figure out which way to hang them?"

"Something like that. Anyway, I think some of them are fakes."

"That could be interesting. Which ones?"

"Well, for absolutely certain, the one with Margaret Thatcher. She denies ever having had dinner with him, or lunch."

"A lot of people would. Unfortunately, you and

I can't. You talk to her a lot?" He was munching on something.

"I e-mailed her and got a response from her assistant. She was fairly prompt."

"She's probably got a lot of time on her hands. You sent her the photo?"

"Yes. I didn't like the look of it. I also think the ones with Frank Sinatra and with Sammy Davis Jr. and Peter Lawford are faked, but I can't prove it. The Gerald Ford one and the Charlton Heston may or may not be, but I think if the others are, then those probably are too, maybe just a better job."

"How about the ones with the Méxicoan business guys?"

"They appear to be the real deal. So my question is, why fake the other photos? If Dos Cerros' interest in him was as a preacher and as someone who rose from the dead, his credibility would not be enhanced by this material. Lawford and Davis have been dead for quite a few years, and a lot of Méxicans would have no idea who they were, particularly young Méxicans. Any ideas?"

"Sure. For one thing, pure egotism. They might have been solely for his own enjoyment."

"Isn't that a stretch? He knew better than anyone that they were fakes. That would be like cheating at solitaire."

"Maybe to impress women. What if Juana Cardenas was a huge Sinatra fan? Maybe she had her own copy of *Ocean's Eleven*, the original version with the Rat Pack, and it just made her weak in the knees to watch it."

"Cody, she's a hooker. Money makes her weak in

the knees."

"It doesn't mean that other things don't as well."

"How about Margaret Thatcher then?" I said. "Why was seeing Brendel sitting across the table from her a turn-on for Juana Cardenas?"

"Proximity to power, and power's an aphrodisiac."

"Well, I think this goes nowhere. Did you run the name Lillian Ballard past your friends in the Chicago police?"

"She's clean. Nothing at all came up."

"Maybe I'll do a Web search. I'll talk to you later."

But I didn't do the Web search immediately because, while I was on the phone, Maya had returned and I soon found myself rubbing her bare back. She was lying on the bed wearing only her jeans and her toes were curled up in an expression of ecstasy.

"I can't get past this picture thing," I was saying. I had told her about the faked images. "It ties in somehow. Cody thinks Brendel was using them to impress Juana Cardenas. I can't quite buy it. What do think?"

"I don't think so either. But maybe there's another reason to fake the photos that you haven't thought of."

"What's that?" My fingers were working on her neck now.

"You've noticed how nothing is what it seems here?"

"Sure. It seems like I killed him. That's the illusion I'm mainly stuck on."

"Exactly. What if Malcolm Brendel was not what he seemed either?"

"I can believe that. Much of his life was fraudulent. Are you thinking he didn't really rise from the dead?"

"That's not it. I mean what if the man killed at Barbara's party, the man whose portrait you had started, was not really Malcolm Brendel?"

My fingers stopped moving on the satiny skin of her shoulders, and the room became oddly quiet. The idea was a stopper, and oddly compelling, but I immediately began to think of reasons why it couldn't be true.

"But if that were so, why wouldn't Stephen Washburn know it? He worked for Brendel for eighteen years. Of course, it would explain the pictures; they would have been altered to prove this man was Brendel and he hobnobbed with the stars. And it explains why nobody in the world outside of San Miguel knows he's dead. That part works perfectly."

"So then Stephen Washburn is in on it too. He has to be."

"Why would he consent to be part of the fraud?"

"You saw the will. You were only focused on the money that came to you, but didn't Washburn get $20,000? That was his pay-off."

"Then who was he? I'm not seeing a motive here for the deception. He was working for Dos Cerros. Why would they not want the real thing? Were they fooled too? I mean, if you're right. It sounds good, but I'm not sure you are."

She stood up and pulled on her bra and hooked it in back. The moment had passed. "Listen, Paul," she said, sitting back on the edge of the bed and pulling on a blue tank top. "I first started thinking about this when we searched his bedroom, before any question about the pictures came up. The odd mixture of toiletry things in the bathroom, some expensive and some just ordinary and cheap. A man who can afford the high quality things would buy them all the time, wouldn't he? He doesn't make odd little economies on a few items. And he doesn't need to mend his underwear either, even if he has someone to do it for him. This man who died, whoever he might have been, was in the process of changing his habits, and he hadn't finished the change when he was killed. He was using up the old stuff, the way a person does who has that economical turn of mind, like you do. He wasn't able to just throw it away if it wasn't used up."

This had bothered me too, especially the underwear, but I hadn't known what to make of it. And I hadn't given the cheap toiletries any thought, because of course, I wouldn't have thrown them away either. They raised no red flags in my mind. I had nearly $700,000 invested now and all my crappy toiletries were still up in the bathroom as I used them up. At least my underwear wasn't mended, although one of my favorite boxers did have a small hole under the waist band.

She stood up and pulled down her top. I put my arms around her and kissed her slowly.

"You're good," I said. "I'm still not sure you're right, but we can't ignore this direction. I'm going on the Internet and see if I can pull up some pictures of Brendel. Maybe there's a difference."

The Internet took its time coming up, the way a lot of things do in México. There's a different sense of pace here, a feeling that, if you're in that big a hurry about something, maybe you ought to go do it somewhere else. When the screen came up, I typed "Malcolm Brendel" in the Google slot. I thought I could hear in the background the sound of somebody way back in the archives getting out of his creaky armchair and shuffling through a ton of dusty old papers, and then a surprisingly long list of sources appeared. I disregarded the 345,200 mentions of him in text entries; what I focused on were the 623 photo images.

I started at the top and opened the listings in order, thinking I wouldn't have to go very far before I got enough images to establish one way or the other whether our man was really Malcolm Brendel. I glossed over the texts and focused on bringing up as many clear photos as possible. Wherever it was available I noted the date on each one as I printed it. I stopped when I had sixteen of good quality. Unfortunately, the newest was from twenty-two years back, dating from his final days in office. He would have been about fifty years old. Scanning further down the list without printing any, I found none more recent.

There are some people, like Lynn Washburn, for example, who carry the same look their entire lives. (I am speculating here about Lynn, but I feel certain of it.) Others change decade by decade into other people. I didn't know which category included Malcolm Brendel, but as I scanned the batch of photo printouts I didn't see any reason to think they couldn't have been of the man who died on Barbara Watt's bathroom floor. The shape of the face, the long, narrow nose, the sharp chin and thin lips; these were all the same. The hair was very close to the way it looked now, but hair can change a lot, depending on who cuts it and how much falls out over the years. The eyes did not match quite as well, but I'd always felt the eyes of the Brendel I knew had been worked on. I leaned back in the chair. It was inconclusive.

Since I was booted up anyway, I decided to do a search on Lillian Ballard, the woman whose funeral card had been in the New Testament and who had no criminal record. I didn't hope for much, and I remembered that Brendel's divorced wife was named Helen Stanton. Maybe Lillian had been an old girlfriend who had kept a place in his thoughts, or perhaps it was the married name of a sister.

Lillian Ballard merited only one primary source, an obituary from the *Dallas Morning News* dated March 17, 1989. It was the usual kind of thing that the funeral director had probably written based on information from the family. No cause of death was listed. She was survived by her husband, George, two children, Alan and Benjamin, and one sister-in-law, Marlene. No siblings were mentioned. There followed a short paragraph about her career in regional theater in Austin, and later, in Dallas. It was anticipated that she would be very much missed. Memorials were requested to go to the American Cancer Society in lieu of flowers. So here was a clue about the reason for her death at fifty-seven.

The other sources were theater reviews where she was mentioned among others as a player. I scanned most of them. They were about evenly divided between a couple of repertory companies and a dinner theater. Apparently she was a good singer. I printed the obituary and two reviews and shut it down, feeling rather sad that this was what was left of her life, for the record, anyway. There had been no pictures. Undoubtedly the surviving family carried something around from her. I wondered if the husband mentioned in the obituary, George Ballard, was still alive.

But there was no connection that I could see. Maybe she was somehow linked to Brendel's private life and we would never know how.

Just as the screen went dark I sat upright and hit the power switch again. George Ballard: the wedding ring in Brendel's bedroom had said GB*LOVE*LH. As the computer cycled through its slow dance of coming to life again, I drew out the front-porch wedding photo from the file and looked at the woman. Was LH Lillian H.? But why was she with Brendel? Now I thought I knew, and Maya was right.

When the screen came up, I Googled George Ballard. He was a bigger deal than Lillian, because the first article was a newspaper feature on a new production of *Death of a Salesman* in Fort Worth, and it included photos. Opening night was June 9, 1994. There was a cast shot, and then further down the page, a close-up of the Willy Loman character. I studied it with special interest, because I was looking into the face of the man I knew as Malcolm Brendel. There may have been an element of triumph in my gesture as I hit print harder than I had to. As the paper slowly inched out of the printer I remembered what I had said to him that day in the studio when I was trying to loosen him up. It had been something like, "And who are we today?"

And George Ballard had answered, "An actor, one to make the Barrymores weep."

He had been playing with me, telling me what he really was, knowing that it would go right over my head. Ballard had planted a clue to add an edgy quality to his performance, but evidently he'd lost control of the last act.

I dashed downstairs with the printout, looking for Maya, and found her in the kitchen, talking on the phone. Her lips formed the words *"mi padre,"* as she put up her hand to keep me from talking. Suddenly she handed me the receiver. "He wants to talk to you."

I handed her the article and took the phone.

"*Señor* Zacher, how lucky to find you there."

"Odd, isn't it?"

"Here is a funny thing that everybody was talking about yesterday in the office. I don't know whether it would be part of your interest in Dos Cerros or not, but permit me to tell you this. In the southern part of the state of Veracruz, near a town called Hueyapan de Ocampo, is a large oil deposit that has been well known since the thirties. It has almost been a joke, since people in the oil business call it 'the Ocampo Sink' because so many companies have tried to extract the oil and lost their investment."

"I see. Why is it so difficult?" And where was this going?

"It is because of the architecture of the subsoil, as we say. The underlying formations fracture the equipment and make the drilling impossible except at a very high cost. It is estimated that crude oil would have to sell for more than $92 a barrel for any company to break even on this field. Naturally the lease has been available for some years at a favorable price, but with no takers. And suddenly now something interesting has happened. The rumor is everywhere yesterday and today that Dos Cerros has bought the lease."

"Why would they do that? Oil is not even close to $92. What is it today? You probably have a screen in the office."

"Ah, well, today the latest quote is at $52.40 a barrel, which is fairly high. In any case, no one knows what Dos Cerros can be thinking. It makes no sense to anyone here. I thought I would let you know because these Dos Cerros people are close to you, right? Maybe you could even let me know what they say." He was chuckling on the other end, as if this were a chatty sort of call with no significance, but I read his thought; I had become an inside source within the industry. From behind me came the sound of bare feet slapping on the tile floor. I turned to see Maya jumping around the kitchen, jabbing wordlessly at the picture of George Ballard in her hand. I thanked Ruben Sanchez, told him I'd let him know if I heard anything, and hung up.

"It's him! It's him! I was right, wasn't I?"

"Of course. Reading all those mystery novels is paying off for you." Next she'd be writing them based on our adventures.

I called Cody and brought him up to date, including the odd information about Dos Cerros and the lease acquisition.

"I'm out to sea on this one," he said. "What possible use to them is a fake Brendel? How hard could it have been to get the real one? Everyone knows he's always been for sale."

"Margaret Thatcher thinks he's in Venezuela or Paraguay. Maybe he's unreachable."

"I think I'll run some checks on George Ballard.

He sounds harmless enough, but you never know."

At this point I began to feel I had to share some of this with Antonio Trujillo. Some, but not all. I wasn't ready to be his fraternity brother yet, or the godfather to his unborn children. But I did owe him something for the $10,000 deposit, and I had even begun to upgrade my lifestyle. I now drank only Plantation rum and I was using a better quality deodorant and after shave, or I soon would be, right after I used up all the old stuff.

After three or four rings he picked up.

"*Bueno.* Antonio Trujillo."

"It's Paul Zacher. How are you?"

"Very well. And you and your lovely friend Maya?" Conversations in México always cycle through rounds of inquiries like these. Failure to do this is one of the reasons Méxicans often feel Americans are rude.

"Quite well, thank you. I hope your family is fine as well."

"Yes, very well, thank you."

"I am calling today to give you an update on my investigation into the death of Malcolm Brendel."

"Wonderful. The head office will be pleased. What have you learned so far?"

"I believe that Malcolm Brendel is not dead, or if he is, he didn't die in Barbara Watt's bathroom." This was followed by a pause, as if he were trying to assemble a response without the word loco in it. He barely succeeded.

"And yet I myself, as well as the police and all the guests at the party, to say nothing of the staff, saw the body, and Dr. Weingard certified that..."

"Of course there was a body. A man named George

Ballard, an actor from Texas, was murdered that night. His age and his physical appearance were very close to that of Malcolm Brendel."

There was a sound much in tone like an obscenity uttered while he had his hand over the receiver. "I am wondering now how it is that we at Dos Cerros could have been taken in by such a man. You are very certain of this?"

"Subject to fingerprint verification, as certain as I can be. Locating the real vice president would also help."

"What led you to think this, if I may ask?"

"Certain items among his belongings seemed out of place. Additionally, some of the celebrity photographs appeared to be fraudulent. I think I might show them to an expert and get a second opinion. The final item was a memorial card left in his New Testament. It was issued for the 1989 funeral of a woman named Lillian Ballard, who turned out to be his late wife, and this information led me to George Ballard. Actually, Maya already suspected that the murdered man was not Malcolm Brendel."

"Well, I must congratulate you on your progress in such a short time. You have been very astute, even beyond what we had hoped. Please keep working on it because I would like to know the intentions of this George Ballard in masquerading as the vice president; we have made a large investment in this project. And, of course, we would wish to know the identity of the murderer so that justice many be done. We are not without influence in the legal system of this country."

I already expected that, and it didn't make me sleep better at night.

"I'll stay on it, and I'll keep you informed."

"Thank you. Now it is so much easier to understand why he did not rise again from the dead. It would be beyond the capabilities of a mere actor. Goodbye, *Señor* Zacher."

I was still thinking about that final comment when I went to sleep that night.

Later, when a strange insistent noise brought me back from dreaming about the next Lynn picture (I think I was planning the background, but these dream-state images were rarely worth anything), I thought at first it must be the alarm clock. "It's the phone," mumbled Maya, her face buried in the pillow. Her tone said, "It must be for you."

The clock said slightly after 1:00 A.M. I hate these late-night calls. It's never anything good, and it always begins with a big adrenaline rush from the ringing. I picked it up anyway. Lynn's hushed voice came from the other end.

"Paul, can you come over right away? There's someone in the house! Dad heard something downstairs, the door, I think, but he doesn't have a gun. I don't want him to go down there. I'm scared. Can you come now?"

"I'm coming. Call the police, but tell them I'm coming too, so they don't shoot me."

I hung up and pulled on my pants and shirt.

"What?" asked Maya.

"Intruder at our other house. Lynn's in a panic." I slipped my .38 revolver into my belt, not bothering to find the shoulder holster, and ran outside to the van. The Cuadrante house was just four blocks away.

# Chapter 13
## Angel Flores

Angel Flores pulled up at the garden side of the mansion on Cuadrante just about half past midnight. After he parked, he dialed the interior light control down to zero. He took his time getting out of the car and closed the door quietly, but without locking it; he wanted nothing to slow him down if there was a problem inside. Flores reached under his light jacket and his right hand touched the small revolver in his belt as he walked up the street and turned right at the corner. There had been no lights visible at the side of the house, and now, passing the front, he could see none there either. The lesser houses along the street were mostly dark as well, as were all the shops.

It was a curious job for Flores; he was accustomed to breaking and entering, well versed in extortion and assault, conversant with kidnapping, familiar with fraud, but never had he been instructed to steal anything as worthless as a collection of photographs. It was not the first curious job he had done for the Chief; shooting at Malcolm Brendel had been another one. Shoot at the man, but hit no one, he was told. Well, he had blown that, but it was not his fault. It must have been fate that the silly bodyguard stood up to return fire just as a bullet was headed his way. Flores knew from long experience that you could not control every factor on a job. Sometimes in a crisis people did stupid, impulsive things. Occasionally they died because of it, or sometimes they got lucky, like Brendel's bodyguard, and survived.

Flores took a leisurely stroll around the block. He did not live in San Miguel and he liked to get a sense of the immediate terrain before he made his move, particularly the most promising escape routes. He saw no one except a couple moving hand in hand down the sidewalk. They turned into a doorway and disappeared. He continued down the street and rounded the corner. Back on the garden side of the house he paused at the recessed gate, hidden from the street light in the deep shadow of the thick stucco wall, and pulled out his tools. It was an old lock, but well maintained. In less than two minutes he closed the gate behind him and was standing silently in the garden. He did not lock it behind him. At the far end on his right was a long carriage house, with one small light on over the door on the left end, but no lights on inside. Probably just a navigating light, he thought.

The seasoned tennis shoes of Angel Flores made a little more noise than he liked as he moved over the gravel path toward the back of the house, but it would have been noisier to fight his way through the vegetation. The steps at the edge of the garden led to a long loggia full of outdoor furniture. At the rear door he used the tools again and let himself into a full-length sun room facing the garden. He paused for a moment and listened. Nothing moved within the house. He took out a small penlight and turned it on.

Opening from the back wall of the sun room was a corridor that he had been told led to the library, the first door on the left. Farther down and opposite the library was a branch of the corridor that went at a right angle toward the carriage entrance. He turned the handle of the library door softly and went in. The room smelled of new furniture. From his jacket pocket he unfolded a heavy black plastic trash bag, big enough to hold a dozen or so small framed pictures. Flores knew nothing about Frank Sinatra or Gerald Ford. He had been told to take them all, and asked to repeat his instructions, which he did.

Accordingly, the photographs he wanted were to be hanging in the empty bookshelves, but shining the light along the rows, he saw no photographs at all, and no shelves either. Simply three lines of picture hangers tacked into the wooden backs of the bookcases. Flores flashed the light around the room. The only other possible place they could be was in a large closed cabinet built into the corner of the library, with doors designed to be continuous with the paneling. He set the torch down on a lamp table so that the beam shone on the cabinet, and placed his left hand on the left door, holding it closed. As he tugged on the right door, it yielded stiffly at first and then suddenly the old mahogany swung quickly toward him, creaking in protest as it came. He jumped back and pulled out the pistol, standing motionless and listening.

At this moment Lynn Washburn sat upright in bed on the floor above, gripping the blue flannel nightgown to her heaving chest, and reached for the phone to call

Paul Zacher. As she dialed, she could hear her father moving about in the next room.

When a minute passed and Flores had heard nothing, he shined the light into the cabinet, disappointed to find it contained only books. Even had they been Spanish books, Flores could not have read them. As quietly as he could, he shifted the books around inside, but the photographs were not hidden behind them. He was contemplating how he was going to explain yet another screw-up to the Chief, when a short, blond-haired man in blue pajamas appeared suddenly in the open doorway next to the cabinet. He held a fireplace poker upright in his hand and his arm moved backward in a swinging motion when he saw Flores.

Angel Flores stepped out from the shadow of the cabinet and shot him twice in the chest. In the small room the noise was deafening, and he immediately heard a scream from somewhere upstairs. The blond man had fallen backward through the doorway into the hall and lay still. Flores shone the light on his face; the man's eyes were open and unmoving. Flores quickly touched his neck and felt no pulse. He was prepared to shoot him again if he were still alive, but he seemed to be gone. Flores picked up the plastic bag and put it back in his pocket, then listened for a moment and heard nothing more from upstairs. Shining the torch ahead of him, he stepped over the body of Stephen Washburn, avoiding the black pool of blood on the parquet floor, and went out through the sun room and into the *loggia*, leaving the door open behind him. It was now certain that this would be his last job for the Chief. He knew he couldn't expect to be paid.

Outside he rushed over the path, the gravel crunching loudly beneath his feet. He didn't care now. Glancing back at the house, he could see a light in one window on the third floor, which abruptly went out. From a street or two away came the sound of a siren racing toward the house. As he threw open the garden gate he came face-to-face with the tall gringo painter he had tricked at the cash machine on the *jardín*. He dropped the torch and pulled the gun out of his belt just as the painter, no less startled, but with his .38 already in hand, shot him in the head from two feet away. Each had the same look of surprise on his face.

In the case of Angel Flores, it was permanent.

# Chapter 14

The sad thing, aside from the fact that I am normally in bed at this time, and now I am not, is that you and your friends *Señorita* Sanchez and *Señor* Cody Williams have at this point killed more people in this town than Pancho Villa did on his unannounced visit in 1919. Consider that." *Licenciado* Diego Delgado paced back and forth behind his particle board desk.

"It can be a tough town, but at least, no one has been raped this time and no stores or banks have been looted," I said, leaning back in my chair. I was not handcuffed and we were not even in the interrogation room. A good sign, so far.

"I am sure we are in your debt for that, but you have not spent a single night in my jail, as yet."

"Beginner's luck," I said, but I knew I was going to have to face the ghost of Angel Flores later.

"And this, at the same time when Mayor Martin is repeating to us every day that San Miguel will soon become the premiere tourist destination in all of México, more, even, than Cancun."

"I hate Cancun. I can't even imagine that many people coming here. I would have to leave."

"But think what you could get for your house." He raised his eyebrows and turned his palms upward toward the ceiling as if to receive a shower of silver.

"Even so. It's not worth it. I like this town the way it is."

"You could rent it out, and then retire. So now you are telling me again that you did not know this man Angel Flores, even though he is the one you gave directions to on the *jardín*. This time you found it necessary to shoot him between the eyes, or slightly above. And this, by the way, is happening in the garden of a $5,000,000 house upon which you own a ten-year leasehold. You are surprised? Yes, I know this." He began to wave his arms again, but with a satisfied look on his face.

"You have seen the will." I shrugged. A lot of people had probably seen it by now. More than I wanted.

"I have made it my business to see the will." He turned to a uniformed cop who was passing. "Bring us two coffees, Ivan, *por favor*."

"Ivan?"

"An old Méxican name." He shrugged elaborately.

"Then you know about the money I inherited, too."

"Yes. It is, by the way, what a *Licenciado* in the San Miguel Judicial Police would earn in thirty-four years."

I really didn't want to go there. Telling him that it was what I would earn from painting in only fourteen years probably wouldn't help. Ivan set two steaming coffees in front of us.

"*Licenciado* Delgado, we have gone over this already, but we can go over it again. I did not need to know this man in order to shoot him. I would shoot anyone who was about to shoot me. You received a call from *Señorita* Washburn saying there was an intruder in the house. She called me at the same time. I'm sure you will find Flores' fingerprints on the door handle and locks, and his hand will test positive for gunshot residue. His gun will prove to be the weapon that killed Stephen Washburn. Plus, Flores is a widely known felon, as you established for me before, after the ATM incident."

"And why was he there? To kill *Señor* Washburn?"

"I don't think so. Why would he need a large plastic bag in his pocket then? He was a burglar."

"What was of value?"

"There was essentially nothing of value. I have been through every item in every room. There were a few dozen books, various articles of clothing and toiletries, some cooking utensils and crockery, but no silver, only stainless steel. But perhaps Flores didn't know that. Maybe he saw what a grand house it was and thought it would be full of valuables. There was the furniture, of course, but that wouldn't explain the bag. He was thinking in terms of something portable."

"I wish you had shot him somewhere less fatal. I wish I could have talked with him. I have made little progress on this case."

"He surprised me. The first thing I realized when I pushed the gate open was that he was about to come through and he was pulling out his gun. Mine was already in my hand. It was a split-second thing. If I had hesitated I would have been the one in the body bag."

"I realize that. But this situation is becoming increasingly difficult for me as an officer of the Judicial Police because now, not only did you have a motive to kill *Señor* Brendel because of the will, but as you have just demonstrated again, you are also ready to kill someone else quite easily. This does not look good for you."

"Let me ask you something. Are you getting pressure to arrest me for the murder of Malcolm Brendel? From your chief? Maybe the mayor? Someone else?"

"I am not able to answer this." He turned away with his arms folded.

"I'll take that as a yes."

"If you wish." He spread his hands apart in a gesture of indifference and looked up at the ceiling.

I stood up and leaned over the desk. "I find it interesting, *Licenciado,* that there has been no public release of the news that Malcolm Brendel is dead. It would be picked up immediately by all the wire services in the States, don't you think?" He nodded slowly. "Is it possible," I went on, "that some order has come down from a higher level forbidding the release of this information?"

"I am not able to comment on this, either, but let me say that such a thing would not be unusual in a case like this. It saves the authorities embarrassment in case the murder is not immediately solved." He shrugged, as if to say, "What can I do?"

"If that is the case, then let me give you something more to chew on."

"Chew on?"

"To think about. The man who was murdered at the dinner party of *Señora* Watt was not Malcolm Brendel." For a moment his face was utterly blank, then the hint of a grin began to form and his eyes narrowed.

"Soon we will be talking about the turnip truck

again, yes? And how I alone was able to stay aboard it? Why would you say this to me?" He slammed his palm on the desk and both the coffee cups jumped. "You cannot be serious."

"I found some of the man's belongings at the Cuadrante house and they suggested he was not the vice president, that's all."

"For example? Was it the photo identity card of another? Because we have his driver's license and it appears to be genuine. Of course, it is from the States, so we cannot be totally certain."

"Nothing like that. There was a wedding ring with different initials on it, and a memorial card from a dead woman who did not have the name of Brendel's wife, but was about the right age."

"His sister possibly. Who can say?"

"But when I looked up the names on the Internet I discovered that this woman was his wife, and that the husband who survived her was named George Ballard. His picture proves that he was pretending to be Malcolm Brendel. He was an actor who looked very much like him, and of course, would be able to play the part. Look up George Ballard on the Internet and you will see." He wrote the name down with his notes. "Look up Lillian Ballard too."

Delgado set his pencil down next to the notepad and folded his arms against his chest.

"You know, I am sure, what I would ask next, because this is not the first crime here to attract your interest. Why would *Señor* Washburn not know this?" Here Delgado raised his finger to me in a way that would have been offensive had it been facing the other way.

"Of all the people involved in this, he alone has been close to *Señor* Brendel for many years. Yet he had said nothing, and when I interviewed him after the murder, he certainly had the opportunity to mention it."

"Don't you find it interesting that he's now dead too? Because I believe he did know, just because, he, of all people, would not have been fooled by George Ballard. Perhaps the person who killed Brendel, or Ballard, also killed Stephen Washburn. I don't mean Angel Flores, or the one who stuck the paint brush in Ballard's ear necessarily, but one who also could have ordered the murder of Washburn. This is probably not making any sense." Delgado dragged his hands over his face as if it was past his bedtime.

"It made more sense for me when I thought he was Malcolm Brendel, and perhaps I will continue to think that until I check out these things on the Internet. We will end this for now. I think you will find that *Señorita* Sanchez and your friend Cody Williams have taken the young *Señorita* Washburn to your house. She was very upset. I will send a crew around in the morning to collect all his things. We will examine them to see if anything bears on his death, and then release them to her. Do you know if her father was all she had?"

"I believe her mother is still alive in the States."

"So at least there is some family for her, even if not nearby. Please have *Señorita* Washburn call me with her mother's address when she is feeling better and I will see that *la madre* is notified. Thank you for your assistance. You should have your gun back in two days, after the tests. Unless, of course, it is also the gun that killed Stephen Washburn. Then we will have another conversation."

"That's not what you think."

"No." He shook his head and yawned suddenly. "It is only procedure." He got up with a weary look and shook my hand as I left.

The city was silent when I came out on the street and crossed the *jardín,* and the sky was black and salted with bright stars. It was nearly three o'clock. I didn't want to think about Angel Flores. I knew he had taken his place with another man I'd killed two months ago, and they'd both be hovering around the edges of my thoughts for a while. It would be time to clean my gun again, once I got it back.

Maya met me at the door and gave me a long hug after I told her what happened.

The atmosphere at my house on Quebrada was grim. Cody and Maya were seated on the sofa with Lynn between them in her blue flannel nightgown. Her comfort suit. Not that it was enough. The corners of Maya's wide mouth were turned downward. Three brandy glasses were lined up in front of them; Lynn's was untouched; the others were empty.

Lynn looked up at me as I came into the room. "I begged him not to go downstairs, to wait until you came, because I knew you had a gun," she said in a small, level voice. Her face was puffy and her eyes rimmed with red. Fiddling with the lace cuff, her right hand was on her other sleeve. A box of tissues sat on the coffee table with a half-full waste basket on the floor next to it. "It was so like him to go anyway. Just like he always had to protect Mr. Brendel's car." She stared at the glasses.

The other two waited for more. After what seemed like a long silence, Cody said to me, "So, they let you walk again. The suspect with nine lives." He didn't smile.

"Reluctantly. I got the sense that there's some pressure from above to arrest me for Ballard/Brendel. Delgado wouldn't talk about it. No one up there cares about Flores. I could have shot him in the back as he lay in bed asleep, moving his crutches aside to get better aim, and still walked."

"Well, remember just the same, here in México you are guilty until proven innocent," said Maya.

"Delgado knows as well as any of us that it's a frame."

"He may not be able to resist the pressure. In México there are big people and there are small people. I am getting worried. What would happen if they arrest you?" she said.

"You and Cody would take my inheritance money and drive off into the sunset in that little Ford Escort of his."

"I can be ready in five minutes," he said. "Which way is west?"

Where would you get friends like this?

"How are you doing?" I asked Lynn.

"I think I should go to bed now. Is that all right? I was mostly waiting for you to be released. I'm glad you're back. If I could sleep a little, I won't have to think about it. Maya gave me a pill."

"Whatever you want. You probably need some rest."

Maya and I took her up to the guest room and we tucked her in. She looked very small in the queen-size bed, lying on her side with her legs pulled up. When

Maya walked out through the doorway I kissed her forehead. "Sleep now," I said. "Things won't seem so bleak in the morning. Maya and I will be just across the hall if you need us."

"Are you all right? You had to kill that man..."

"I'll be OK. I'll get over it."

Downstairs we assembled in the dining room and I poured myself a small brandy.

"I was so much more ready to accept the murder when I thought it was Brendel," said Cody. "It seemed like we wouldn't have to dig very much further for a motive with him. But with Ballard? Just an old actor playing another part. What could it be? Could the killer really have thought he was Brendel?"

"I don't have any idea, and Delgado had much the same reaction," I said. "But I know what Angel Flores was looking for. I was thinking about this on the way back tonight. It had to be the celebrity photos. What else would he want? It's interesting that besides me there are only three people who knew they were fake; you two and Antonio Trujillo."

"So you are working for the bad guys," said Maya. "Do you know this?" Her look said, Maybe you should go back to painting. "Too bad he's so good-looking. But why wait until now to take those photos, because he must have known all along they were fake?"

"As long as no one else knew, he could afford to leave them in place, and it was even better if he did," said Cody. "It was Paul's eye that identified the problem. Probably Dos Cerros thought they were too good for anyone to spot."

"But you see where this goes—if Trujillo used

Flores to retrieve the photos, it means he also used him to shoot at Ballard outside this house the day of the painting session," I said.

"And it also means that it was Trujillo who set up you and Barbara with Flores outside the bank," said Cody. "No one in the bank would acknowledge bringing the security tape to the police. It had to be someone with some real pull to make that happen. Maybe with as much pull as Dos Cerros."

"So why am I working for the bad guys then? What do they want from me?"

"That's easy," said Cody, giving me an indulgent smile. "They want you to tell them everything you know about what's going on as soon as you know it, so they can stay ahead of you on this, like tonight. They bought everything you know about the case, or can find out, for ten grand."

"And I'm a guy who, with this house and the money from the insurance and the estate, is worth about one-and-a-half million bucks, but now I'm nothing but a cheap date."

"They could have just asked me that," said Maya, taking a delicate sip of her brandy.

"Well, you know what? I can turn this upside down too. I'll feed Mr. *Señor* Fancy Pants Trujillo so full of bullshit it'll turn his eyes brown."

"They are brown already," said Maya, "with flecks of gold, and shaded by long, long lashes."

"I think these are the big people Maya was talking about earlier," said Cody. "It's people like Trujillo who run things here."

"Wait a minute," I said. "This can even go back a

step further. If all this is true of Trujillo, then why not think that he killed Ballard too? He was there. We don't have a motive for him, only I have that, but we have means and opportunity. And we know he's involved in a cover-up, in the attempt to frame me."

"Which might still succeed," said Cody. "We need to sit down with Barbara as soon as possible and have her reconstruct what she can remember about the minutes before the body was found. She may have the key to this."

"Wouldn't Delgado have already done that?" asked Maya.

"I'm sure he tried, but what has he told us about it?" asked Cody.

"Nothing. We don't know what the police are thinking. Delgado wouldn't get into that with me tonight."

"There you go," said Cody. "He may have an excellent reason for that."

I was up at eight, a little foggy, but I had slept well. Going to bed so late had kept me from thinking much about Angel Flores. We enticed Cody off the sofa with the aroma of fresh coffee. By 9:30 we all were showered and coherent and I had reached Barbara and told her we needed an urgent sit-down. She invited us for breakfast. Any opportunity to be a hostess again. I opened the guest room door a crack and saw that Lynn was still out of it, her long body curled up in a ball, so I scrawled a quick note for her and left it on the kitchen counter by the coffee.

Casa Watt is an extraordinary place in any light, but this morning it was especially inviting as we sat at the small round corner table in the dining room. Barbara looked fresh and put together, and her new houseboy, Javier, served French toast and bacon and an enormous bowl of sliced mango and papaya with lime slices.

"This is wonderful," she said. "I didn't know if I would ever have any guests again after last weekend."

"How are you doing with all of this?" asked Maya.

"Not that well. I was in shock most of the week. I was paralyzed; it brought Perry's death right back to me. I couldn't do anything. If Javier hadn't been here I probably would have starved."

"I don't suppose you tried painting again? It can be very therapeutic," I said.

She shook her head. "The thought of having a brush in my hand makes me sick now."

"I can see that."

"I haven't been able to go into the studio. Fortunately Cody came by a couple times to see me. I spent a lot of time sleeping too. I couldn't even answer the phone; not that it rang that much." Javier came in with refills on the coffee. "Javier, could you bring in the urn with the rest of the coffee and then leave us for a while?"

In a few minutes he returned with the coffee urn and cleared what dishes he could, and then disappeared.

"OK, bring me back into the loop. What's been happening? I didn't want to talk in front of him."

Cody brought her up to date on everything that had happened until last night, and then I filled her in on the deaths of Washburn and Flores.

"Wow! So you killed that man who was behind us at the ATM? And he had just shot Mr. Brendel's driver? And Malcolm Brendel was really an actor named George Ballard? I almost think I've heard that name, even though I was never in Dallas much. I just don't understand what's going on. Why kill an actor?"

"Bad performance?" said Cody.

She looked at him for a moment. "But he convinced everyone, didn't he? He really wasn't that bad."

"He convinced me," I said. "But the real reason I called and coerced you into giving us breakfast is that we'd like to reconstruct what happened just before you went upstairs after the body was discovered."

"I think I can help with that."

"Go back to when you were first aware of a problem upstairs."

"OK." She closed her eyes.

"What made you aware of it?"

"I heard the voices as I stood at the archway to the foyer. I had come from the veranda and crossed the great room after I told the musicians they could take a break. People were milling around."

"Then who were you talking with?"

"That big man, the good-looking one."

"Trujillo."

"Yes. I know! He looked up the stairs first, which is why I focused on what was going on up there. Otherwise there were several conversations going around us. I could have paid attention to any of them, I guess."

"Did he accompany you coming in from the veranda?" asked Cody.

"No. No one did. He was already standing at the

bottom of the stairs."

Cody gave me a significant look. "What were you talking about?"

"The party. He was thanking me for having the party for the vice president."

"And then?"

"I started hearing voices from upstairs, words like 'bled out' or something like that. I ran up. I don't think I said anything to Trujillo then, I just bolted up the stairs. When I got to where they were standing, Paul moved a little to let me pass and I saw him—I don't know what to call him now—on the floor. I might have screamed, I don't know."

"Did Trujillo follow you right up?" I asked.

"I...I don't think so, but I was completely focused on what was happening up there. What are you thinking?"

"That if Trujillo already knew what had happened, he wouldn't have needed to go up," I said.

"Let's go back a bit to before you spoke to the musicians, before you crossed to the veranda," said Cody. "What were you doing?"

She put her hands over her face and thought for a moment.

"I'm sure I told this to *Licenciado* Delgado. He would know. Oh! I was in the kitchen talking to staff about what drinks to serve and whether to open more champagne."

"How long would that have taken?"

"Maybe three minutes, no more. I looked around a little, just to see that everything was going all right."

"How about before you went into the kitchen?"

"I was talking to someone about the food, about the steaks, I think. Oh, it was Sally Mason. She wondered where I got them; she said she could never find them here."

"Was Malcolm Brendel near you or in view during these few minutes?"

"I didn't notice. There was so much going on, and if you're the hostess, you don't always give your full attention to the social part. People were spreading out, gathering into little groups and I wanted to make sure everyone was covered by the servers."

"How much time passed between when you got up from the table and when you ran up the stairs?" I asked her.

"It's hard to say precisely, but I think ten, maybe fifteen minutes at most."

"And Brendel—it's hard not to keep calling him Brendel—got up when you did?"

"Yes. That's why I stood up. Is this helping?"

"I'm not sure. I think so," I said.

"One last question," Cody said. "During those twelve minutes or so, did you see anyone go up the stairs?"

"No, not even Brendel. Not until I heard the commotion on the landing. But think about it. You've got twenty-five guests, and nine inside staff. I don't count the car valets or the musicians, or the security. If you're me, what you're watching for is that the staff is covering everybody, that no one is standing around like a wallflower without someone to talk to, that the musicians are playing the right things at the right times, and that everything moves as it should. If someone chooses to use the bathroom upstairs, it's not likely to register."

"Isn't there another stairway coming from the kitchen?" asked Maya.

"Right, for the staff. But any of the guests could have used it."

"I don't think Brendel did, but the killer might have."

"Let's look at that again," I said.

We all walked back into the kitchen, which was roughly square, with a center island and stainless steel cabinetry and counters. It was clearly a staff room. Barbara would never be talking to guests here over her shoulder as she chopped onions, and they wouldn't be leaning against the sink counter as they listened with a wine glass in their hand.

Only if you were kitchen help would you enter through the swinging door from the dining room directly or from a small, inconspicuous doorway under the grand staircase which led to the kitchen and staff area by way of a hallway. The same hallway led to a service entrance on the north side of the house. It also gave access to the servers' break room where Delgado had done his interviews, immediately adjacent to the kitchen, and just past that, the staff staircase and bathroom.

"So anyone using the service door from the outside could go directly to the second floor without passing the kitchen, too," said Cody.

"Except that the outside door is always kept locked unless we're receiving a delivery."

"Was it locked the night of the dinner?"

"I didn't specifically test it myself, but I know one of those two big security guys did when they first came in. Of course, someone on staff or even a guest could have unlocked it later without being noticed."

"And you could also get to the servants' stairs by coming through the small door under the main staircase, without passing the kitchen."

"Right. It's how the staff would come and go to answer the front door, for example, without coming through the main rooms."

When we got back home Lynn was up and drifting aimlessly through the house. She still wore the flannel nightgown.

"How are you doing this morning?" I asked, putting my arms around her.

"OK, I guess."

"Do you feel like eating something?"

"Just coffee, I think."

I put on some coffee and found a banana. I set it in front of her on the island counter, but she didn't touch it.

"I'm going to send Trujillo on an errand," I said to Maya. "Only this time the people on the receiving end will be armed and ready."

"What are you thinking?"

"Listen in," I said. I dialed Delgado's number at home.

"Sorry to bother you on a Saturday," I said. "I hope your family is well?"

"Very well, and thank you. How is *Señorita* Washburn this morning?"

"A little better, not much. We will keep her here for a while."

"I am glad you called, *Señor* Zacher. I have just heard something from my brother-in-law, the deputy mayor, that is cause for concern. The rumor is that the chief of the judicial police will soon be ordered to arrest you for the murder of Malcolm Brendel, or George Ballard, if you prefer."

"I see." I was not surprised. This had been coming for a while.

"If this happens, we will have no choice but to comply. You did not hear this from me, but you will not wish to be here in San Miguel when the order comes through. I have been able to protect you from this until now, where many others would already have been arrested, because I believe you are being set up, and also because you and I have a certain understanding."

"Thank you."

"But, as I have said, if the court orders this, through the chief, I can do nothing to stop it. My job would be lost."

"I understand. We will be ready for it on this end. But there is something I wanted to run by you and get your opinion. I believe now that Antonio Trujillo and Dos Cerros are behind the visit of Angel Flores to the house on Cuadrante."

"*Madre de Dios*! Soon I will need body armor. I hope this is not true."

"But it could be. I would like to perform a simple experiment. If I am wrong, it will be harmless to everyone. I will report to *Señor* Trujillo that two witnesses saw Malcolm Brendel sending a text message on his phone after getting up from dinner the night of his death. I will say that I believe it may reveal something about his killer. Now, Brendel's personal effects, his phone, his wallet, and his clothing, they are still being held by your office?"

"This is true. Now we will wear the target?"

"Exactly. And it will be most instructive to see if someone comes after the phone, and how."

"And in any case, *Señor* Zacher, it would not be you coming after the phone, because, as the heir, you would be receiving it anyway in a few days, once these things are released. There would be no point."

"Right. Only the murderer will need the phone now."

"But, none of this is true, then? I mean about the text message?"

"Totally false."

"Because I have seen the report from the cell phone, and the numbers it dialed and received, and there were no text messages at all. The only numbers were those of Stephen Washburn and the two security men."

I thanked Delgado and hung up, looking at Cody and Maya. Lynn had gone back upstairs with a book while I was on the phone, bringing a cup of coffee with her. I believe it was not one of Maya's murder mysteries.

"Pin the tail on the donkey," said Cody. "This time it's them."

"This is a good thing, but now we must flee?" asked Maya.

"I think it's best. I understand Guanajuato's lovely this time of year. I'm going to see if I can reach Trujillo. Can you start packing? And explain to Lynn that she can stay here as long as she wants? I'm sure she's not ready to go home yet. Cuadrante must still be an ungodly mess."

Cody followed her upstairs to talk to Lynn. I dialed Antonio Trujillo and tried to generate a sense of excitement at the new information. After we exchanged the usual formalities, I said, "We have uncovered something new. It may be important, or maybe not. I've come up with two guests at the dinner party who saw the man pretending to be Malcolm Brendel sending a text message just minutes before he was killed. I'm thinking that if we're lucky it might identify the man who asked to meet him upstairs. I think he may have suspected something. Just a chance. Anyway, the judicial police are still holding his personal effects, but I talked to them earlier and they'll be releasing them to me in a few days. I didn't say anything about the text message. I thought this was something we could handle on this end as soon as I get hold of that phone. Then we'll know for sure what's going on here." I was wishing I could see Trujillo's face as I spoke.

"Well, this is very interesting, and you are sure no one mentioned it to the police?" he said slowly.

"I cautioned the witnesses to say nothing." Always the loyal employee of Dos Cerros.

"You are thinking that the message can be recovered from the cell phone?"

"Absolutely. Knowing him, it would not have been a cheap phone. It would have that feature." Maybe they all do. I didn't know. I didn't care much for them and I often left mine behind just to be out of touch.

"Excellent work, *Señor* Zacher. Please let me know when you receive his effects."

"You'll be the first to know." Of this I was certain. He would know before I did if this went as planned.

I flipped my phone shut, but before I could get it back in my pocket it beeped. This time the familiar voice on the other end did not identify itself or go through the usual México courtesies.

"They are getting ready to come for you. It is time to go, *mi amigo. Hasta luego.*"

I flipped the phone shut and ran up the stairs. Maya was just finishing the piles of clothes and toiletries on the bed. I threw them into the suitcases and slammed them shut. Cody's gun was already in my bag.

"Don't use it on any cops," he called after us as we ran down the steps. "Delgado can trace it to me." Lynn waved silently from the hallway above. We were in the artmobile in ten seconds and burning away from the curb. There was no conversation until we were on the Celaya road, moving past the glorieta.

"Now we are fugitives," she said, pulling her hair back into a pony tail. Her lips were tight. "I came from a good family in México City—you know this. We lived near Chapultepec park. My father has a Ph.D. We were not *ricos*, but we had the respect of many. One evening when I was eight years old we entertained the oil minister for dinner. I sat on his lap. Imagine. And now this."

"And you have a master's degree," I said, trying to be helpful. "However, your sister's a bit of a tart. Not to contradict your basic point."

"Yes. Half-sister, please. And now I am running away with a gringo who is wanted for murder. I must have made a wrong turn somewhere."

"True. But this gringo has a pure heart and a clear conscience. And he does not much care about the opinion of others, usually."

"You decline to be arrested."

"Should I submit to being charged with murder? Like you said, here you are guilty until proven innocent. And you have Dos Cerros leaning on the process. I would never get out, I could never clear myself. Trujillo would be cooking up new pieces of evidence against me every day. The best way is to not allow myself to be put in jail."

"Couldn't Dr. Weingard help you?"

"He would be pushing one way and Antonio Trujillo pushing the other. No contest."

"What are we going to do?"

"I think we'll settle in Guanajuato for a few days, until Trujillo steps into the trap we set for him. Then we'll see what happens." We were on Highway 51 approaching Santa Teresita. I was trying to avoid the thought that things were spinning out of control. Maya was looking past me out the window. She pointed suddenly.

"There is the house; that's where I was being kidnapped in July." Another comedown for a girl from a good family. Where would it end?

Eight kilometers farther we turned onto the road to Guanajuato. This was not the only route, but it was a well-maintained road and I was hoping it was less likely they might have anyone looking for us here yet.

"If we are caught, will they arrest you too?" I asked.

"No. In México it is understood that a loyal woman would flee with her man. Anything less would be ignoring her duty. Because the police understand this, they would only shoot you. Perhaps it's time to check your will, now that you are getting so much respect from Fidelity Investments."

I didn't respond for a while. I didn't have a Mexican will, which I knew was a mistake.

Everything I had would go to my parents, which didn't seem right when Maya and Cody were about to start a new life together.

"I'll think about it when we get back. When we get to Guanajuato, we'll find an out-of-the-way place to stay, one where we can park the van out of view. A place that's quiet and somewhat selective."

"We won't use our real names?"

"No."

"I have an idea," she said.

"What?"

"Bonnie and Clyde Barrow. What do you think?" She thrust her chest out and put her hands behind her head. This is what she imagined blondes always did, maybe from Barbara.

"It's been done before, but I like the attitude."

"What's your idea?"

"Marta and Geraldo Segundo."

"You got that from Geraldo Rivera?"

*"Si."*

We were passing the cut-off for Xoconoxtle El Grande. My feeling is this: if you can't pronounce it, don't stop there, because, after all, how could you tell anybody where you had been? Of course, I could do the El Grande part. It's probably a charming place. We'd never know; we flashed past it at one kilometer over the speed limit. The next stop was Santa Fe. I was tempted to stop, just to compare it with the Santa Fe in New México, but we didn't have the time. I had in my mind a neighborhood in Guanajuato that I'd only heard about. An out of the way, full of summer mansions and consulates sort of place, above the town, up by la Presa de la Olla, the reservoir that supplied water to all of Guanajuato City. The big bonus of the idea was that it was full of state government offices, and state cops. Who would look for us in the very bosom of the enemy? And I later planned to be in the bosom of Marta Segundo. Yes, artists are quite properly distrusted by the community at large.

Half an hour later we came up on the eastern side of Guanajuato and connected with the *Paseo de la Presa*. It curved around the hills for three or four kilometers and passed the governor's offices and a large monument inside a circle and then became renamed as Marques de Rayas. We climbed a gradual slope beside a park and then passed a large dam—*la Presa de la Olla.* Then, after passing another park above it, *Parque de las Acacias,* we looped over the top and started down the other side. About halfway down Maya spotted what I was looking for—*la Quinta de las Acacias.*

It was an old summer home from the twenties, judging by the architecture, with rows of shuttered windows facing the street. Just beyond the building was a driveway with off-street parking behind. Exactly what we wanted; a little privacy for two weary travelers. I pulled the van into the lot and parked up against the building. It would stay there during our visit; I planned to take cabs or walk.

"It looks like a lovely place," Maya said. "Is this where we're staying?"

"If they let us, I didn't make a reservation."

"It looks expensive."

"I think it is. Salma Hayek stayed here once."

"And you are hoping to sleep in the same bed she did?"

"It could happen."

We walked around to the entrance, and the manager was able to find us a room overlooking the narrow park across the street. I sat down at the writing desk while Maya unpacked a few things, and I stared into the mirror above it. A moment later I felt her cool fingers on my shoulders. She had an odd look on her face.

"You've done it this time, haven't you," she said. There was no judgment in her voice. I found I couldn't respond right away. To have her go from the lighthearted chatter about Salma Hayek, to laying it out so simply before me had the effect of bringing to the surface everything that had been seething inside of me. She moved around to my side and I buried my face on her shoulder. A car went by, maybe two, as I breathed the soft warmth of her skin through her cotton shirt.

"I think I'm really frightened now," I said, "for the first time. I didn't feel like this even when I killed that federal officer as he held a gun to your head."

I don't know how much time passed, but as we were about to leave, my phone rang. It was Cody. The sound put me back in the present.

"You missed them," he said.

"Damn."

"That's what they said."

"How many?"

"Two uniforms. Polite, disappointed. They kept their guns holstered. No sign of Delgado or Rodriguez. They looked around a bit, just enough to make sure you weren't here. I said I didn't know where you had gone, that you had called me and asked me to stay with Lynn because she wasn't ready to go home yet. I don't think they understood the flannel nightgown. I was also unable to say when you'd return."

"That's my position too. We're in Guanajuato, just about to check in at our bed and breakfast."

"Do you think that's far enough away?"

"You never know. I don't plan to drive while I'm here, so they won't be spotting the van. How's Lynn doing?"

"Right now, alternating between weepy and resigned. She's still in the nightgown. She said she doesn't think she can ever live at Cuadrante again. I can understand that. I didn't tell her that her father wasn't the only person murdered there this year."

"Good move. If you have a chance, get hold of Rigoberta, our cleaning woman, and see if she can find someone to clean up the library over there. The garden too, where I shot Flores. Her number is on a card on the refrigerator. We'll check in with you later. Let me know if anything pops down at the police station." I had a strong sense that something would.

# Chapter 15
## The Big Man

On Sunday, the day after Paul and Maya inaugurated their stay in the queen-size bed at La Quinta de las Acacias by pretending she was Frida Kahlo and he was her exiled revolutionary lover, Leon Trotsky, Officer Hugo Peña reported to *Licenciado* Diego Delgado at the central station on Calle San Francisco, overlooking the *jardín*.

"They have made contact with me this morning," Peña said. "The messenger was a woman. Very nice too, but I didn't recognize her. I think I would have remembered."

"Did she address you by name?"

"No. She merely asked me what time my shift ended. I thought at first she might be wanting to meet me later."

"Interesting. How much did she give you?"

"Ten thousand pesos to leave the rear door unlocked at the end of my shift."

"Excellent. I was hoping it wouldn't be any more than that. As we discussed at the meeting this morning, a matching amount from our mordida fund will be in your pay envelope at the end of the week. Can you describe her?"

"Yes, small stature, Méxican, slender, well dressed."

He went down the list from memory, ticking off each item on a different fingertip. "Small gold loops in her ears. About twenty-eight to thirty years old. Attractive. Wearing tan slacks, nicely tailored, and a white sleeveless top with white sandals. Coral toenails and matching lipstick, her..."

Delgado made a gesture of impatience.

"On foot?"

"Yes, I saw no car. After we spoke she went into a shop on the *jardín*, next to the photo place that also sells Cuban cigars. She must have left by the rear, through the courtyard, because I waited for a while down the street but she didn't come back out. I didn't want her to see me following her, as you ordered."

"You have done a fine job with this, Hugo. Your loyalty to the department has served you well today. We will be working late tonight."

After Hugo Peña left, Delgado sat at his desk for a while with his chin in his hands. Méxican judicial police are as deeply sensitive to politics as they are to crime. He was now walking a thin line between the heavy-handed influence of Dos Cerros and the certainty he felt in his own mind that Paul Zacher was being set up. It was true that Zacher was a gringo, an interloper in this charming *bajio* town, and that the Dos Cerros group, however insensitive and pushy, were his own people; at least, that narrow segment of his own people that had power and wealth. It was also true that this was not the particular segment that included Diego Delgado. And there was something in his makeup that urged him to tweak the collective nose of Dos Cerros, if he could get away with it, and side with Paul Zacher, gringo or not. After all, Zacher had always treated him with respect, had never been pushy, and lied to him only when necessary. It did not get any better than that with gringos.

Slightly after five o'clock he left his desk and had a snack down on the *jardín*. Sitting on a cast-iron bench, he watched the crowd circulating among the ice cream vendors and balloon sellers. He felt a pleasant buzz of anticipation. It was rare that criminals came to the station of their own accord. When one of the pigeons from the crowd at his feet landed next to him on the bench, he dropped it a few crumbs and decided to go back up to his office and wait.

At the top of the stairs he encountered Officer Ignacio Ramos, a ten-year veteran of the regular police, who generally had a quick hand and a cool head.

"Cancel your patrol tonight and stay here in the office with me and Peña. I'm expecting company."

The police office, which served the central and western parts of the city, was laid out in a rectangle on the second floor of a venerable building that had played a role in the War of Independence in 1810. Tall windows overlooked the *jardín* and the streets surrounding it. Rows of desks filled the room. Doors in the wall behind led to a shower and break room, and three interrogation rooms, all windowless. Behind these was a row of holding cells and the evidence room. From this room a door led to the second-floor open walkway facing the interior courtyard of the building. This door had no exterior latch and was always kept locked. It was strictly against regulations to use this door, except for exit in case of a fire. At six o'clock Delgado unlocked the dead bolt and lifted the steel bar from its brackets. Regulations crashed and burned.

They had already put on bulletproof vests.

Along two walls of the room were racks of storage bins, each one labeled on the front edge with the name of a case or victim. Earlier in the day Delgado had spent some time on the Internet and confirmed Paul Zacher's supposition that the dead man was George Ballard. On the bin marked "Brendel," the name "Ballard" had been added below, in parenthesis.

Delgado seated himself in the corner of the darkened room within easy reach of the light switch. Supply and file cabinets partly shielded him from view of the outside door. To his left, the door to the break room was open, but that room was unlit as well. Waiting there out of sight was Peña, while Ramos looked down through the tall windows to the street in front. At seven o'clock they changed positions and Delgado sat in the break room, out of sight of the door.

At eight, Delgado moved to the front windows facing the plaza, stretching his legs and looking out on the increasingly busy streets. Under the bank arches a group of mariachis broke into a tune he had heard a thousand times before. Groups of tourists photographed the brightly lit spire of the *Parroquia*. Ten minutes later, as he bent over to re-tie his shoe, a car directly across the street from the station burst into a mushroom of flame.

"Beengo," he said to himself, yanking the knot tight. "We have you, my friend. We are a long way from the turnip truck tonight."

Ramos came running in from the break room, gun

in hand, having seen the flash reflected on the walls and heard the explosion, and Delgado made a sweeping gesture indicating he should turn around.

"Leave it for the firemen," he whispered. Delgado waved them both back into the break room and he took up a position in the chair in the evidence room.

Five minutes passed before a knife edge of light appeared along the door frame. There was no sound. The door opened further and in the light penetrating from the courtyard he could see the profile of an enormous man slide through the doorway and switch on a penlight that played back and forth slowly across the evidence bins.

"Do not move, *Señor,*" said Delgado calmly, turning on the overhead light as he spoke. But the big man turned at the sound of his voice and fired in his direction. Delgado felt the slap of the side of his suit jacket as the bullet passed through it and he fired dead center into the man's huge chest, a target he could hardly miss. At the same moment Ramos and Peña appeared in the break room door and each fired two rounds. The intruder spun around, hit the wall, and slumped to the floor into a spreading pool of his own blood.

When Delgado reached him and kicked his gun away the man was wheezing and crimson bubbles gathered at his lips and nostrils. One leg began to move spasmodically and then was still. Ramos reached inside his black jacket, now oozing blood that seemed almost as black as his shirt, and pulled out the man's wallet and gave it to Delgado.

He shook it open and read the driver's license, but he had already recognized the man.

"Gaspar Frutos. This man was a security guard for the man known as Malcolm Brendel. I wish he had not chosen to shoot."

In the States when an officer shoots someone in the line of duty, he is placed on administrative leave. In México, he is issued replacement bullets.

# Chapter 16

By Monday morning Maya and I had worn off a fair amount of shoe leather trekking up and down around Guanajuato. The city was built across a series of ravines; we had seen no level sidewalks. After touring the Diego Rivera museum house we had gone up on the ridge above town to see the Pipila monument, where some kid managed to pull two ten peso coins and a luggage key out of my front pocket without me noticing it. With skills like that, I can't believe he didn't go for my wallet. He clearly had no idea he was messing with a fugitive on a murder rap, or he would have been more careful. We'd had a great dinner Sunday evening outside at the Hotel Santa Fe, directly on the intimate and welcoming plaza, the *Jardín de la Union*. What works so well is that there is only one side of it bordered by a street with car traffic; the other sides are pedestrians only.

Although I'd visited Guanajuato in the past, I'd never gotten a sense of how it was laid out and how to navigate it. Maya had taken on this task, so we had nearly everything we needed, except any information about what was happening in San Miguel. Early in the afternoon we found a sidewalk cafe on Obregon opposite the Basilica. Maya ordered two coffee drinks and I dialed Cody.

"Williams."

"It's the gringo on the run. What's happening?"

"Nothing much, aside from two big things. There was a car fire on the *jardín* last night, no injuries, and Lynn changed out of her nightgown. I think that's a good sign, the last one anyway, although it may have just been a case of wash it or burn it. We sat up on your roof garden and watched the column of smoke while we drank a bottle or two of your wine."

"Nice. Next you'll be painting her. Hear anything from Delgado?"

"Nothing.

"I wonder what's going on? I almost feel like calling him, but it wouldn't be quite proper, you know, being a fugitive on a murder rap and all."

"Since when was propriety a big deal to you? You're a painter."

"I'm just thinking of him, of his career. He wouldn't want it known that he talked to me."

"I'll call him and let you know."

"How's Lynn doing?"

"Standing up straighter. She didn't go into a tailspin this morning when she got up. She got a little loaded last night, which helped her to vent a bit. She got into a thing about when they lived in Topeka..."

As I listened I was watching a police car cruise slowly down Tenaza, on the left of the pumpkin-colored basilica across the street. As it neared the intersection it pulled over to the curb, and I saw the driver place something up onto the steering wheel and study it. Then he looked over our way. I touched Maya's wrist and nodded at the car.

"Time to go," she said quietly, picking up her purse and pulling on her sunglasses.

"We've got a situation here, Cody. Call me later." I tossed some pesos down on the table without hearing his last sentence. Moving along the sidewalk behind us was a crowd of tourists, each person with a camera, and led by a guide speaking rapidly in what could have been Japanese. We plowed through it, provoking a few startled looks, and even though I was eight inches taller than anyone in it, the crowd gave us some cover as we passed through. On the other side was City Hall, and we ran through the lobby toward the back wall, hoping there might be a rear exit.

God sometimes smiles on artists, but mostly not; they're not his main clientele. Today was a good day, however, and there was an exit at the back that gave onto a small alley wedged tightly between two buildings. About a hundred feet down was Alonso, one of the main streets of downtown Guanajuato. A main street meant there would be a cab stand nearby.

A peculiar virtue of Guanajuato is its network of tunnels formed by an underground river over thousands of years. Once the river was diverted, the improved tunnels provided a subterranean road system of great efficiency, far more than any above ground in the city itself, which was designed for burros, carts, and carriages. Adjacent to the cab stand, what could be more handy than one of the tunnel entrances? This is why, as we piled into the rear seat of the cab, I was pointing and screaming, *"Tunel, tunel, muy pronto, señor!"*

"Another crazy gringo," the driver probably said to himself as he tossed his newspaper on the seat beside him. But he did pull quickly away from the curb, even managing to produce a slight squeal of the tires. Most taxis in this part of the country are well-used green and white Nissans of the non-squealing variety. The only squeal you'd normally hear traveling in one of them would be when it broadsides a hog.

Amid a sudden blare of horns the driver jammed the cab into the line of traffic entering the tunnel.

"You are getting good at this," said Maya. I couldn't tell whether she was talking to me or the driver.

I looked out the rear window as we disappeared through the opening and saw the police car coming around the corner onto Alonso from Estrella, and turning our way. But there was too much traffic moving through the tunnel for any great burst of speed. Just before we rounded a wide curve a couple hundred yards farther in, I saw the police car behind us, maybe fifteen cars back. Another half block into the curve and we were stopped by traffic.

Ahead, the dim lighting brightened in a small area on the left. I touched the driver on the shoulder and pointed.

"Is that an exit?"

"Only for the people. It is a staircase. It gives ventilation as well."

I tossed a twenty-peso note on the seat beside him and pulled Maya out through the door. There was a narrow sidewalk along the tunnel wall; and the air was yellowish green with exhaust fumes. We dashed toward the brighter light; behind us, the police were out of sight behind the curve. We were invisible to them, and the traffic was not moving. If we could make it up the stairs into daylight before the cars began to move again...

The cars next to us started to creep along again, but suddenly the opening in the wall was before us and we skipped up the stairs and emerged opposite the Plaza del Baratillo, with its big fountain in the center, and, fortunately, its big cab stand on the northwest corner.

In twenty seconds we were inside another one of the green-and-whites.

"Governor's Palace, *por favor.* Paseo de la Presa."

"But that's not where..." Maya started to say, and I placed my finger on my lips.

"We'll walk the rest of the way," I whispered to her in English. Few Americans came here. I thought it was because the town was so confusing to navigate. The driver probably spoke no English because he had little use for it. She nodded, understanding my reasoning.

We jumped out next to a military guard and paid the driver and headed up the street after waiting for him to drive off. We struggled a bit going uphill on the stoney pavement. Although concrete works well as a highway surface here and to hold buildings together, it has not yet been identified as a sidewalk material in most of México. We were coming up to La Quinta de las Acacias when my phone went off. It was Cody.

"Hey, desperado, there's a lot going on here, so let me take this up again. I assume, since you answered, that you're still on the loose. I'm not as nicely connected to the *policia,* so it took me a while to pry it out of them. Anyway, the car fire last night was just a diversion for a break-in at the evidence room at the *jardín* station. A big guy came in the back door, expecting all the cops would be out front dealing with the fire, but Delgado and two others were waiting for him. He decided to shoot it out and now he's dead. It's a friend of yours; I think it's the one you used to call Suit Bag, Gaspar Frutos. He was on duty at Barbara's dinner."

"So it worked."

"Yes, and Delgado's already gotten his account records from the bank. Suddenly they're eager to cooperate. Frutos was a Dos Cerros employee, only indirectly, in a sense, because his payroll checks all came from Grupo Catalina, their security division. You'll remember the name from that phonebook note at Casa Victoria. Or maybe you don't, your memory may be somewhat selective about that evening."

"Don't remind me. Any cops hurt?"

"Delgado took a bullet through the side of that shiny brown suit he always wears. Didn't hit his body."

"Damn, how's he going to replace that?"

"He'll probably just get a little reweaving done on the holes. He's already taken the Grupo Catalina connection to the mayor and the chief judge and they've killed the order for your arrest. You're a free man, provided you haven't piled up any additional charges in Guanajuato."

"I've never seen the police move that fast here. Free at last. This must be too much for even Dos Cerros to cover up."

"It looks like it. Also you got a call here on your

land line. It was a woman; she wouldn't identify herself or leave a message. It wasn't Barbara, and Lynn was here with me. I figure it must be someone wanting to pose nude."

"Could be. There's a long line. Some people get impatient."

"So anyway, the chaos here is clearing up. You can come back any time. You had some problems with the cops there?"

"I'm pretty sure we were spotted, but we dodged them. It might be time for a lunch celebration and then we'll head back." I flipped the phone shut.

"What do you think, Marta Segundo, baby? Shall we celebrate?"

"I know a place up in Valenciana. It was the mansion of the count who owned the silver mine. He was so rich he personally paid for the cathedral. Now his house is a restaurant."

"That must have been quite a mine."

"It produced one-third of the world's silver for 200 years. And it's still operating, but not as much."

There were clearly signs of a prosperous past all around us; the rows of old mansions on both sides of the park and reservoir, the fact that all floors in the house where we were staying were made from Brazilian rosewood. I had done some woodworking when I was in my early twenties as a way to finance college and I estimated that just the material for the floors would cost more than $200,000 now. If it was even available in that quantity.

We packed up quickly and checked out. Soon I wouldn't have to be Geraldo Segundo anymore and

I'd be able to use my credit card instead of paying cash for everything. We looped around the edge of the city and headed northwest on Highway 110 to Valenciana. It was all uphill, but it wasn't very far. Our mood had definitely lightened.

"Is it better now?" I said.

"It's better not to be Marta Segundo, or Frida Kahlo."

"You liked it well enough yesterday."

"That was yesterday. But it was exciting to be in bed with Leon Trotsky; our family has always been politically conservative."

"But now we're back."

"Yes." The hills rose precipitously around us and we finished the trip on a long snaky road, tucked in against the cliffside. At the top, a small village with an oversized cathedral looked out over 360° views. Two thousand feet below Guanajuato rose and fell over the steep hillsides. Not a great walking town without hiking boots and pitons. At our left stood a golden limestone mansion, early eighteenth century, with the architectural details now blurred by time and rain, but to us as inviting as it had ever been to its builder. Over the door a tablet read, "La Casa del Conde." We parked along a high wall enclosing the platform that held the cathedral as long thin streamers of clouds raced past. I left Cody's gun in the car. Any more confrontations at this point could be settled with a food fight.

An elegant entrance led us to a paved courtyard with tables under umbrellas and a softly murmuring fountain. We found a table with good shade and settled in.

"It's good to be on the right side of the law when

you kill someone," I said, feeling more mellow.

Maya placed her hand over mine. "You're so sweet, Paul. You worry about things like that."

"I do. I'm thinking now about no longer running from the police. It's been hard to relax. I think it would affect my painting over time."

The waiter came over with a *molcajete,* a three-legged black lava mortar filled with guacamole, and a basket of chips. We ordered margaritas and then studied the menu. Maya looked at me over hers.

"Do you think it's over now?" She smiled hopefully.

"That's what you always ask. I always say yes, but most of the time I'm wrong."

"I know, but I'm a historian. I want to place this securely in the past. Having it in the present makes me uncomfortable. These are big people. Can you see that? I'm not sure I can live with this all the time."

"Well, it seems like Dos Cerros has backed off. But that may have to be enough. Why they wanted to frame me for killing George Ballard, or even why they even wanted him dead, we may never know. My guess is that they're going to be occupied for a while covering their tracks on this, and I don't know how far Delgado can get with them. His jurisdiction is limited and they have a lot of highly placed friends. He told me before this ever got started that they had the ear of the president. Delgado has turned out to be a valuable ally on this one, but at the end of the day, he's just a small town judicial cop."

"I would like the shrimp enchiladas, please," she said to the waiter, who had appeared over her shoulder.

"What are you going to do when we get back?"

I asked. "Arrachera, *por favor, medio rojo*," this to the waiter.

"I've got a stack of shorthand notes to transcribe. That'll take a few days, then back to the archive. Are you going to do another Lynn picture?"

"I think so. I've got a good profile idea. I also think she doesn't know what to do yet, so if it's all right with you, let's keep her around for a while. She doesn't seem like she'd do well alone right now."

"I don't mind, but she might be stronger than you think."

"Women usually are. Think of Barbara. All she went through being widowed and now to have George Ballard murdered at her dinner party."

"I've thought about her enough, but you're right."

We took our time with lunch and afterward crossed the road and toured the cathedral. If there was an undecorated surface I couldn't find it. It seemed way over the top to me, but I guess if you have the money... It was good to be finished with the fugitive thing; I don't mind being slightly at odds with the law, but I didn't enjoy being chased. Somehow my anxiety had not altogether disappeared. Cracks were starting to form in the facade of the Dos Cerros plot, but I couldn't make myself think they were down and out, partly because I still didn't understand what it had been about. But México is like that, you don't always know what you're looking at, and after a while, you come to accept that.

We arrived home at about five o'clock to find the house deserted, with no one in the garden or the *loggia*, although it was a perfect evening. However, after I brought in the luggage I discovered a corkscrew on the sink counter in the kitchen. A cork was still attached.

"That Cody is an operator," said Maya. I hadn't heard that term in a while. "I thought he was in love with me."

"Love the one you're with," I said, shrugging. "Cody remembers the sixties. To the rest of us it's just a vague blur on the historical continuum. No matter what angle you look at it from, it's always out of focus. Besides, Lynn needs someone right now, and Cody probably doesn't mind being needed because no one has needed him for a while. Anyway, you've got me, and Geraldo Segundo, and Leon Trotsky."

"But only one at a time."

We left the luggage and I pulled two glasses out of the cabinet and followed her up to the roof garden in time to watch the lowering sun spread a brilliant wash of red and pink over the western hilltops. Cody and Lynn were seated at a circular mosaic-topped table with a bottle of wine and two glasses between them. The umbrella in the center was tilted to give them perfect shade. I'm not sure whether Lynn's pale skin had ever been touched by the sun. She was wearing white shorts and a halter top. When she saw us, she got up and ran over.

"They're back," she said over her shoulder to Cody. "And the cops don't want them anymore. Isn't that great?"

We both hugged her. "How are you doing?" Maya asked.

"Oh, I'm better than I was when you left. Cody's been a big help. And he can cook too. I've been pretty useless."

She probably thinks she doesn't even mourn well, I thought.

We joined them at the table and told them about Guanajuato and our tunnel escape.

"It can be a real advantage to not have a car in that town. You're just that much more flexible. If you're a fugitive, I mean. What else has happened here?"

"Well, we finished your wine," said Cody, "so I had to go out and buy more. You owe me $20. And Barbara called after I talked to you. She's still feeling kind of blue and would like another painting lesson."

"And I'm ready to start picture number two, if you still want to do that," said Lynn.

"How about the clean up on Cuadrante?" asked Maya.

"Rigoberta's brother-in-law has a commercial cleaning business. He'll be taking care of it tomorrow morning."

"I guess it's over, then," said Maya. This was her mantra.

"It's not over until someone is in prison for killing Ballard," said Cody. "Paul may be in the clear, but this case is still open." Maya said nothing.

In the morning I found Lynn in the kitchen and the coffee already made and fairly good. She was wearing her blue flannel night gown.

"It looks like you're ready," I said.

"Whenever you are." She managed a smile. Her hair was perfectly flat on both sides and parted in the middle.

"You've got the look I want, provided you haven't gained a lot of weight."

"Actually, I've lost a couple of pounds over this."

"We can wait with it, if you don't feel up to it. It's kind of soon, you know?"

"It's better if I'm doing something, I think. And it doesn't require much concentration. You do all the work. Let's try it."

After breakfast I called Barbara to set up a noon lesson and then Lynn and I adjourned to the studio. Maya had set up her notes in the dining room and Cody was packing up to go back home. I took a long length of dark blue cloth and spread it over the platform. Over that I put a small silk Turkish prayer rug for her to sit on. It had a subtle pattern of blues and pale golds; the blue picked up the color of the cloth beneath. She came over to the platform and pulled off the nightgown.

"Ta dah," she said. "Here we are again. Do I still look like a model?"

"Exactly like a model. Today we're going to be slightly more modest. I want you to sit on the prayer rug, facing right. Knees up, and your arms just below your knees, pulling them in toward your chest. Almost protective, in a way. That's right, but your head faces me, chin resting on your right shoulder. Your hair goes equally over both sides. I want to see the part clearly. Perfect. This may strain your neck a bit, so we'll take more breaks."

I studied her for a while. The long hollow in her thigh below the bone was perfect, and below her arm was the small curve of the underside of her breast. Her arm covered the nipple.

"This is it," I said. I began pulling out the paints and selecting brushes. There was a slight curve to her back and I could count all her vertebrae.

"What are you calling this one?"

"Lynn Two. How about that for originality?"

"How about Lynn Too? Like 'also.'"

"That would work." I poured out some thinner and mixed a couple of washes. "Have you had any thoughts about your dad's funeral?"

"I know he wanted to be cremated. They haven't released his body yet, but Cody called *Licenciado* Delgado and he said he would call City Hall and order death certificates for me."

There was a heavy silence in the studio, and I got up and put on some Stan Getz, the *Cafe Montmartre* CD. Working for another hour, I blocked in the shadows around her body and under her arm.

"What are you going to do now? Have you figured it out? You'll have that money that your father got from Brendel's will, right, the $20,000?"

"I'd like to stay here and continue with that writing course at the Bellas Artes, even though I've missed a couple of sessions now. Cody says I can get the money as soon as I have the death certificate."

"Do you know if there's any insurance?"

"I think there is, but I haven't gone back there to look through his things. I guess I'll be all right if I can just get through all this stuff."

"I think the police collected all his effects already. They were going to look for some reason for the shooting other than burglary. But don't be shy about asking for help from any of us. We know the ropes down here pretty well. I'm sure Maya would go to the police with you when you're ready, if you feel like you'd rather have some feminine company. She's a sympathetic person, most of the time."

I began working on her face. A tear had formed at the corner of one eye and started to slide down her cheek, but I edited it out. There's something about a tear in a painting that says cheap emotion, although there was nothing but real pain in the moment. It also didn't fit the idea I had of her today as a kind of construction, the long legs and arms and the line of her back, with the direct gaze coming at the viewer from the top of the frame. The long, flat hair was part of that as well. And her narrow feet with their shallow arches.

When we finished around eleven o'clock I gave her what I thought was going to be a gentle hug after she put her nightgown back on, but she clung to me fiercely for several minutes. I cupped the back of her head in my hand and pressed it into my neck. I told myself that at least she still had her mother.

"How's your mother doing?" I said, after along moment had passed.

"She's all right. They weren't even in contact much anymore. She's got someone she's been with for a couple of years. I think they might get married."

After I cleaned up, I was coming back downstairs when the doorbell rang. On the step was a uniformed man who handed me an official-looking letter and had me sign for it. I looked at the envelope as I closed the door. It was from my close friends and employers at Dos Cerros.

There were two pages inside, one in English and

one in Spanish. Across the top of each page was written, TERMINATION OF LEASE AGREEMENT.

It went on to say that the ten-year lease on the property at Cuadrante 13A was now terminated for two reasons. One, the person named Malcolm Brendel, who had signed it, was actually George Ballard, and therefore the contract was null and void. And two, the contract specifying forty taped broadcasts in promotion of the religious time share community called El Monte Sagrado, which was the payment for the lease, had not been delivered.

I was given ten days to vacate the property and remove my effects. The last paragraph contained the name and number of an attorney in Veracruz who would answer any questions I might have or receive any protest. It was signed by José Lucero, vice president of Urban Property Management. He was also the one who had signed the lease for the company.

So, I was out on the street and relieved to be there. The big house had always been an embarrassment to me. I had no intention of ever living there, nor did I know what else to do with it. The idea of subletting it had crossed my mind, but I didn't want to be a landlord. I didn't want to add a third business to painting and detecting. Wonderful restoration that it was, it didn't feel like a friendly place, given its recent history, or one that could be easily adapted to my needs. I had not even given it much thought in the recent chaos.

Lynn had not come downstairs. Maya was off to the archive, so I made myself a quick lunch and watered some dry spots in the garden. When I went upstairs to say goodbye to Lynn, she was in the shower, so I left a note for her and headed up the hill to Los Balcones, and Barbara Watt.

Javier, the houseboy, let me in. I liked the idea that Barbara had permanent staff now. I had pictured her bouncing off the walls there with nothing to do but count her money since the death of Ballard had ruined her social life.

"She's up in the studio, *señor*," said Javier. "She is expecting you."

I went quietly up the stairs, hoping to catch her at work, but I couldn't help glancing into the bathroom where Ballard had died. Of course, it was immaculate now. I wondered whether she had used it since, or ever would again.

Moving down the hallway I tried to avoid making any creaks in the parquet floor. The studio door was open, but she was not at the easel. Instead she stood looking out the window over the steep upper edge of the city, wearing a denim skirt and a pale blue shirt. Her arms were folded. She turned around as I came in.

"The professor is here," I said. I couldn't read her look.

"I'm glad you came." Her voice was thoughtful. "I've been standing here staring out the window, watching the light change. Do you see how each shadow on the hillside deepens as you get further down? I noticed that for the first time this afternoon. I think I've been noticing more things since I started painting."

There was a halftone of melancholy in her tone, but clearly, at last, it was art talk. The expanding awareness of degrees of shadow. Maybe we were going to have a good session today, without the usual deflection into the possibilities of exploring our sexual sides. I was up for it. I could talk art until everyone around me was dead and buried from boredom. Then she came close to me and put her arms around my neck. Her breath was like honey and orange blossoms. There were times when I wished I was not a painter and so acutely aware of how everything looked, because what I was seeing now was how finely made she was, the exquisite detail of her neck, the curve of her chin and the miniscule lines in her perfect lips. The moist tip of her tongue between her teeth.

"Do you know what always cheers me up when I feel down like this?" she whispered.

"Do I want to know?" Of course I did, I just didn't want to appear to want to know.

"I think you do. A little action."

So much for foreplay, or art. She looked deeply into my eyes.

"How little?" I said, looking into her eyes. "I could maybe pinch your butt once or twice, but that's about it."

"That's not going to do it today, Paul Zacher. I was thinking, what if you screwed my brains out?" Her lips were about three inches from mine, and I realized I was bending over slightly.

"Interesting second choice, but too risky. I might like it."

"I guarantee it." Her fingers sent a none-too-subtle message telegraphing down my spine. "Do you remember that I have blond pubic hair? Tastefully trimmed? I know your visual memory is flawless. Think about it." She did not crack a smile as her face came half an inch closer.

There seemed to be no safe way to answer this; none

that I could come up with in the next half hour, anyway.

"You should remember; you spent hours looking at it fondly when I posed. Do you remember that soft place behind my knees that you enjoyed painting so much? Do you remember how perfect my breasts are?"

"OK, I may have a marginal recollection of these things. It's not something I dwell on."

I tried to take a step backward but she didn't release me.

"Because if you did we'd be in bed at this very moment, wouldn't we? Can't you allow yourself to think about it? We could be lovers. You're free now, the cops have given up on you. I could be here for you whenever you wanted me. We could do crazy things. We'd wear each other out. I'd be sore all the time, but I'd cope, because I'm a trooper."

I lost the connection with whatever answer I was dredging for as her mouth met mine and my arms pulled her against me. The heat coming off her body was intense and my sense of caution evaporated in the taste of her kiss. All the oxygen left the room in a rush.

After what seemed like a long time I pulled away from her and closed the door.

"What about studio discipline?" I asked weakly. "Remember that?"

"It's my studio, and I'll set the discipline. That means I can do whatever I want."

She began to unbutton her shirt, and no bra came into view. But I already knew she wasn't wearing one by the way her breasts felt against my chest. I closed my hand over her fingers.

"No more," I said. "If you got me to sleep with you, you'd never see me again."

"Either that, or I'd see you every night. And I think I know better than you which one it would be."

"We'll see. Why don't we paint?" There was a small pause as she considered it, then her glance wavered. She looked back at the window, then seemed to brighten, and walked over to the easel and started pulling out some tubes of paint. "Are you still painting that stick girl?"

"The first one is finished. We've started another one."

"With her legs open?"

"How did you know about that?"

"Cody told me. He looked at it when you were gone. I thought it sounded kind of rude. I wasn't brought up that way in Montgomery, Alabama."

"I didn't think it was rude."

"You wouldn't." There was a slight edge to her voice.

"You're sounding like Maya now. She thought it was kinky."

"Would you like to paint me like that?"

"Would you want me to?"

"No. It seems kind of personal. I'd show it to you though, if you want." So much for changing gears.

"Thank you."

"You're polite. Maybe you would want to put your mouth on it?" she asked softly, moving closer. "That special moist place?"

"I'm not going to pretend that I wouldn't."

"And would you rub that little hump on your nose in my cleft?"

"Of course."

"What if I came on your face? Because you know I would. Probably twice."

"Are you trying to give me something more to think about? Because what I'm thinking now is that you might want a little more red here." I pointed to the reflection of the paint tube on the cup. "Give it a bit more punch. It's awfully good, though. Another thing you might do is deepen the contrast of the left side. Your cup is lit on the left, so it will move the cup forward in the picture if you darken the background there. Then on the right, where the shadow begins to grow, lighten the background. It'll give more definition without getting too linear. When was the last time you worked on this?"

She looked at me for a moment, not certain she was ready to give up, then picked up a palette knife and pointed to an area at the base of the cup.

"The day before the party. I felt like I was on a roll with it. Then everything crashed the next day. I think I told you that I couldn't touch a brush for a while. Cody tried to help me get back into it, mainly for therapeutic reasons, I think."

"You two are getting chummy."

"He was there for me, and it's good to have a man around. I appreciated it." She paused a moment. "But don't worry, I'm still saving myself for you." She smiled sweetly.

"Cody's in love with Maya. He has been for a long time. She encourages him."

"Another one. Is there something I don't know about Méxican girls?"

"Probably. There's certainly a lot I don't know."

"It makes me sick that you're in bed with her every night. All that black hair. Don't you ever get tired of it?"

"You're going to boost the highlights on the leading edge of the pedestal, right?" I was ready to move on.

"I hadn't thought about it."

"What I do at the very end is scan all the highlights, and I often end up bringing them a bit higher. And when you do this, keep your paint thick, because when it dries it will still stand up and the edges will catch the ambient light in the room. Don't make them smooth, skip over it with your brush held edgewise and the paint will be kind of blobby."

"Blobby?"

"A technical term. Indicates wide variations in texture."

She worked for a while and I watched over her shoulder. I didn't touch her, although I wanted to kiss the back of her neck.

She sat down on her stool and regarded the picture for a moment.

"Try getting back from it a bit. I used to know a painter who had a reducing lens with her at the easel so she didn't have to move away. She also had a mirror she could place at the top of the canvas so she could look at it upside down. It's a good way to check your composition. But moving back ten or fifteen feet does the same thing."

"I'm listening, but I just thought of something else. A funny thing has happened over the last few days." She turned to face me.

"What's that?"

"The stock of Watt Industries has gone up about fifteen percent. I've looked for news, but there hasn't been any. I've made about six million dollars." She frowned.

"Tough. Oil prices keep going up, though. Doesn't it seem reasonable?"

"I guess, but it made me think that if I could be up six million so easily, I could also be down that much. Then were would I be?"

"You'd be a person who had only thirty-four million, instead of forty-six. I see your point. You'd be down by the *jardín*, dressed in rags, and holding out a cup to the tourists. You're awfully attractive, though. I think you could do some good business."

"You're sweet." She put both her hands on my cheeks.

"Let me ask you something." It was a subject I felt reluctant to bring up, but there might be something in these price fluctuations. "What was Perry working on before he died?"

"Well, he had acquired a few new things, coins mostly. I think you saw some of them at that party back in February. Then there was that gold and emerald rosary, a shipwreck piece. I thought it was a bit gaudy."

"I meant for Watt Industries."

She paused for a moment, thinking.

"There was an acquisition he was very hot on. A company called BorMass-Tec. Some engineers from Louisiana had a promising new technology, I'm not sure what it was. Perry's conversations to me about business were usually a little vague. But nothing had been finalized when he died. It fell into James' lap to handle it. I don't know whether it ever went anywhere."

"Thanks. I think we're probably finished for today. I've had about all I can take."

"Am I that hard to take?"

"You're hard not to take. That's what wears me out."

I put my hands on her shoulders and kissed her neck, and then her ear and her cheek. I felt her warm breath on my skin. I touched the fine blond hairs at the edge of her face. Yes, I was losing it. Again.

When I got home I fired up the Internet, still feeling the taste of that long kiss on my mouth as the computer booted. A whole series of images from my visit passed through my head as I waited for the screen to fill. There was nothing on BorMass-Tec.

In my Rolodex I found the number of Calmen Houck, a kid I'd been to school with in Ohio who'd gone on to become a power-hitter stock broker at Smith Barney in Cincinnati. I'd never had the money to be his client and I didn't plan to now that I had a little more, but we'd been in contact occasionally over the years. Once on a visit to San Miguel five years ago he'd bought one of my still lifes.

"Cal," I said, after his sales assistant put me through. "It's Paul Zacher."

"Still in exile?"

"And loving it. I can't see myself ever moving back. But I've got a question for you. I've been hearing something about a startup out of Louisiana called BorMass-Tec. You got anything on it?"

"Well, they're not publicly traded, I can tell you that. It's all privately held, but their technology has been causing some talk about acquisition or an IPO, if it falls through, otherwise I wouldn't know anything about them. Are you messing with the oil patch now?"

"No more than I have to."

"Let me see what I can find. Hold on." There were a couple moments of silence, and then, "Wait, here we are. Sure, I see what's going on. They were acquired by Watt Industries down in Houston, let me see, it finalized just the middle of last month. There's been some nice buzz about it, and Watt has had a great pop from it, something like fifteen percent. You know that Perry Watt died earlier this year? I think he was only about forty-five years old."

"Forty-seven," I said. "And I did hear that."

"Stock took a big hit from it, back in February. It was coming back nicely, though, even before this Bor-Mass-Tec thing."

"Do you know what they have? The folks at Bor-Mass-Tec?"

"Not exactly, but I assume it's a drilling technology. Looks like the owners got a block of Watt stock and management positions inside on the deal. That's all I've got. You looking hard at Watt? Maybe you know something?"

"You could say that, but you know what they say, buy the rumor, sell the news."

"Feel like shorting it?"

"Not yet. I'll keep you posted. Thanks, Cal."

# Chapter 17

After my near miss with Barbara, I called Diego Delgado and invited him for a drink with me at Harry's New Orleans Bar when he got off his shift. Harry's is not favored much by Méxicans and I doubt Delgado ever came around much, but it has great oysters, the smell of jambalaya hanging in the air, and a bartender who knows his stuff and is quick at it. The wide range of tequilas was the hook for Delgado.

I slid onto a bar stool just after four and ordered a Plantation rum. Just as it came Delgado climbed onto the stool next to me and placed a powerful hand on my shoulder.

"Ex-fugitive Zacher, I believe. You are enjoying your new freedom?"

"Thanks to you. How are you, my friend?"

"Good. Better than good, really. The department bought me a new suit. What do you think?" He held out his arms.

It was a cheap brown suit indistinguishable from the last one, only less shiny at the knees and elbows. It could have come from K-Mart, like his desk.

"Elegant," I said. "You'll never miss the old one. What are you drinking? You look like you could use a double Don Eduardo Anejo."

"You have the insight of a connoisseur, my friend, and the cash to support it, I believe."

"This is true. How is your family?"

"Very well, thank you. My son begins the university this week."

"Congratulations, but more money, right?"

"Fortunately, he has a partial scholarship. We also have some money remaining from what *Señora* Watt gave us during the summer when was I injured. She gave more than we needed to get by."

"She's a brick, isn't she?"

"A brick?" His hand with the glass stopped in midair. Some of these metaphors don't travel well.

"A person of great solidity. Someone to depend on in a crisis."

"She is like family to us." He took a strong pull at the tequila and closed his eyes. "And so beautiful. She is golden, like a fine tequila. Her face is like...You are close to her?"

"Often too close, but she is like a sister to me."

"I understand. When I spoke to her at the unfortunate party, I felt very bad about what had happened in her home. She was much saddened by it. And being a widow, of course, it was too much."

This was the opening I was looking for.

"Is there any progress on the investigation?"

"Well, as Señor Williams probably told you, we have identified Gaspar Frutos as an employee of Grupo Catalina. So there is that connection to Dos Cerros."

"How about Antonio Trujillo?"

"The Dos Cerros headquarters in Veracruz has informed me that *Señor* Trujillo was called away quite suddenly to assist with a problem with a resort project in Belize City. So, however urgently we would wish to speak with him, we cannot get an arrest warrant based on what we have, even if no one was interfering. And even if we had one, there is no extradition from Belize. It would help only if he returned and we picked him up."

"And is someone interfering?"

"Not that I know of. They would hardly need to at this point. If *Señor* Trujillo chooses not to return, there is little we can do without more information. And even if we had it, we could only use it to pressure Dos Cerros."

"What are you going to do?"

"The usual things. We are digging into Frutos' background. We are trying to find a connection between Angel Flores and Dos Cerros or Grupo Catalina. We have nothing much from the dinner party interviews. The killer chose his moment well. No one was observed going upstairs except you."

"Are you finished at the Cuadrante house?"

"Yes. We had finished by the following day."

"Dos Cerros has canceled the lease on it. They are turning me out."

"You are surprised about this?" He looked at me appraisingly.

"No, not once I thought about it."

"But you still have the money."

"Yes."

"I wouldn't spend it just yet. Maybe it would make sense to move it out of the country."

"To the States?"

"Perhaps. Or you might think about the Cayman Islands."

"I still have the $10,000 deposit from Trujillo as well."

"That I think you might keep. Dos Cerros is too much in the spotlight right now to bother you about it."

"Good, because I spent some of it already on my flight from justice."

"You were in Guanajuato?"

"Yes."

He nodded slowly. "I received a call from the police there. They weren't certain that it was you. But *Señorita* Sanchez was with you?"

"Yes."

"I am happy there was no confrontation there. They are not as quick or as clever as the police here. And I know you do not hesitate to shoot."

"Clearly. This is why I left San Miguel."

"I have something of yours." He reached into his coat pocket and under cover of the edge of the bar, pulled out my .38 revolver and passed it to me. After I put it in my belt he dropped five bullets into my hand.

As I walked back home with the pistol hidden under my shirt, I wasn't wondering what the next move would be; I was wondering how there could be a next move. The police were better equipped than I was to go after Dos Cerros, but they seemed stopped. I felt uneasy about having made such a powerful enemy without realizing why, but apparently they weren't trying to kill me. That would have been fairly easy. I was on the streets of San Miguel at all hours, and often with no one around to witness an attack. One shot from a moving car would be enough.

Maya was home when I got there and kissed me as I came in.

"How was the *Licenciado*?" she asked.

"Stumped."

"Stumped?"

"You don't know that one. Out of gas, up against a brick wall, dead in his tracks."

"In other words, he is not able to bring down Dos Cerros."

"That's it."

I spread a newspaper on the kitchen counter and pulled out the gun.

"You are going to kill someone else now? I had hoped we were finished."

"Just for practice." I pulled out the cleaning kit and the phone rang. Maya picked it up and then handed it to me, raising her eyebrows as if to say, Who is this?

"Paul? It's Victoria Mendez."

I held it to my ear with two fingers. "Look, if you want to share another glass of champagne, I think I'll pass," I said.

"Now you're making me feel bad."

"You feel bad? You're not the one who spent the night in a field full of dog shit."

"That was your choice, darling."

"I guess I wasn't thinking clearly. What's on your mind? Not another painting, I hope."

"No, I'm just feeling that I ought to make it up to you for what I did."

"Remorse? When did you acquire a conscience? Who are you working for, anyway?"

"You're being awfully hard on me. Don't you remember the good times we had? I can remember a time when you were awfully eager to get into my pants."

"You weren't wearing any. It wasn't that hard."

"But you were. Anyway, if you still want to talk to Juana Cardenas, I can arrange it. That's why I called."

"Tell me more." This did pique my interest, since I had nothing else going.

"She's moving back to Casa Victoria tonight. I'm bringing her over at eight with some of her things. I can leave the door unlocked for you. I won't tell her you're coming." I heard a sort of purr in her voice.

"Why would you do that?"

"Like I said, I think I treated you badly. I want to give you a real chance to talk to her. Just to get it off my conscience." Enough other things on it already, I thought. Probably not much room for anything else.

"I'll think about it. Thanks for the information, Victoria."

"And Paul? Please don't tell anyone about it. She's kind of shy because of Malcolm Brendel's death. She's still in mourning."

"I understand."

If Victoria thought I was going to fall for this, then she had preserved a considerable amount of naiveté despite being in a tough business.

"Who was that?" asked Maya.

I filled her in quickly, leaving out some of the details from my last visit, and called Cody.

"Williams."

"The game's not over, Watson."

"Meaning?"

"I just got a call from Victoria Mendez saying Juana's coming back to Privada de la Luna tonight at eight, should I wish to have a word with her."

"She must think you're really a sap."

"I can't think what would have given her that idea. I was very impressive at our last meeting."

"Right. Did you get your gun back?"

"Earlier today. I had a drink with Delgado."

"Want some back-up?"

"That's why I called. I'll pick you up at ten minutes before eight. It'll be two saps with guns."

When I picked up Cody in front of his building, it was fully dark, and we cruised down Prolongation Aldama to El Cardo, then followed Ancha de San Antonio into *centro*. There was little traffic out on la Aurora, and we found a parking place across the street just past the entrance to Privada de la Luna. The roasted chicken place was doing a good business.

"What do you think?" I asked.

"I've got my universal key set with me. I think we enter through the house annex where you spent the night of your visit and come back over the roof. If this meeting is the real deal, I'll stand guard under the arches while you talk to her. If it's not, we'll be able to find out just what it is. But I've gotta tell you, I don't think it'll be Juana Cardenas who's waiting for us."

We waited a minute until there were no cars in view, then crossed the street. It took Cody longer than usual to get through the lock.

"Not been used for a while," he said. "It's stiff, but it's coming. I shot it full of graphite."

The lock gave way with a groan as if being resuscitated, and then we were inside. In the glow of our flashlights the entry was dank and trashy, with patches of discolored plaster alternating with exposed rough stone. Three irregular openings let the night sky in. In the great room a jumble of cardboard boxes sagged rotting into the tile floor. Two broken chairs sat in a corner. No door hung in the frame that opened onto the loggia. It was a fixer-upper, as the realtors would say. It would probably go for less than half a million.

Once in the courtyard we turned off the flashlights. In the far right corner a stairway led upward and we climbed it without expecting to see a roof garden. There was no moon, but the sky was slightly lit by city lights.

"Watch for soft spots or holes," I whispered. Cody weighed about 240 pounds. I could see him suddenly disappearing.

We crept along the street side of the roof until we met a parapet four-feet high between the adjoining houses, and paused for a moment. A single light was visible across the courtyard of Casa Victoria. It was the illuminated doorway of room three, slightly obscured by the beaded curtain. Juana's room, where the white plastic tray had melted in my lap. There was no movement or sound from that direction.

We slipped over the parapet and I dropped to my knees and felt the roof surface.

"Much better," I whispered. "It feels nearly new." Below us and to the right there was a creak, as if someone shifted in a chair. We waited unmoving for a moment. Then Cody made a "Follow me" gesture about six inches in front of my face and we moved farther along the roof, hugging the wall on the street side. When we had gone about twenty feet I could make out the form of two jeans-clad legs extended and crossed under the overhang below. They did not belong to Juana Cardenas. A slightly paler area at the top of the legs suggested hands, and in the hands a subtle silvery glint.

Cody placed his palm flat against my chest and pushed me back toward the parapet. He was shaking his head. We edged our way over it onto the old house's roof. About halfway to the stairs he whispered, "Are you in the market for a shoot-out? Because that's the only way we're going to find out who's down there. We can't come around through the courtyard and go through the opening in the wall, because then he's got a clear shot at us. The same is true about coming down the stairs on his side. What do you want to do?"

"I don't want a shoot-out because I'm already getting heat from Delgado about exceeding the death toll of several revolutionary movements. We could wait in the van for a while and see if this guy gets tired of waiting. He must be using the Privada de la Luna entrance, because the one we used coming in hadn't been used in a long time."

"A stakeout?"

"Why not? He's the only connection we've got going. Not to mention the fact that now they're trying to kill me instead of just framing me. Maybe you noticed." We went back to the artmobile.

"How are we going to get coffee and donuts out here?" he asked.

"There's that roasted chicken place, but I doubt they've got donuts."

"The chicken would be too sticky anyway. Let's

tough it out."

I called Maya and told her it was a set-up and we were going to wait for the guy with the gun to come out and then follow him. "It's a stakeout," I said. I didn't have to explain the word; she'd seen the movie. She started to tell me about the cute little butt that would be waiting for me in bed when I got back, but I cut her off. "Keep it warm," I said.

"So what's he doing now?" said Cody after I hung up.

"He's probably wondering why I didn't have the guts to take Victoria at her word."

By ten o'clock there had been no movement from Privada de la Luna. From where we were parked we could see the entry to the annex house as well.

"Now you're remembering how boring this is," I said.

"You don't forget. Let's take it in shifts. You want to start, or should I?"

"Why don't I take it until two, and then you take it until six?"

Cody got out and climbed into the second seat. Moments later soft snoring began.

There's not much stimulus on a street like la Aurora after ten, but at least it was easy to focus on the two entries. Nothing moved. I thought about the Lynn Too picture for a while, trying several background ideas in my mind. By one-thirty I was pulling my eyelids out and snapping them back against my eyeballs. It worked. At two I woke Cody and we changed places.

"How are you doing?"

"I couldn't sleep."

"Right. See you at six." I dreamed about a still life of coffee and donuts, and the trick was getting the steam right as it came off the two big china mugs. I had let the paint surface over the cups set up good and hard first because I knew I wouldn't get the steam right on the first try and I'd have to wipe if off. Probably more than once. The donuts were all right. They were chocolate frosted. Then someone was pulling at my hand with the brush in it, and the steam dragged off sideways, like it was in a high wind.

"Six o'clock," I heard Cody say.

"Don't do that when I'm painting."

"Right. I'll remember that."

The darkness was still thick, and we sat talking about who served the best coffee in town. We settled on Cafe Opera, across the street from the Angela Peralta theater.

By the time the profile of the hills on the eastern side of town began to take shape, we had gone through who was the best auto mechanic, who baked the best *bolillos*, whether Los Balcones was a better place to live than Ojo de Agua, and who had the best reason for wanting me dead.

Just then, on the opposite side of the street, the morning street sweeper moved into view, taking his time, pushing along his accumulation of debris. He wore the usual blue coveralls but with a nonstandard neckerchief tied over his head.

"The day begins," said Cody. "That guy in the brothel is probably still sleeping like a baby."

"So he knows we're here."

"He didn't come out. He might have spotted us from the roof, although I'm pretty sure he didn't hear us inside."

The street sweeper turned in at Privada de la Luna and disappeared, leaving his pile on the curb.

"Best antiques store?" I said.

"That's not fair. I don't have any antiques, except my badge. Best cop?"

"Retired or not?"

At that moment the sweeper emerged from Privada de la Luna, added his pile to the previous one, and continued down the street.

"Not," he said.

"I'd say Delgado. It seemed like Rodriguez got himself shot too easily in that little dustup in my entry last summer. Delgado's tough and honest, even if his ethics are a little iffy."

"You can be honest with iffy ethics?"

"It's México. He might take his share from a stash of stolen goods, but he'd never put you in jail if he thought you weren't guilty. Witness how he was with me. And he'd never touch drugs. That's the distinction. Trust me on this. He kept me out of the slammer."

"I know, you see things differently. But remember, you got him out of prison. He owes you."

Just then I saw the sweeper lean his broom against the annex house and jump into a car parked at the curb. "Bingo," I said, starting the van. "Call the emergency number and tell them to collect an injured sweeper in Privada de la Luna. I think our boy's got his uniform." I waited until the car pulled away and turned the corner before I pulled out and inched down to the intersection and peered to the left. He was about a block down, threading his way through a little *barrio* on Castinblanque. There was no traffic at all and no way to be unobtrusive. We could have had an illuminated sign on top of the van saying, "Pursuit Vehicle." This went on for a while and I maintained my distance. Just a couple of gringo tourists in a place where there was nothing to see. Then he turned right on Ignacio Ramirez, gathered speed slightly, and, when he crossed Anastasio Bustamante, floored it in a run for the Dolores Hidalgo road. I knew he was serious when he hit a chicken stepping out between the parked vehicles, and the bloody feathered body sailed over his car.

There were about ten car lengths between us when we hit the highway, skidding as we swung around to the left, and now we had other cars to contend with. Ahead of us were two buses, three or four pickups, two of them with laborers in the back, a motorcycle, and a hearse. Just as I passed the hearse, hitting over eighty miles an hour, the dried wad of chewing gum that filled the bullet hole in my windshield blew out and hit me in the neck. Then the hole began to make that annoying whistling noise again. It got worse the faster we went until Cody pulled a piece of gum out of the glove compartment, chewed it rapidly, and filled the hole again. It sticks better when it's wet.

There were only four vehicles between us and the guy in the sweeper suit, and there was enough traffic coming into town so I couldn't get any closer. Suddenly there was a shrill whistle coming from deep in the fields ahead on the left and I realized we were approaching the rail crossing. A gap had opened in front of the sweeper and he accelerated into it, just crossing in time, as we slowed to a stop and waited for the train. It was a freight, and it looked like it stretched from here to Veracruz. Game over.

Eventually we got back to Quebrada to find Maya up and relatively functional, standing barefoot in the kitchen, hair covering one side of her face, pouring a cup of fresh coffee.

"How was it?"

"Well, we never really had a chance," said Cody. "We chased him up onto the Dolores Hidalgo road, and then a train got between us and it was all over. You just can't do a chase properly without a siren and lights because nobody will get out of your way."

"I know that crossing," she said. "When I go to the archive I always leave a little earlier or later, because that train's a mile long."

"How did you sleep?" I asked, pouring two more cups of coffee and then rubbing her shoulders.

"Great. There was no one nibbling at me all the time." She pulled her hair back and kissed me.

"Must have been boring."

"Did you see him clearly?"

"Not really." I sat down at the island. "He was wearing a street sweeper's uniform and a kerchief over his head."

"At least he didn't get a shot at you."

"I just realized something," I said. "Speaking of still being alive. The $100,000 life policy on Brendel is gone. Pffft. It wasn't really Brendel. It's over. He must be alive somewhere."

"It's a good thing you didn't try to claim it," said Maya. "Then somebody else would be coming after you now. But what did this guy want?"

"He wanted to kill me, that's all. The frame job is over. Now they're just hunting."

"It's your abrasive manner," said Cody. "Lack of proper training in the fundamental niceties of detective work. Rough edges. You ought to pay attention to my refined manner when I work. You could learn something."

"You don't think it's still Dos Cerros?" asked Maya, properly ignoring this.

"I think it always was Dos Cerros, but now Trujillo's gone underground in Belize and passed the torch. I just don't know who's got it."

# Chapter 18

## Antonio Trujillo

Antonio Trujillo sat at his rosewood desk in the Dos Cerros construction office in Belize City. The air conditioner purred softly at a low speed. Coming from Veracruz, he was not much troubled by the heat. His two broad corner windows gave views of the harbor full of sailboats on the left, and on the right, the escalating structure of *Cielo de los Pescadores,* the new condominium project of Dos Cerros. Currently the ground crew was pumping concrete onto the fourteenth story level for floors. The project was almost two weeks ahead of schedule. The day had been going well until the phone rang.

"They can't do that," Trujillo almost yelled into the receiver a moment later. "Without the BorMass-Tec system the Ocampo Sink is just another dismal swamp, but one which we paid 200 million pesos to lease."

"Yet that is exactly what they have done," said the icy voice on the other end. "Their argument is that we have blundered on the Brendel project, and then withdrawn. And there is worse news. They will be offering the technology to Tres Valles Exploracion."

"Shit! But maybe we can salvage something. What if we offer the lease to Tres Valles then?"

"It would have to be at a steep loss. They know that

they would be the only bidder once they have the technology. It limits the competition. Listen, Antonio, this was your project. To say that the *jefes* are displeased would be to deeply understate their position. Unless you can salvage this in some way, well, your ass is grass, as the gringos would say. You would be lucky to be a dishwasher on our next resort project. I suggest you get back to San Miguel and straighten things out. Get hold of the others and see what can be done. You're the only one who can save this."

"But, as you know, the police there would very much like to speak with me, because of the death of Frutos and Flores, to say nothing of the chauffeur, Washburn."

"A small obstacle to a man of your talent. I'm sure you will find a way. And don't be taken in again by that devious painter. That cell-phone trick was too costly. I hope I need say no more, because I don't plan to. I'll be waiting for your report." There was a click at the other end.

Trujillo sat for a moment staring at his immaculate fingernails, then touched a button on the edge of his desk. A tall, elegant young woman appeared at the door with a notepad in her hand.

"Sir?"

"Guadalupe, please book me a seat on the next flight to Leon, Guanajuato, changing in México City. Use the Morillo Castaneda name and get me that passport out of the safe."

"Yes, sir,"

"The very next flight, understand? Leave the return open. And order a car to meet me at the airport.

Not a Town Car—get me something less obtrusive. I won't need a driver."

"Anything else, sir?" She was rapidly taking notes.

"Yes. Book me into Casa Sierra Alta up in Atascadero. It's a bed and breakfast; the number's in my Rolodex. I'll be there through Sunday. And ask Santos to handle the concrete inspection reports tomorrow. Pull him off whatever else he's doing. And cancel my appointments for now through Friday."

"When shall I say you'll be back in the office?"

"If I'm not back Monday, I probably won't be coming back. Reschedule nothing until you hear from me."

Her eyebrows went up. "Yes sir." She left the room.

Antonio Trujillo had no intention of being a dishwasher at a Dos Cerros or any other kind of resort. If a little blackmail was what was needed here, then, after all, it was only business. And Trujillo did business better than most.

He picked up the phone and dialed another number. After a brief conversation he left the office and went home to pack.

Settling into his wide leather seat on the plane, he sipped his glass of white wine, which the cabin attendant had served before half the coach class was seated. Now that he was faced with possible expulsion from Dos Cerros, his mind went back over his career. He had come to the company fifteen years before with a fresh MBA diploma in his briefcase and a confident smile on his face. His imposing presence and film-star good looks had greased his way from purchasing construction materials, in which he made a name for himself by eliminating the normal graft associated with this position, to leasing and promotion, and finally, to major project management.

He had begun the Brendel Project with considerable reluctance because he correctly saw it as a venture meant to provide unique technology to the exploration division, with no particular benefit to resorts and properties, which was the only branch of the company he had ever worked for. It was simply not his field. The criminal aspects of it gave him no ethical problem, but he regarded it nonetheless with distaste from a business perspective. Framing or murdering people was not his way of doing business. He didn't see the point of it; it added another cluster of unknowns to any deal. But his boss had been clear about the nature of the opportunity it presented, and its peculiar terms. Ballard, as Brendel, had to be plausibly connected to El Monte Sagrado to obtain the oil field technology. Trujillo was the link. Now he knew his instinct to avoid it had been correct; it was about to bring him down. If he failed in this last attempt at rescue, he'd be without a job and exiled in Belize, unable to return to México without facing prison. He flagged the attendant and got another glass of wine.

But Antonio Trujillo had not arrived at his present position by being a pessimist; he had always been up to the task. His powers of persuasion had never failed him, and recalling this, his outlook improved. Precedent did count for something. It explained why he was where he was, and why he would remain there.

If everything went well in San Miguel, he might even be able to spend some time with Victoria Mendez, his sweet young gringa girlfriend, whose body tasted like ripe strawberries.

Three hours later, Trujillo left the Aeroméxico plane in Leon and passed through customs as Morillo Castaneda, a resident of Cuernavaca, México. The passport stated his age to be forty-one, his height 1.85 meters, and his weight ninety kilos. If the San Miguel police had alerted immigration to watch for him as Trujillo, there would be no problem. He had left his dark business suits in Belize City and traveled in carefully pressed jeans and a buff-colored, short-sleeve shirt with a subtle stripe in the weave. He could have been a tourist.

After collecting a leather suitcase from the luggage carousel, he advanced to customs, palmed a switch at the entrance, and a green light appeared, signaling to him to move through without inspection. Near the parking lot exit, he spotted a man in a dark uniform carrying a placard that read "Castaneda." Trujillo nodded to him and the driver led him to a black Jeep Cherokee and gave him the keys. Then the driver walked over to the cab stand, selected the nearest cab, and rode off.

Trujillo placed his suitcase between the front and rear seats, and adjusted the front seat to accommodate his long legs. One minute later he emerged onto the highway in the direction of Silao, and then took the left fork in the road for Guanajuato. In a little more than an hour he was checking in at the Sierra Alta on the heights of Atascadero, overlooking San Miguel.

Once he had put his clothing away and set up his toiletries in the bathroom, Trujillo made a call to the Villa Rivera Hotel to confirm his upcoming meeting. But the person he was trying to reach had already checked out.

# Chapter 19

The next day I began with another long session with Lynn. *Lynn Too* had become a vision of a woman injured by events impossible to predict—not a stretch for this model. The pose was more enclosing and self-protective than the first picture, the face shuttered in vulnerability. We worked for nearly four hours, which is a long session for most models, and for most painters as well. The picture was moving along fast, with the face and hair nearly finished. There were no hands to do in this one, because as her arms went around her legs just below the knees, the hands were out of sight. When we were finished, I picked up her nightgown and handed it to her.

"You were great today. Good stamina. How are you feeling?"

She stood up and pulled the nightgown over her head. "It's getting a little better. It's nice to have something to do, then I don't think about Dad nonstop anymore. I've been trying to think about the future. I even had a couple of ideas about my book."

"Your murder mystery?"

She nodded. I started cleaning up when she disappeared behind the screen to dress.

"Who did it?"

"I don't know yet."

"How can you work like that, without knowing how it ends?"

"That's like life, isn't it? I've been dropping a few clues as I go, and I'll use only the ones I need at the end, and not the others. Isn't that the way things are in reality? Some things are meaningful, and some aren't. Anyway, this way I can't give it away, because I don't know myself."

"That makes sense, I guess." I didn't know; I never read mysteries. There was plenty of serendipity in my paintings, but I always began with a clear view of how it would look finished, and if the picture didn't end up there it was because I'd come across something better as I worked. Just then the phone rang.

"I'd like to speak with Paul Zacher, please." It was a woman, young, not someone I knew. It certainly was not Victoria Mendez. Maybe this was the woman who had called earlier.

"This is Paul."

"I have some information for you. It's very important."

"Right." I may have sounded a bit cynical.

"I don't think you understand what I'm saying. Someone is going to try to kill you."

"Actually, I do understand that part. Anything else?" Lynn emerged from the screen and waved at me as she crossed to the guest room.

"I have something to show you that will help you understand this."

"I'd like to know your name. Tell me that first."

"I can't. I want you to meet me, then you'll understand why I can't identify myself on the phone."

"What do you have in mind?" Another trap was looming.

"Do you know the three arches, as you come up the hill into Atascadero on Santo Domingo?"

"Of course."

"Meet me there tonight at exactly ten o'clock."

"Listen, miss. This is all very mysterious and important, I'm sure. But I've been seriously sandbagged a couple of times on this case and I don't intend to have it happen again. Have you got anything more specific?"

"How about George Ballard?" She hung up. I felt my hand slipping from the side rail of the turnip truck as I lost my balance and went over the tailgate. Clearly, this was one meeting I had to attend, but not alone. I called Cody and asked him to come over for a strategy session, and located Maya in the garden sipping a fruit drink and reading a magazine article on colonial interiors.

"Cody's on his way over. Let's throw something together for lunch and talk about a meeting we're all going to tonight."

I went into the kitchen and started putting together a big salad with sliced carrots and hearts of palm and a mix of mesclun, arugula, and endive from our garden. I whisked up a new batch of balsamic vinaigrette for dressing, took three Negra Modelos out of the refrigerator, and moved it all out onto the table in the *loggia*. Just as I was setting the beers down Cody appeared with Maya, hand-in-hand. After I served up the salad I filled them in on the call.

"Did you get the number she called from?" asked Cody.

"No. It came in on the land line."

"Young, old, Méxican?" asked Maya.

"Young, American, possibly slight southwestern accent, not very pronounced. Her manner was vaguely frightened and definitely serious."

"The police have not released anything about George Ballard," said Cody. "We told Barbara and she agreed to keep quiet. Obviously she had a right to know, since he was killed in her house. Other than that, none of us has said anything, right?" He looked at each of us. We shook our heads.

"OK. Either your caller is an insider, or maybe she overheard something and she doesn't want to place herself too much at risk. Probably, from your description, it could be the same woman who called while you were in Guanajuato. It's not Victoria Mendez and it's not Juana Cardenas, because she must have an accent. Someone from inside Dos Cerros, possibly? An American employee?"

"I think we do the meeting," I said. "I was going to blow it off until I heard the name George Ballard. Let's drive up after lunch and look over the terrain."

Santo Domingo goes steeply up the eastern rim of the basin that cradles San Miguel, crossing the beginning of the Querétaro road, and then rises more sharply until it passes through the center of a triple stone arch whose purpose I should probably know, but I had never paused to read the bronze plaque that explained it. On the left are a series of detached villas, and among them, exactly at the left edge of the arches, is Callejon Atascadero, a tiny street that looks like a water course, too narrow for cars and too steep for motorcycles. You could make it up and down on foot if your hamstrings were in good shape.

At the other end of the arches is a right turn going up into Privada de Santo Domingo, which gives access to a townhouse complex that fronts the street above a high retaining wall. Slightly past the Privada and on the same side of the street is a concrete platform with half a dozen garbage cans. We pulled off the street next to these and got out and walked around.

"Tough place to control," said Cody. "It would have been better to choose a place way out in the open."

"Great, but just as I was deciding I wanted to do this, she hung up."

"Maya, can you see that area of shrubbery farther up the hill and near the edge of the pale yellow house? From that point you can see the south side of the street, which will be the only part I can't see, because I'm going to be up on the townhouse wall overlooking the arches. I'll give you a police whistle and if you see anyone hiding or approaching when Paul pulls up, blow it hard. That'll mean it's an ambush."

"I'll come up in the artmobile and stop at the right arch to talk to the woman," I said. "I'll have my gun, and you'll have yours up on the wall."

"So if you hear anything from Cody, or the police whistle, move out very fast," said Maya. "Cody can cover your back."

"It looks plausible," I said. "Unless they've got someone in one of the houses with a rifle. But then they might hit the woman."

"And if there's no woman here, don't stop, just accelerate through."

It seemed like a lot of risk for a little information, but, since we were dead-ended, a little might turn out to be a lot.

Back on Quebrada we had a conversation with Lynn. I felt it was time to clear her things out of Cuadrante 13A. It was clear she wasn't going back there, even without the eviction notice from Dos Cerros.

"My lease at Cuadrante has been terminated," I said. "Do you feel up to moving out your things? You can stay here until you figure out what you want to do."

She shook her head slowly. "I can't go back there, even for that."

"We'll pull your things together, then," said Maya. "Is everything in your room?"

"Yes. And there's my suitcase there too. Thank you so much. I'm sorry to be such a burden."

I called Trujillo's office in Veracruz; I knew he was in Belize City, but I just wanted to let his staff know we were gone from Cuadrante. I preferred not to talk with him anyway.

It was four blocks to the mansion, in the "good" part of town, but we drove anyway because I didn't want to carry the suitcase that far. The house was silent and empty, not the first time I'd seen it that way. We let ourselves in through the back at the sun room. I couldn't help looking in on the library. The crew from Rigoberta's brother-in-law had done a good job cleaning up, but there was still a dark shadow on the parquet floor. Blood had seeped between the wood pieces and now outlined the edges in black. Nothing to do for that but rip out a portion of the floor; and of course, nothing would be available to replace it that matched. It was a good thing Dos Cerros hadn't collected a damage deposit from me.

We found Lynn's room on the third floor. Maya pulled out a tired suitcase from the armoire and began emptying the dresser. I took out a few dresses, jeans and shoes, and laid them on the bed. Last we cleared the bathroom of her toiletries. There was no make-up, not even a lipstick. Going out through the garden gate, I genuinely hoped I would never see the inside of that house again. I had taken everything from Ballard's effects that I wanted. I didn't much believe in bad karma, but really, enough is enough. On the way home we stopped at the post office and I packed the keys from my pocket along with Lynn's in a small box and mailed them to Dos Cerros. Maybe the next tenant would be an upstanding citizen with no legal issues.

At nine-thirty Cody and Maya left in his Escort to take up their positions by the arches. I checked my gun, emptied it and reloaded it, spun the cylinder, and then placed it in the map pocket in the driver's door of the artmobile. I didn't intend to get out of the van. At five minutes to ten I closed the front door and drove off.

Halfway up the hill I crossed the Querétaro road and entered that stretch of Santo Domingo where it narrows between house fronts on the left and a length of wall on the right where the hillside climbs much higher. Suddenly a blue Ford sedan careened past me down the hill, going way too fast for the available space. "Idiots," I said under my breath.

I slowed to a crawl as I approached the arches, but instead of a solitary woman I saw a dark-haired woman with a tall, heavily framed man. Maya and Cody.

"They took her," Maya said, leaning into the driver's window. A blue Ford sedan. Two men jumped out and snatched her just as she got to the arches."

"I couldn't get the license number from up on the wall," said Cody. "They were moving too fast."

"Damn, I saw them passing. Did you get a look at her?"

"I did," said Maya. "She walked right past me. It was Rebecca Watt."

"Rebecca Watt? Are you sure?"

"I remember her and James from the party."

"She was on foot?"

"Coming down the hill."

"If she's staying at a hotel up here, there's only one place it could be—La Puertacita. Get in."

Just below the top of the hill stands a gem-like small hotel with spa and swimming pool and townhouses attached. It's all white stucco with bougainvillea streaming over the sides. In the courtyard sits an ancient oxcart filled with even more bougainvillea. Inviting enough for even a Watt to stay in. We parked in the courtyard and entered the lobby. An immaculate young man in a white jacket was covering the desk.

"We'd like to see Rebecca Watt," I said. If I had asked if she was staying there he would have frozen up.

"I'll ring her room, sir, but I believe she went out a little while ago." He called her room and got no response, as I expected.

We thanked him and left. I drove slowly back down to the arches and parked, trying to digest this. We got out and walked around the arches. "Where was she standing?"

"She was on that end, just coming up to the arch," said Maya. Cody was on his cell phone, punching in the number for the police. At the far end of the third arch the streetlight caught the gleam of white from a sheet of paper on the ground, and next to it a flash of metal. I bent over to pick it up. It was a room key with a plastic tag that read La Puertacita. Rebecca must have emptied her pocket as she was pulled into the Ford. The paper, or rather two stapled pages of an agreement, was more interesting. I stood under the street light. It was a photocopy of a contract between George Ballard and Dos Cerros, detailing the terms and payments for his residence in San Miguel, in the role of Malcolm Brendel, unscripted, entirely improvised, and very well paid. It was signed by Antonio Trujillo.

I passed it to Maya, and Cody flipped his phone shut and read over her shoulder.

"And what," I said, "is the link between Rebecca and Dos Cerros?"

"The obvious one," said Cody. "They've got her now."

Maya's hand found mine.

We walked off the rest of the area, but there was nothing more. The surface was fully paved; there would be no footprints or tire tracks, it hadn't rained in weeks. Lights appeared coming up the hill and a white Chrysler of the judicial police pulled over behind the artmobile. Diego Delgado got out.

"This is not my shift," he said. "But the name Watt aroused my interest. What do we have?" Peña, whom I had met before, got out of the passenger side and began to look over the scene. "Did she say anything to the kidnappers? A name, for example? Something to suggest whether she knew them?"

Maya shook her head.

I told Delgado about the anonymous call I had received earlier in the day and Cody and Maya filled him in on other details of the kidnapping. I handed him the key and the papers. He studied them for a while without making much progress and then asked me to translate and explain several legalistic phrases. I didn't understand it all either.

"I believe I understand some of this. Look at the date; almost two months ago. They are drilling for much trouble now," he said, with a grin. "I believe this might bring them down. It is unfortunate that Trujillo is in Belize. What was the *Señorita* Watt wearing?"

"Jeans, I think," said Maya. "Soft shoes, like running shoes, or trainers, dark top and a jacket, like a man's sport coat, I'm not sure of the color. It might have been brown."

Delgado made a few notes.

"It's possible that Barbara Watt may have a photo of her. It's worth asking," I said. "I'm sure you remember Rebecca Watt from the party."

"Of course. The daughter of Perry Watt. Let me know if you hear from her again, but I think this is not a ransom case. I'm going up to La Puertacita. It's possible someone saw the blue Ford following her. Good night."

Peña made a palms up gesture that indicated there was no further information to be had from the scene, and they got back in the car and headed up the hill.

We were back at Quebrada before ten-thirty, gathered in the living room. I pulled out an old cognac I had bought with the Dos Cerros money and poured three glasses. None of us felt like calling it a night, but it was hardly a celebration, either.

"Another stunning coup for the Zacher Agency," I said. "We can't even get information from someone who wants to help us."

"You are sounding bitter now," said Maya. "Some things are fated not to be." Not her usual position on fate, which I knew she thought was rubbish. She was only trying to make me feel good.

"That sounds like a Méxican point of view," said Cody. "It would be nice to make our own fate sometimes. We need to take the offensive."

I checked for messages on the phone, but there were none. Probably too soon, even if someone wanted us to ransom Rebecca.

"I feel like we are that close to opening this up, but I just can't make the leap," I said. "I can feel the meaty hand of Dos Cerros in this, even with Trujillo gone, but why Rebecca? How did she get hold of that contract? But even more, how did she know about Ballard?"

As we chewed on that for a while I put on a fine guitar album by Baden Powell. True, it was Brazilian, not Méxican, but it was close enough.

"Will they kill her?" asked Maya.

"Clearly, she knows too much. If they know she had the contract copy, then they'll also know she didn't have it with her in the Ford. They may figure out that we picked it up and then they'll come after Paul."

"Nothing new there," I said.

The doorbell rang. I pulled out my gun and looked through the peep hole. It was Delgado.

"Come in," I said. "I still have some of the Don Eduardo Anejo."

"You are so kind. Of course, that would sustain me in these late hours." He came in and greeted Cody and Maya.

"Please have a seat." I poured him a tequila and sat down next to Maya.

Delgado took a long pull at the glass and set it down empty. "I have back come tonight because of something with your name on it that we found on the bed in the room of *Señorita* Watt."

He took an envelope out of his new brown jacket pocket and handed it to me.

"Naturally, I would wish you to open this in my presence. Unless you might feel it could be a *carta de pasion.*" He grinned slyly.

"Unlikely in this case. Maybe we caught a break," said Maya. "Let's see what she says."

The letter was addressed to me, including the street and number, as if she thought she might have to mail it at some point. I slit it open with my finger.

Dear Paul Zacher,

No one could be more surprised that I am writing to you than I am myself. Ever since my father's death in February I have hated you more than anyone on earth, even that scheming slut who married him. I've seen her looking at you, and I know you are sleeping with her now, and probably even before he died. I was pleased that you would both be going down together.

But if you've opened this you already know that I was prevented from meeting you at the arches, and there are some things you must know as well.

Everything that has happened since the arrival of "Malcolm Brendel" in San Miguel is the doing of my brother, James. He hired that aging hack George Ballard to impersonate Brendel, knowing that the vice president would be out of the country for an extended period. His plan (when he was still sharing his plans with me in the beginning), was to fake the death of Ballard in such a way that it would humiliate Barbara completely, and appear that you had been responsible. He would then withdraw Ballard from the scene. He created the Fidelity account and the insurance policy to give you a strong motive. Having the victim appear to be a former vice president would pressure the México police to take action. All the evidence would point toward you. If it had worked you would have spent the rest of your life rotting in a stinking Méxican prison. I was OK with this.

You'll think I was callous or even vicious for participating in this, and you are right to think so. But I have reached my limit, and that point was when James killed Ballard at the dinner party. The bungling of Dos Cerros has now driven James over the edge. He had promised them an exclusive on the new BorMass-Tec drilling system in order to have the use of their resources here, but he has withdrawn that offer, and I'm sure they will be coming after him. He's gotten very reckless, and the message I was to have given you tonight was that he has determined to kill you no matter what the cost. He is staying at the Villa Rivera Hotel. Like Dad, whom he worshipped, he can't tolerate failure.

I wanted you to know I've rethought my part in this. Even revenge has its limits.

Rebecca Watt

My first instinct was to eat the letter, or failing that, to eat a key part of it in the first paragraph, but there was no subtle way to do this. So instead I quietly placed it in Maya's outstretched hand. About ten seconds later, my next instinct was to get a towel from the kitchen and wipe off the old cognac she had thrown in my face.

"There are perhaps some areas of controversy in this letter?" asked Delgado, delicately mopping a few drops of cognac spatter from his cheeks and lapels with his handkerchief.

"Nothing we can't straighten out, *Licenciado*," I said. "You know how México families are."

"Now calm down, darlin,'" said Cody, who had risen and wrapped his restraining arms around Maya as she was actively searching the room for other things to throw at me.

"Maya," I said, turning to the side to avoid a knee in the groin and placing my hands on her shoulders as she struggled in Cody's grip. "It's not true. It's just not true. This is Rebecca's perception, based on Barbara's look, not on any factual knowledge. I have not slept with her, and I never will."

Gradually the spring inside her relaxed. Cody felt the tension go and released his grip, and Maya sat down again. Her eyes were blazing, but she had not said a word, which I knew was an extremely dangerous condition. On lesser issues she could turn the air vermilion with obscenities I often didn't even recognize, just like any other upper-class Méxican girl of good family and proper upbringing.

"Are we OK now?"

She nodded slowly, but her lips were still tightly compressed.

I translated the letter sentence by sentence for Delgado, and I saw his eyebrows go up several times. "Of course, I know this could never be true about Paul and *Señora* Barbara Watt," he said to Maya. I poured him another Don Eduardo Anejo, filled to the brim. "First we must notify the airports to watch for Antonio Trujillo's return." He pulled out his cell phone and made a brief call in the foyer, then returned. "Something that bothers me about this is that there would most likely be no case made against Paul Zacher if there were no body. She says that Ballard would be withdrawn from the scene once his death was faked. It is theoretically possible to be convicted of murder in México with no body, but it is extremely rare. I cannot remember such a case, although I am certain it has happened."

"I wonder if James only told her that to bring her in on it, intending to kill Ballard all along. Once she was in, it would be difficult for her to withdraw, as you see by her letter," said Cody.

"That makes more sense. She was taken in by him. I can see no crime from this letter in itself that we could charge her with, aside possibly from conspiracy. I wonder if she would be a willing witness, now that she is so upset by what has happened?"

"The thing will be to find her, if she is still alive," said Maya, now in reentry. I poured her another cognac.

"Maybe we can find James Watt," said Delgado. "Interestingly, the Villa Rivera Hotel is not far from the mansion, at Cuadrante number 13A. I will send someone to check on this, although I expect he's gone by now." He went outside and spoke briefly to Peña, who was still in the car.

During this conversation Lynn had not emerged from the guest room. When Delgado returned he said good night and asked that we call him if we heard anything.

After he left, Cody came over and put his arms around both of us. "Can you two be civil now?" he asked.

Maya's hand found mine. "I think so."

After he left I went upstairs and took a shower while Maya cleaned up the glasses and turned out the lights. When I opened the door to the bathroom she was standing there wearing only a big smile and a matching pair of dimples. "I think I know how to make it up to you," she said.

I don't normally think about other women when I'm in bed with Maya, but that night I found myself thinking partly about Rebecca Watt.

# Chapter 20

## Antonio Trujillo

Antonio Trujillo headed down the hill from the Casa Sierra Alta for his meeting with James Watt at 9:45. When he had reached Watt earlier in the day from Belize City, James had protested in his arrogant way that there was nothing left to discuss. He had already promised the BorMass-Tec system to Tres Valles Exploracion, he said, and Trujillo and his blundering organization had only themselves to blame for it.

Trujillo had responded that there was one more piece of unfinished business between them, and it was too sensitive to discuss on the phone. After a pause, Watt had agreed. The meeting was set for ten at Harry's New Orleans Bar, not a place often frequented by the San Miguel police. As Trujillo wound his way down Santo Domingo, he unknowingly passed Maya in the shrubbery of a villa on his right, and continued below Cody Williams perched on top of a wall on his left. His Jeep Cherokee meant nothing to either of them, and he did not pause at the arches. They meant nothing to him.

Although the sun had been down for more than two hours, the evening was still warm. The difference between the average high in the warmest month and the average high in the coldest month in San Miguel is only 12 ° Fahrenheit. Today the mercury had reached

78°. Trujillo had worn a light jacket only to conceal the gun in his belt.

He had one card left to play. While he did not know that Rebecca Watt had copied the contract with George Ballard, Trujillo did know that the police had ample reason to bring him in for a serious conversation, especially after the death of Gaspar Frutos. He planned to tell James Watt that if he did not return exclusive use of the BorMass-Tec system to Dos Cerros, he would turn over all the documents in the George Ballard fiasco to the police and give them a full statement, issued from his desk in Belize City. Since Belize had no extradition treaty with México, it would mean permanent exile for Trujillo, but Belize was not Siberia. He would even be able to slip into Veracruz now and then, using the Morillo Castaneda passport. But this would be his final visit to San Miguel.

It was a Wednesday evening and most of the remaining traffic in the city was centered on the Jardin, and the surrounding cantinas and restaurants. Harry's was at Hidalgo 12, about half a block away. Trujillo found a rare parking place around the corner on Mesones and sat for a moment in the car, watching the activity on the street. He saw nothing to worry him. Choosing a moment when there was no one in view, he moved swiftly down the sidewalk and into Harry's. The only car to pass him was a blue Ford sedan.

In addition to the large bar area in Harry's and the main dining room facing the street, there is a smaller annex room, partly closed off, but still with a view of the main action. Trujillo settled into a corner from which he could see most of the long bar as well as the entry. When the waiter entered, Trujillo refused the menu and ordered a Don Julio Anejo tequila.

By 10:15 he had finished his drink and was feeling a mild apprehension creeping over him. He no longer had the resources of Dos Cerros at his back and he was beginning to wonder if he should have been more explicit to James Watt about his intentions. With only one card to play, he had to play it exactly right.

At 10:20 he ordered another drink and a plate of chile rellenos. He tried to recall the last time he'd been stood up. Quite possibly it was in high school when he asked one of his history teachers out. It was her loss. He shrugged.

By 10:45 he had finished eating and the bar was mostly full. He got up and walked through the crowd on the off chance that he had not seen James Watt come in. Watt was not there.

He sat down again in the annex room, now nearly full as well. His mind went over a series of options, none of which was promising. He could go back to his superiors and suggest they use their government influence to get the BorMass-Tec system barred from México, perhaps on some phony environmental grounds. But they had left it up to him to solve this; to go back to them now would be viewed as failure compounded by weakness. He could find Watt and break his neck, but that would only go so far toward fixing the situation, although it might feel good. He ordered another tequila. In the end, his only option was to find Watt and give him the pitch. Trujillo thought he knew where to look.

# Chapter 21

In the morning we awakened early. It seemed like there was something urgent to do, but I didn't know what it was. I rubbed Maya's neck a little, but she was still a bit tender from our reconciliation the night before, so it didn't go anywhere. Around nine I called Barbara and told her there was something I wanted to show her, something that would explain a lot about what had been going on. She said she'd come right over.

When she arrived, we were still drinking coffee and I poured her a cup. Before Delgado had left the night before, I had copied the letter from Rebecca and now I placed it before Barbara. She stared at the small, crabbed writing for a moment, looked at the signature, and then began to read. At the end of the first paragraph she gasped and looked at Maya, folding her hands on the letter, a look of dismay on her face.

"Maya, I have never slept with Paul. I hope you realize that. I can't deny that it's crossed my mind, but it just never happened. He's always said that you were the only woman he wanted."

"I know that now," she said. "But when I read it last night it was a shock. I thought that Rebecca knew something that I didn't. Don't worry about it."

"This letter explains the whole thing," I said. "I was supposed to meet Rebecca last night at the arches and she was going to tell me about this and show me Ballard's contract, but she was kidnapped before I got there and the police found this letter in her hotel room."

"So this whole thing was only to humiliate me and put you in prison. It nearly worked. My future as a hostess is certainly ruined, that part went as planned."

"And if Delgado had bought into it, I'd be in prison now. But he never did. James must have thought that Delgado is not nearly as smart as he really is."

"How could they hate us so much?"

"You already knew they blame you for breaking up their family. If you add blaming me and Maya for Perry's death, it's a good recipe for hatred. But clearly Rebecca got in over her head."

"Of course, James has always been arrogant and headstrong," she said. "He loves to manipulate people."

"Which is a common trait among people who are handed everything. People who pull themselves up by the bootstraps seem able to maintain a more common touch," said Cody.

Lynn appeared in the doorway, showered and dressed.

"I heard some of this," she said. "Can I read that?"

"Are you ready to think about this now? It's going to be difficult."

"I think I am." I introduced her to Barbara and she sat down and read the letter.

"Wow," she said when she finished. "This is strange stuff. Who is George Ballard?"

I told her about the contract between Ballard and Dos Cerros.

"So that was never Malcolm Brendel at all?"

"No."

"But my father must have known about it." Her face wrinkled up into a blend of dismay and confusion.

"Yes."

"I can't believe it. No wonder he was worried. So the will was merely a way to pay him $20,000."

"Exactly. They purchased his cooperation. But I'm sure they told him the same thing they told Rebecca; that the murder would be faked. No body would ever be found."

"Remember when I told you he thought Brendel was up to something? But he was still playing along with them. Why kill him?"

"There was no reason to kill him," I said. "Dos Cerros sent Angel Flores to retrieve the celebrity photographs, which were fakes. Your father interrupted him. If they had felt more certain of your father, they could have called him and warned him not to interfere. But, of course, Ballard was already dead at that time. They must have felt it was too risky to let your father know. If he was having second thoughts, he could have had the police set a trap for Flores. If Flores had been taken alive, he might have sold them out."

Barbara got up and placed her hands on Lynn's shoulders. "I'm very sorry about this," she said. "It's a lot of old Watt family business that we all thought had been laid to rest. I never thought James would be capable of this."

"Remember when you told me about having the

party?" I asked. "It was the day of your first painting lesson. Whose idea did you say it was?"

"It was Harry Weingard, the consul. He called me and said how nice it would be if they could introduce Malcolm Brendel around to the expatriate community, and how the consulate didn't have a large enough space to do it. But he wouldn't have anything to do with this. Would he?"

"I'm going to see if I can reach him." I found the number in *Juarde,* the gringo directory. The secretary put me through. I wasn't surprised he was so available; the consul's job is mostly a sinecure for party faithful.

"Dr. Weingard, it's Paul Zacher."

"Good morning. Have you solved the murder yet? How is it going?"

"Well, there's movement, I can say that. I don't want to get too specific at this point. But I have a question for you. I'm interested in how the idea of having a party for Malcolm Brendel came about. Did it originate with you?"

"Actually, it didn't, although I was thinking about trying to organize a small reception of some kind to introduce him around and make him feel at home here. The problem is that we just don't have a facility for that here in the Consulate. You've been in here; it's just the two rooms plus storage down on Hernandez Macias. And I don't have the budget to rent a hall for a party. It was a relief when Antonio Trujillo called me and suggested that Barbara Watt might be a good candidate to host it, so I called and asked her. It was also Antonio's idea to see if she would be willing to ask Perry's kids to come, it being for the vice president and all. It seemed like a nice gesture."

"Did you know Antonio Trujillo before?"

"No. Well, I had talked to him once before. He had called me as a courtesy to let me know that Mr. Brendel was moving down here. A very nice man, and a power in Dos Cerros, I believe."

"Can you recall when that was?"

"Not precisely, but I think it was about three or four weeks before the party, so it all went rather quickly."

"You've been most helpful, Dr. Weingard. Thank you. I'll let you know how it all shakes out." I wasn't ready to announce yet that Brendel was really Ballard, and apparently the police weren't either. They still hadn't made a public announcement of the murder.

I hung up the phone. "Trujillo set it all up." I said to Barbara. "He's behind the call to you from Weingard, and it was his idea to invite Rebecca and James. It sounds very much like conspiracy to commit murder. I'm surprised, now that I think of it, that Delgado didn't get into this with you at the party."

"He must have just assumed it was all my idea. That would normally be the case, wouldn't it?"

"It would. It's just that had he asked, and found out the reason the party came about, he would have had Trujillo right there, instead of sitting in Belize City."

"Easy to come up with that now," said Maya. "But it only came to you now to ask the question yourself."

After Barbara left, Maya went to the market, and as I tidied up in the kitchen I looked out the window and saw Lynn out in the garden reading one of her mysteries. Seeing her like that made me connect a couple of threads. I opened two Negra Modelos and came out and sat beside her.

"Agatha Christie?" I asked, handing her the beer.

"No. Much later. It's by Michael Connelly. *Lost Light.*"

"Don't know him. Is it the kind of thing where nothing is what it appears?"

"Not entirely, but there is an element of that in this one." She looked at me carefully from under her straw hat and sipped her beer.

I relaxed into one of the cast iron chairs and gave her a casual look.

"I suppose that's common enough in books, but what about real life? Imagine when people close to you are not what they seem, but something else entirely. Don't you think that's the scariest thing of all? I know I do."

"Horrible." Nodding, she closed the book and fiddled with the hem of her shorts.

"It's the kind of thing I've been trying to deal with all through this Ballard murder."

"I know. The identity thing of Ballard being Brendel."

"I think I've got most of it cleared up, though. But not all of it. That's not unusual. There are still a few missing pieces."

"Not all of it?"

"No. One thing in particular that's been in the back of my mind for a while puzzles me. It's something about you."

"What's that?" Her voice became very small.

"The way that I got hired to do the Brendel portrait.

That's how I came into this whole thing. I think you know what I mean, don't you, Lynn?"

"What are you saying?" Her eyes became very large.

"I'm saying that I don't think you just ran into me in the line at that house sale on Cuadrante. And you were never told to ask around at the Bellas Artes for a portrait painter. I think you were asked to connect with me any way you could, weren't you? I'd like to hear the truth."

She was silent for a moment, looking toward the back wall at the bamboo. She had rolled that hem on one leg into an extremely tight rod.

"You're making it sound much more sinister than it really was," she said, shifting uncomfortably in her chair, her toes curling in her flip-flops. "Mr. Trujillo just told me that they wanted you to do the portrait, they had already decided on it, but that I should not say that the idea came from them. I didn't know why. I thought maybe they were thinking you'd charge more if the contract came from Dos Cerros directly, and I could see that. Not that you would, but only that they might think that. They had me go down to Galeria Uno and look at your photo so I'd recognize you. Then when you were in line and talking to that man with the white hair, I came up and asked the woman behind you if I could cut in line. I said I was your cousin."

"How did they know I was at the sale?"

"They had someone following you, I think. How did you figure this out?"

That would have been Angel Flores, I thought, but I didn't want to say it to her.

"Something I realized when I was painting you. You

have an unusual body and a look most painters would love. Yet you made this display of maidenly modesty when you came to pose. I couldn't believe no painter had ever asked you to do it before. What really gave it away was that you always knew when it was time to break. I think you've spent a lot of time posing, isn't that right?"

She nodded slowly. "I did in school. It was easy because there was a big art department and they always needed models. I'm sorry, Paul. Once we got started I really liked you and I looked forward to our sessions together. And then when Ballard was killed, everything got so awful I thought I could never tell you the truth. I convinced myself it would never come up. It seemed like such a small piece of this. I wanted to stay close to you so I could hear about the investigation. I thought it could help me with my book. Now you think I'm part of the other side, don't you?"

"No. A lot of people got pulled into this, and Dos Cerros only told each one the bare minimum of information. No one knew the whole thing except James Watt and Antonio Trujillo. Your father is an example of what I'm talking about. So, no, I don't think you're part of the other side. Think about this; I worked for Dos Cerros as an investigator. In fact, I still do."

"So you're playing both sides."

"I had to. There was so much evidence piling up against me I had to get into it just to get out of it."

"I feel responsible for that. I know I put everybody at risk. But you know what's worse?"

"I believe I can guess. It's your father, isn't it?"

Her head fell forward on her chest and tears began to stream from her eyes. "I can't get past this part of it. Not only did I put you and Maya at risk, but if I hadn't started this in motion he wouldn't have been killed. I was the catalyst for the whole thing. I can't ever forget that."

I got up and put my arms around her. "Lynn, if it hadn't been you, they would have found another way. And you couldn't have seen what was coming; it looked to you, and to me as well, like just a portrait job. You know how I'm always looking for work.

"Are we OK then?" She pulled away and looked at me. "Not that I am."

"Of course. I just needed to clear that up."

"And we'll finish the picture?"

"Yes."

"And do I still have to wear that dumb nightgown when I come out from behind the screen?"

"Yes, always."

# Chapter 22

San Miguel is quite a distance from Belize City, so I was surprised that evening when I looked through my rear view mirror at a stop sign and saw Antonio Trujillo behind me in a Jeep Cherokee. If he hadn't been under a street light I wouldn't have known it was him. When I crossed the intersection he came slowly down the street behind me, and then pulled over to the curb in front of a small grocery store, one of those *tienditas* that has only about a thousand pesos worth of inventory. I moved farther down toward the corner and parked, then flipped on my cell phone and reached Cody.

"Williams."

"I've got Trujillo, believe it or not, parked on San Francisco between Nuñez and Juarez. He went into one of those hole-in-the wall groceries. What are the odds of that?"

"It's a small town. Are you driving?"

"I'm parked ahead of him. When he pulls out I'll stay with him. Why not call Delgado and see if he wants to put someone in place at the Cuadrante house, just in case that's where Trujillo's going?"

"Got it. I'll be over there myself in a couple of minutes. Keep me posted."

In three or four minutes Trujillo came out of the store entrance, paused in the shadow of the doorway while he looked up and down the street, and then got into his car. He was carrying a plastic bag that looked it might contain a couple of bottles of water and a few smaller items. Once back in his car he did not immediately pull out and I couldn't see what he was doing without getting out of the artmobile, so I sat and waited as well. Maybe he was having a snack.

It was fully dark now. I knew Maya was expecting me back home, but I didn't want to use the phone to call her in case I had to get back to Cody. I did have my gun.

As Trujillo pulled away my phone rang.

"Where are you now?" Cody said.

"Trujillo just pulled out, and as soon as he passes I'll get behind him. Looks from his signal like he's going to turn left."

"OK. In about one minute Delgado will be inside the garden, and they'll have an unmarked car toward the front."

"I'm moving now. There's a car between us. Where are you?"

"I'm on Pila Seca, just before it changes to Cuadrante. I'm trying to park, if I can find a space."

"He's heading down Recreo now toward the bull ring. I think he might be intending to come around to the garden side from Terraplen. He must have his own key. If he turns up along the garden wall, I'm going to stop here. I don't want to spook him."

He made the turn. I parked the artmobile on Terraplen and looked around the corner. He had parked, but was still in the car. I didn't move. I couldn't see Cody up on the far corner, but I knew he must be there. A minute or two passed.

Trujillo's car door opened and he got out, closing it softly. He was a few steps from the garden gate. He had left the bag in the car, but appeared to have a water bottle in one hand. He paused briefly to work his key and then went through, shutting it behind him. Immediately Cody and a uniformed cop came down the street from Cuadrante, and I moved up toward the gate. When I got closer, I recognized Ignacio Ramos from working with him on the codex case when Maya was kidnapped. All three of us had our guns out.

The gate swung open and Delgado came out, looking pleased with himself. He stepped aside while Trujillo followed in handcuffs, and behind him was Peña with a gun trained on Trujillo's back. When the taller man passed I could see over Peña's shoulder that a light was on in one of the third floor windows. Bingo, as they say, even here.

"Where is she?" I asked, placing my hand on Trujillo's shoulder. He turned to me with a look of contempt on his face.

"Don't be an idiot. I don't know what you're talking about."

"What's that light up there?"

"I have no idea. Like you, I just got here. Now I am leaving."

Delgado said to Ramos, "Put him in the car with Cisneros and then secure the front entrance. We'll go in this way."

We waited until Trujillo was in the unmarked car

and Ramos had crossed to the front of the mansion before we went into the garden. Peña checked the carriage house, but it was locked up and dark. The four of us climbed the steps to the *loggia* and tried the door to the sun room. It was not locked. Careless, perhaps arrogant. I thought I knew who might make a mistake like that. We moved noiselessly through the room toward the corridor. Above, the house was silent.

As we checked the adjacent rooms and then paused in the foyer, Delgado looked through the glass in the entry doors to see that Ramos was in place. We moved up the grand staircase. Delgado and Peña were in the lead, Cody and I followed. On the third floor I pointed out Lynn's former bedroom.

"This was where the light came from."

Delgado tried the handle, but it was locked. He pounded on the center panel and yelled, "Open up, police!" There was a muffled shout from inside in response, a woman's voice.

"Help me! The door is locked." But we knew that.

"I've got my kit," said Cody. "Let me get at it. Get a light on in here." As I found the switch, Delgado and Peña moved back and Cody bent over the lock, trying various narrow blades and picks. The seconds passed. I wondered briefly why he didn't kick it in; maybe it was respect for a historic property. Then there was a grunt from Cody and the door flew open. He lunged into the room, his gun drawn, and Delgado and Peña followed. There was a scream of relief from Rebecca, but at that instant the next door on the hallway opened quietly and James Watt rushed out from Stephen Washburn's room. His face was contorted with hatred when he saw that I was still in the hall. I leaped after him, but he wheeled and his foot connected solidly with my knee. It buckled and I went down. As I got to my feet my knee was screaming in pain, but I hobbled down the marble stairway after him. He turned at the base of the stairs and headed down the hall toward the rear of the house, disappeared through the library door, and slammed it shut. As I came limping down the hallway I heard a key turn in the lock. Cody and Delgado were right behind me. Delgado drew his gun and tried the knob, then stepped back and waved Cody forward.

He worked over the lock and we waited. There didn't seem to be any point in shooting out the lock and I wondered if James was going to kill himself now that he was cornered. I could hear nothing from inside the library. It had no door to the outside, but I remembered two windows facing the street, and it was probably an eight-foot drop to the sidewalk, not a problem for someone James' age. Then I also remembered that the windows were covered with a steel grill. If James got one open, he would have no where to go. Now we had him.

The door swung open and we all rushed in. Both windows were still closed, but no one was in the room. Delgado tried the handles on both of them, but they were latched from the inside. We stood for a moment and looked at each other, then at the bookcases, the cabinet, the ceiling. Cody pulled the cabinet doors open, which made a sound of protest, but there were only the same stacks of books inside. Time was racing by, and we had nothing.

"This can't be," Cody said. He knelt and looked

up the fireplace flue, but it was too narrow for a man.

"He's not here," I said, stating the obvious with great clarity. "There must be another exit we're not seeing." Delgado dropped to the floor and began tapping the parquet with the handle of his gun, listening for a hollow sound.

I looked at the design of the paneling. The walls were embellished with rows of mahogany raised panels set into frames, a shorter one below, and one taller above, and then a third row under the ceiling. Each frame was divided vertically from its neighbor by a narrow decorative strip, about every thirty inches. At three feet off the floor a chair rail with a radius edge went all around the room, protruding an inch and a half from the panel frames. Starting in the outside corner, I ran my hand under the chair rail until around six feet in I found what I was looking for, a recess on the underside. I pulled the rail firmly toward me and in the wall a latch yielded with no sound and the panel frame swung open. I stepped into a space within the thick masonry wall, pushed on the back of the panels I was facing, and walked through into the similarly paneled dining room. Naturally, the room was empty.

"Very slick," said Cody. We rushed through the dining room doorway into the foyer.

Ramos was waving furiously as we unlocked the entry door.

"He came out into the foyer and then ran up the stairs."

The four of us wheeled and started back up the staircase.

"I'll search the second floor," yelled Delgado. "Peña,

you stay with Rebecca Watt. Paul and Cody, search the third floor. See if he got out onto the roof." He flew into Brendel's bedroom at the front of the house as we continued to the third floor.

The servants' level was a maze of rooms, some on the interior and without windows, others facing the garden or the side street. A lucky few faced Cuadrante and had a view over the facing buildings. Peña ran for Rebecca's room and Cody passed him going down the hallway to start at the far end. I turned left down a narrow corridor and started in the corner of the rooms at the front.

There were no closets, of course, because that was an amenity that postdated the house. Some of the rooms were unfurnished, others had beds and a few even had armoires. Wherever I found these I flung the doors open. I saw no sign of James, and heard no footsteps other than my own.

Two bathrooms served the entire floor. James was not in either of them. In the last room at the front of the house there was a door in the inside corner of the room, larger than the door I had come through. But there had been no door in the adjoining room on the shared wall. As I crossed the room I heard above me a low scraping noise, as if something were being dragged across a floor. I opened the door soundlessly and looked in to see a staircase with worn wooden treads and a handrail, more steep than normal; I had found the attic.

I had never seen an attic in San Miguel, but I had never been in another house here quite like this, either. It had a feel more European than Méxican; it could have been a townhouse in Madrid or Seville, or Brussels, for that matter. Eighteenth-century townhouses have a similar look.

Afraid that the stairs would creak, I placed each foot at the extreme edge of the tread, where it was supported at the line of the wall. The treads held without creaking. If James was waiting at the top for me I'd be a perfect target. When I was three steps from the top I heard another scraping sound, then a bump like metal hitting wood, and a low grunt. I paused, listening. There was nothing more.

At the top, I looked around in darkness. There was a line of small windows at the street side, and another pair on the side over the carriage entrance, but the only light entering was from street lights far below. The smell was dry and musty, with overtones of disturbed dust hanging in the air. I was on a small landing, with three doors before me, all standing open. Edging over to the opening on the left I saw a line of what I at first thought were headless bodies, and I froze, straining to get a clearer view. But as my eyes got accustomed to the darkness I realized they were dressmaker dummies, and that across the room were three racks of clothing, draped with dust covers. I dropped to my knees and scanned the area beneath the clothes for feet, but there were none.

The light was better in the second room, which held a few pieces of upholstered furniture, a doll house, three large bird cages in scrolled baroque designs, and about two dozen large trunks of different shapes lined up along one wall. I debated whether I should start opening them, but I didn't want to risk the noise of creaking hinges and rusty latches. I could come back if I found nothing else. My recollection of this kind of trunk suggested they were full of compartments anyway and wouldn't provide a hiding place for a man.

The last room held more furniture, and against an open window facing the carriage drive, the footboard of an iron bed leaning against the sill. On the top rail a stout rope was knotted securely over the bar, passing out the window. I tugged at the rope, but found no tension on it. James was gone, and I climbed through.

Outside the window I found myself on a flat segment of the roof about four-feet wide running the length of the house from Cuadrante back to the garden. This explained why we'd never seen the attic structure from the street. Looking up from below, it was set back far enough from the cornice to be invisible. At no point did the narrow street permit someone to get far enough away to see it. But it would have been visible from the upper floor of the neighboring buildings. I got to my knees and looked over the edge. Below me was the carriage drive, tight against the neighboring house, and for about thirty feet the drive was covered at the first-floor level, one edge of the arched roof structure anchored to the mansion over the carriage door, and the other resting on the garden wall of the house next door. The rope end rested on this canopy with about six feet extra. James was not in view. I shoved my gun into my belt.

At this point I paused. I would be an easy target coming down the rope, yet to run back down inside the house and then hope to rouse someone next door who might not let me in to search his garden would lose valuable time. What was the likelihood James was waiting for me to drop into his cross-hairs? Or was he now running? What decided it for me was that James did not know it was me coming. He had seen at least three of us, and he thought I was injured. It tipped the scales in favor of flight, so I gripped the rope and began to let myself down. Because of the cornice overhang, I was about three feet from the house itself. I knew I was depending on the quality of John Schleicher's restoration effort here; if the cornice crumbled I would drop suddenly six or eight feet and be slammed against the house. But it had worked for James, and I kept the rope in the same place.

I was halfway down, and no one had fired at me, when my feet, entwined with the thick rope, encountered resistance; I found myself standing on a bracket of some kind. I bent my knees and put my hand down to feel the broad seat of a swing, padded with what felt like velvet, although I couldn't see it in detail, and on the other end was another bracket, followed by more rope. I thought of Victoria and the "fun" room in the carriage house briefly, then slithered to the bottom.

The carriage drive was modestly lit from the house lights and I could see that James was not there. I scrambled over the arched canopy covering the drive and scanned the neighboring garden. In the darkness were large shapes that might have been stacks of pipe or timbers, possibly forms for concrete work. There was the lighter circle of a well in the center, and mounted on the back wall, which was illuminated better because it caught some light from the mansion windows, was a sculptural fountain in the form of a large shell. Standing on the upper scalloped edge, about to swing his body over the top, was James Watt. I don't think he saw me, but if he did, he didn't pause.

As he disappeared I dropped to the ground inside the garden. The surface was a minefield strewn with construction debris, chunks of stone and lengths of wood, small piles of tile fragments and cutoffs, mounds of hardened excess concrete, coils of rusty wire. There was no way to get over the back wall except through the sleeping house or by the same route James had taken, and if he had seen it was me coming after him he would probably be more willing to fire. I leaned against the wall and pulled out my phone and speed-dialed Cody.

"I'm next door across the wall of the carriage drive," I whispered. "James is over the same wall east of me. He's probably heading for Terraplen if he can get through one of the houses. See if you can get some people out there." I didn't wait for a response, but flipped it shut and climbed up the fountain. Once again I was in target position. There was nothing to do but go for it.

I banged my injured knee on the edge going over and grunted as I landed on the ground. I hadn't paused to look around because I came over so fast, and I now found myself in a field of dim figures, many taller than my head, some gesturing oddly, others carrying what might have been baskets and vases. I hit my ankle on the base of one and realized I was in a large group of garden statuary. James and I had apparently landed in the backyard of El Jardinero, a garden implement store on Terraplen. This was confirmed when a single shot rang out, careened off a tall woman in front of me with a metallic ding, and buried itself in the body of a satyr at my left, with the sound of lead hitting plaster. I did not see the muzzle flash, so I had no idea where James was.

A light came on in the courtyard to the left, but almost none of the light came this way. In the little that came into my side of the wall I could see a large wooden box filled with glass balls of different colors. As I waited in the silence I picked one up. There was a parting of the statues just ahead of me and I leaned forward and rolled the ball briskly over the gravel toward the back wall of the store. It was a good shot; I heard it skip down the lane and shatter against what must have been a step under the overhang. I hadn't been bowling in quite a while, but I guess you don't forget. There was no response from James.

Then, as if in response to the noise, I heard a door open, a soft grunt, and something fell on the tiles with a heavy metallic sound. It could have been a gun. Then nothing more. I couldn't believe James opened the rear door by himself, nor did I believe he would grunt and lose his gun. He must have gotten the drop on someone. I rolled another ball. It went off the gravel course and bounced off something else without breaking, probably the base of another plaster statue. Again, nothing from James. I counted to sixty slowly and started to move.

The garden store was still dark and as I came through the door I heard Cody say quietly, "Paul. Put up your gun," and a penlight came on. I came further into the store. Cody and Delgado and Ivan were standing by the open front door.

"What happened?" I whispered.

"Ramos brought Trujillo back to the station and Ivan Carillo came with another car," Delgado said. "Peña went in first just as Carillo came up. When he opened the back door Watt was waiting. He took Peña with him."

"Where are they?"

Delgado made a gesture. I looked narrowly around the door frame and saw James and Peña walking up the street about half a block distant. Gripping Peña's collar, James had a gun to the officer's head and he was looking back our way. When they got near the corner James hit Peña in the back of the head with the gun and he fell like a rag doll to the pavement. James jumped into a parked car.

"Now." Delgado said to Cody. "Peña's down!"

As we ran out, the blue Ford squealed away and turned left at the corner.

"Give me the keys and get help for Peña!" Delgado yelled to Ramos, and raced for the police car. Cody and I pulled out right behind him in the artmobile.

When we came around the corner the police car was about fifty feet ahead and I couldn't see a blue Ford, but Delgado must have seen the direction James took. We flew straight up toward the Queretaro road, running in the wake of Delgado's siren and lights. We had the advantage of height in the van, so every time we went over a speed bump or came over a rise I could see over the police car and then I finally caught occasional glimpses of James's car.

"Call Maya," I said to Cody over the pounding of the cobblestone pavement and the engine noise. "Tell her we've got Rebecca and we're chasing James out of town."

The road was not very wide at this point, and I was able to stay with Delgado pretty well by being close in behind him and leaning on the horn whenever he pulled out to go around someone.

"I can't get hold of her." He flipped the phone shut. "So what kind of a thing was that, to have a secret door in the library?" yelled Cody. "I associate that kind of thing with smuggling or Prohibition."

"They didn't have Prohibition here. That was a gringo idea. I think that this is nothing more than a staff idea. Remember when that house was built? 1740 or thereabouts? It used to be fashionable to have servants be able to move from one room to another without traveling through the public areas. Which in this case meant being able to serve drinks to gentlemen in the library after dinner without going through the foyer. That's all it was. Not sinister, routine, but James knew about it. We didn't."

Cody grunted as he hit a speed bump hard.

"How would we have found it?"

"Barbara showed me a picture once of the Watt family compound in Houston. It's a Georgian-style house. Eighteenth-century floor plan. A modern builder might easily have put a concealed door in there, too. It's a tradition in that kind of architecture."

We moved past the traffic circle in front of Gigante, weaving in and out of the traffic.

"And he would have had ample opportunity to get familiar with the place when they were setting this up," said Cody.

"And James had to be the source of that *Asesino*

message," I said. "Or one of his staff."

"Looks like it now. He was trying to soften you up."

Delgado was slowing down, but I couldn't see why. Suddenly James flew off the road to the right, running between two moonlit gate posts with his lights off. We were no more than four or five kilometers out of town.

"What is this?" I said.

"I think it's *Rancho Sinagua*."

"What good is a ranch without water?"

"It belongs to some guy from Texas named Pritzker. He was going to make it a movie ranch, but then he got sick and went back home. The name's just a joke, because it's poor land for agriculture, but I guess it's picturesque in daylight."

We bounced over the road, curving in and around several dry arroyos, and losing sight of James in the process. There were half a dozen side paths he could have used. The moon slid into a series of spotty clouds and didn't help much. Delgado pulled over to the side and got out, holding his arm in the air. I followed him in and cut the engine. We listened for a while. There was nothing.

"You and Cody cover the right side, and I'll cover the left. Fire a shot if you see the car," said Delgado.

We climbed up the shallow embankment and moved over the uneven terrain. I could barely make out a mixture of flat areas with scrubby vegetation and clumps of small trees, then gullies and washouts from what little I could see in the deep shadow. My knee was better, but still slowing me down. There seemed to be no point on the landscape where we could look out over any distance, but I wasn't sure. James wouldn't have had his lights on anyway.

We paused for a moment and immediately a low rumble started from off to the left; how far I couldn't tell. Gradually the rumble took on definition as a cyclical kind of thwack, thwack, thwack sound and gathered speed. And now I knew what I was hearing as lights appeared rising above the edge of the hill.

"The sucker's got himself a helicopter," said Cody. "That's it. He probably called him from the road and the pilot had it warmed up. I think we've seen the last of James Watt for a while."

The chopper lights rose swiftly into the air and swung off in the direction of Querétaro in a wide loop. James was probably waving goodbye to us. Delgado came up behind us, putting his weapon away.

"Can't shoot," said Delgado, as if he were afraid I was going to. "It's not good to kill the pilot."

"Dang," I said.

We drove at a normal speed back to Quebrada.

"He'll have enough high-powered lawyers around him at home to stave off extradition indefinitely," said Cody. "He won't be able to come back here any time soon, but he won't be seeing the inside of any Mexican jails either."

"So he did kill Ballard, as Rebecca thought."

"I think so. Trujillo seemed too collected and detached that night to have done it. Probably too smart too."

"Why do I feel partly responsible?"

"I can't imagine. Any problems James's father had were his own doing. You just uncovered them. It's a case of kill the messenger if you don't like the news."

# Chapter 23
## Victoria Mendez

On the day after he had ascended into the darkened heavens and left his pursuers behind in the barrens of *Rancho Sinagua*, James Watt lay naked with Victoria Mendez in bed at his rented townhouse at the La Puertacita Hotel compound, where he was registered as Michael Faraday. Had Victoria known more about the history of science and technology, she would have appreciated the irony of this, but her skills were anchored in more intimate things. The morning sun spilled through the tall second-floor windows and dappled their bodies with the clear upland light. Their clothes lay in a pile on the *barro* tile floor. James leaned his head on one hand, and with the other, pulled back the sheet from her body. He moved it slowly down her back, over the enticing arch of her perfect butt, tracing the small scorpion tattoo on the left side, and down her thigh and the hollow behind her knee until he could reach no further.

"You've got a lot of nerve, James," she said. She turned her head toward him.

"What? Shouldn't I be doing this?"

"There's nothing wrong with what you're doing.

I meant about staying here after that close scrape at Cuadrante."

"A simple thing," he said, smiling. "Hide in plain sight. Everyone thinks I headed for the nearest airport and went back home in a private jet. I had Jacobs file a flight plan for Houston and then take off in the company plane from Querétaro an hour after I lifted off from *Rancho Sinagua*. No one would ever think I stayed."

"Didn't the police try to stop him?"

"Oh, they searched the plane. Jacobs said he didn't know where I was. They thought he was a decoy and I was flying from somewhere else, possibly one of the private landing strips out in the hills.

"You're too clever by half some times."

"It doesn't take much in México. Anyway, it's what I do best, moving people around in new directions. In this case, that means a wild goose chase. I wanted another day with you to get our business taken care of. I'll go back tomorrow and no one will notice. They'll be moving all the paperwork back to the dead-end files."

"So the loan for the renovation is transferred to my account?"

"Just as we agreed. There's enough to convert Casa Victoria into the finest bed and breakfast in San Miguel. But tell me something. Why go legit? I thought you were doing well enough as it is. Not that hospitality isn't a good business. I guess you've already been in it for a while, in a way."

"That's the way I am. I'm tired of being the bad girl all the time. You can see that. The expatriate women won't even look at me on the street. Like I told you before, I'm ready for some respect in this town, and I plan to get it."

"Not just in the morning?"

"No. Now and always." She gave him her special smile.

James shifted a little on his side. "I'm a little stiff after last night. How about your legendary back rub?"

"No problem."

James lay on his stomach. Victoria sat on his buttocks and moved the heels of her hands over his back along both sides of his spine. He sighed softly. Then she moved her hands onto his shoulders and began to knead the muscles as she thought about Antonio Trujillo. The seventeen-year difference in their ages was much more to her taste, although young James had been sweet in his way on the few times he had paused long enough to really see her. But he lacked the solidity, the mature mass of the older man. Being in bed with Trujillo was like being taken by an angry stallion. Now she had no idea when she would see him again. It would be up to Dos Cerros to get him out of jail. All this because James had decided to renege on the technology deal. His youth made him capricious. Victoria was the same age, but she had left capriciousness behind long ago. Now she was into strategic planning.

Her hands slid back down along his spine. "Here's a knot," she said, probing a spot to the left of his vertebrae, about a third of the way down. "Can you feel that? I think I can make it go away. Shall I try?"

His only response was an affirmative grunt, his face buried in the pillow.

With her left hand she withdrew a knife with an

eight-inch blade from beneath her own pillow and, leaning on the handle with both hands, thrust it deeply between two ribs directly into his heart. His back rose in a great wracking arch and then he collapsed unmoving on the bed. She sat for a moment waiting for more, but it was finished. Setting one foot on the floor, she got to her feet and wiped a single smear of his blood from her inner thigh with the corner of the sheet.

"Good night, sweet James," she said quietly. "You've served your purpose well. But now it's over."

Moving to the desk, she opened his briefcase and found the loan agreement she had signed the night before. Kneeling naked at the fireplace like a vestal virgin before the sacred flame, she lit the gas jet and burned the papers to a fine ash.

CPSIA information can be obtained
at www.ICGtesting.com
Printed in the USA
BVOW08s1003040517
483141BV00001B/19/P